INTO
THE
SUNKEN
CITY

INTO THE SUNKEN CITY

DINESH THIRU

HARPER TEEN

An Imprint of HarperCollinsPublishers

For Ruch

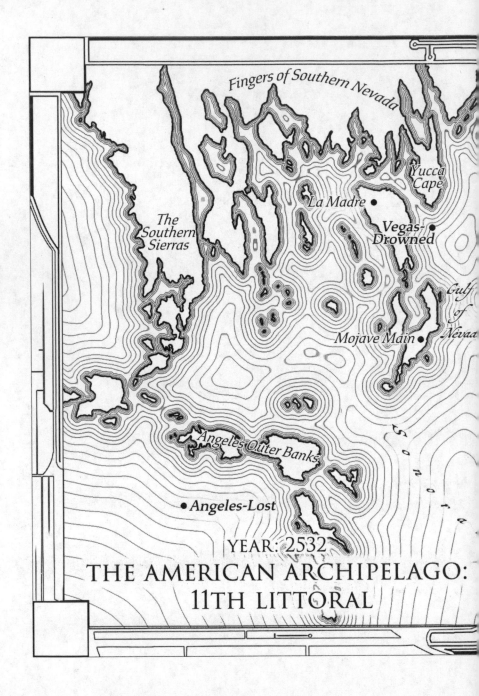

Fingers of Southern Nevada

Yucca
Cape

La Madre •

Vegas- •
Drowned

The
Southern
Sierras

Gulf
of
Nevaa

Mojave Main •

S
o
n
o
r
a

Angeles-Outer Banks

• Angeles-Lost

YEAR: 2532

THE AMERICAN ARCHIPELAGO:
11TH LITTORAL

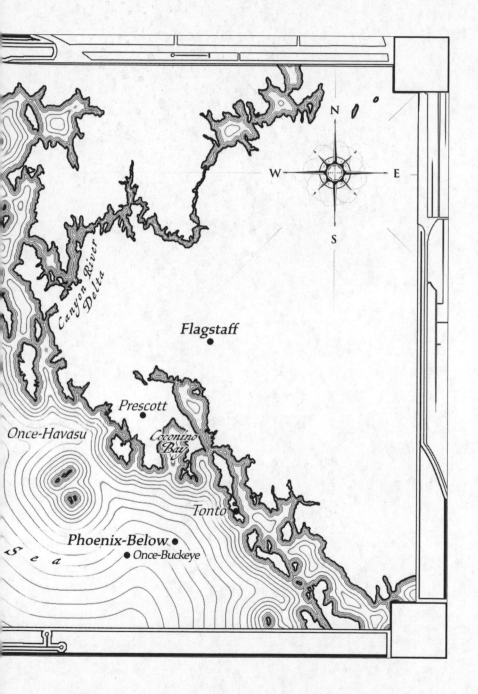

INTO
THE
SUNKEN
CITY

In the immediate nearness of the gold,
all else had been forgotten. . . .
—Robert Louis Stevenson, *Treasure Island*

1

I swore to myself I'd never do this again.

Rain rips down on a diagonal, battering the bay and our floating three-slip dock. It's midnight, and I sit here jerking on my wetsuit. One leg, another, a shimmy into the waist, plunge my arms down the sleeves, zip up the back, fingers into gloves. The neoprene molds over muscle and bone, comforting me, telling me this is right, this is safe, secure.

But nothing about this activity is safe. And Thara, my sister, would actually kill me if she knew I was here, doing the very thing I made her promise never, *ever* to do herself.

Small drops tonight, but the rain pours down fast and hard, and the resulting sound is like an ever-present hiss. Warm air, though. No surprise for August in Southern Arizona.

I collect my remaining items, stuffing a dry bag with my mask, weight belt, headlamp, and watch, and I place a giant monofin beside it. Then I wait for him.

Spume mounds in fluffy piles next to me, the smell wafting over the dock, all salt and decomposing fish bits. I suck up that pleasant air, conducting breathing exercises to ready my body for the higher carbon dioxide levels. Behind me, the wind shrieks up a massive bluff that cuts a hook around the bay. Atop that bluff is our inn, the dilapidated, five-story structure that is my life and burden. I was raised an innkeeper's daughter. Now I keep the inn myself.

I can't say I keep it very well.

Which is why *this*—the suit, the water, the plan. Beyond reckless to try it—with no recency, no acclimation. It's been almost three years since I journeyed below. But I turned eighteen last month, and now I'm on the Navy's recruiting lists. If I don't pay their monthly conscription tax, they snatch me up, and then I'm serving three years in the Pacific while my fourteen-year-old sister is torn from our parentless home.

Won't let that happen.

So, I'm breaking all my promises and compromising my honor and whatever other shreds of dignity I still have left. Tonight, I'm going to freedive into one of the recently drowned homes in Coconino Bay. I'll return with something worth selling. Otherwise, no point returning at all.

A honk pierces the wet air, and I turn to see a pale-yellow spotlight. Taim's utility boat pulls up along the dock.

He looks every bit the newly admitted Coast Guard cadet

with his shoulders rolled back, one hand on the wheel, his indigo poncho rippling against his tall, unbent body. For some, the rain beats you into submission; for others, it makes you rise up stronger.

I unlatch my eyes and hurl the dry bag and fin into his eight-foot boat. Then, three steps back, a short run-up, and I leap off the dock, landing right beside him as the boat rocks beneath us.

"Jin," he says, a smile creasing his lips.

I nod back. "Taim."

Off to a great start. We can say each other's names. This won't be excruciating at all.

"Do you want to talk about it?" he asks.

Short answer: *No.* I absolutely do not want to talk about it. Taim was accepted into the American Archipelago Coast Guard. He's moving two hundred miles northwest. He'll be stationed in the Gulf of Nevada for eight months (who knows where after). *And* he did not tell me about any of this until two weeks ago. So yeah, there's shit to talk about.

I shrug. "Nothing to say."

Taim swivels his head and his penetrating eyes search mine. He is so beautiful with his rounded cheeks and long lashes and glistening dark-brown skin. "There's more I'd like to say." He pauses. "But we can do that after the dive."

So beautiful . . . and so very annoying.

"Let's just go," I say. "And cut your lights. Don't want Thara spotting us if she's up."

He shakes his head. The sheer amount of disapproval this man gives off. Should have broken up with him months ago.

"You *should* be using one of the atmo suits," he says. "Safer that way."

Thara and I own two atmospheric diving suits, hard-shell exoskeletons that let divers sink up to five thousand feet and withstand the pressure. They were Dad's pride and joy (after his kids, of course). We used them for wrecking, mostly in Phoenix-Below. I did my first dive as a little girl, just five years old.

Taim knows damn well why I'm not using an atmo suit, though. He should shut his pretty, rusting face, and never bring that up again. Because here's the thing: Taim was down there when Dad died. I don't blame him, but he was there and now those two things can never be separated.

"This is just a freedive," I say. "I do it once, pay off the tax, and I'm done."

"And next month's payment?"

Clouds above—shut up.

"Are you gonna drive this rust heap, or do I need to swim there?"

Finally, he pushes the throttle down. Rain lashes my face as we cruise out across Coconino Bay. I gaze behind me, and I can see the inn's orange neon-tube sign flickering on our roof: The Admiral Bhargav Hotel VACANCY.

Bhargav was my father's name. Admiral was not his rank. Highest rank he made in the American Archipelago Navy was petty officer second class. He thought *Admiral* would serve as a better brand for an inn. He was right about that.

Taim aims the boat north, toward the bay's apex, where the homes just went under in the last few years. Shallowest there. He keeps the spotlight off, so the only glows are from our distant sign, a few sleepless homes that dot the cliffside, and a faint rope light that outlines the boat's gunwale.

"Eight oktas tonight," Taim says. It's a nonsense comment about the weather. Means that there's full cloud cover, which there always is. The only variant is nine oktas, which means there's so much mist and fog that the sky's obstructed from view. Nine oktas and you're inside the cloud. (Considering that you're breathing, I suppose the cloud is also inside you.)

Still, I glance up at the black, starless heaven. You can't see the clouds right now, but they're there. They're always there. Five hundred years since the Stitching, since the clouds first fused a foggy shell around Earth, and now the rain falls every day of every week of every year.

"You ever think about it? " I say. "Seeing the sun."

Just speaking those words, I'm transported into a memory. Six months ago, Taim and I, lying with our backs flat on the inn's slanted roof. The rain only stops for a few hours total each year, so Taim and I climbed out, lying shoulder-to-shoulder, sandpaper shingles beneath us. Must have been thirty minutes we lay there, staring up at the empty clouds, wide-eyed and foolish. At the end we promised ourselves that, one day, we'd make it up above those clouds—together.

It was a careless, impossible dream. Only about two hundred peaks (mostly in the Himalayas and Karakoram) even pierce the canopy. I should have known Taim didn't take it seriously. He leaned in close, nibbled my ear, and breathed hot air against my neck, saying, "Imagine the warmth."

I shiver, thinking of that memory—the thought of Taim's lips on my skin, yes, but also from the gravity of it. There's something magical about those moments when the rain stops. The whole world grinds to a halt. The impossible is achieved, and in the remaining silence, it feels like anything can happen.

I open my ears to the world now, and there's no silence. Just the cacophony of the rain. Tings and pings and dunks and plunks as it crashes down, washes us out, muffling the world—so loud, sometimes you think the rain wants you to just lie down and give up.

I look back at Taim, and he's staring out across the bay, the wind playing with the tightly curled tendrils of his topknot. *Maybe he didn't hear my question?* Except I know he did, and at last, he turns back to me. "Seeing the sun—that's your dream,

Jin, not mine. You want it so badly? Do something about it."

It stings—the command in his voice, the shame that gnaws at me for not having the courage to try. Maybe he realizes it came out hard, because he reaches a hand to my waist and rubs his thumb across the neoprene right where my sun tattoo is. It was a silly thing—a little black sun, triangle rays, inked into that dimple of flesh below my back-right waistline. I got it after we made our sun promise. "My badass tat," I teased, showing him the next day. "You should get one too." Of course, he never did, and that reminds me—this tender touch is something of boyfriends. Not ex-boyfriends.

I turn away from his hand, reach into my dry bag, pull the watch out, and check the geo-location. "This is good," I say. "Cut the engine."

The hemispheric cliffs of Coconino have a break at the northernmost point, and a road (now boat ramp) used to travel from there down into the valley. Fifteen years ago, when Dad retired and bought the inn, the bay was just forming. Rain's come down hard since then, and sea levels have risen about four hundred and fifty feet. Last of the valley went under three years ago, and it's a sharp reminder that the inn will be under one day too. Rain didn't always come down this hard. They teach the timeline in school. Started out a few feet of rainfall per year, then ten, then twenty, now thirty feet a year is what we get to live under.

The utility boat comes to a stop, and I hook on my weight belt, watch, and headlamp. Then, without a word to Taim, I jump into the water, holding my fin in one hand.

"Wait," he shouts, ripping off his poncho and shirt. "I'll come with you."

I pause for a moment, tracing the contours of his chest with my eyes. Last time I'll see *that*. I smile, thinking how strong and smart he is, knowing you always dive in pairs. Not tonight, though. Only I can do the time and depth required.

"Put your shirt back on," I say. "I'm going at least a hundred feet, and I'll need five or six minutes."

"Five or six? Okay, get out of the water," he says, dropping a wetsuit he just pulled from an aft deck dry box. "That's way too dangerous. You told me fifty feet and three minutes max."

I shove my feet into the monofin and call back to him. "Knew you wouldn't take me if I told you the truth." With that, I turn away, draw several slow breaths, and pour out a massive exhale to clear my lungs the way Dad taught me. Taim screams from the boat in the background, "Stop!" and I'm afraid he's going to leap in and grab me, but he makes a mistake. I hear a rustle on the boat, know he's digging for his fins, and that's it—my lungs are empty, this is my moment. I inhale again, a giant breath, lungs at max capacity, then I drop the mask and propel myself forward into a duck dive.

My fin shoots out of the water as I get full vertical for the descent. I'm completely under a second later, flicking on my headlamp. Visibility's good right now with the tide coming in, and I can see about twenty feet in any direction I'm facing. The water's chilly, and it'll only get colder the deeper I go, but the wetsuit will insulate me fine. The real issue is the pressure, and I move a hand to my nose, pinching and equalizing as I thrust the fin like a dolphin's fluke. The monofin is a gigantic, glorious prism. Three feet wide and long, it powers me into negative buoyancy (about thirty feet) after several kicks. Still nothing's in sight, and the pressure eases on my skull as I equalize, shoving the back of my tongue up against my throat, half pinching my nose, driving air out of each nostril over and over.

Pressure equalization is critical and one of the most dangerous parts of a freedive. A hundred feet down, I'll be compressed under four atmospheres. If I don't equalize perfectly, then it's ruptured middle ear, blown capillary in my eye, facial spasm, blood in the lungs, or any number of other problems.

I should have done a warm-up dive to half my depth goal. Safer, but I knew I didn't need it. There's just something about this body that made me born for this. Dad used to poke fun: "You have rubber ribs and nothing inside your head. You are built to handle the pressure, my little sea creature." I know he was proud of me. And down here, he's all I can think of.

There are a million questions I'd ask Dad, but most resolve

to one: Does he approve of the life I'm living? A life where my focus is on the inn, on Thara and getting her through school? It feels like the answer should be yes; I'm putting Thara first. But it's come with sacrifices. I dropped out of school, I stopped diving. Which was what Dad loved. So, in the end, all I can think is that he wouldn't be happy.

And that—is a deeply unsettling thing.

The shadow of a structure comes into view, and within seconds it materializes into a metal-shingled roof, encrusted in bird's nest corals and pink anemone. A smack of moon jellies glow a faint purple on the far side, and I still my body as a large southern stingray skims right over the roof. They're harmless if you leave them alone, but the whip-like tail has barbs that I don't want anywhere near me.

It carries on, though, and I drop below the roof, glancing at my watch. I'm one hundred and twenty feet deep and a minute expired. That leaves me with three minutes inside, and a minute for the return. I could try for multiple dives, but it requires long rest intervals to rebuild my oxygen levels, and I don't have the time. If Thara wakes up, and I'm not there, she's going to be waiting for me at the dock.

I imagine her sitting there, feet in the water, orange trench on, long black hair soaked through. People say Thara and I don't look alike, but it's crap. We look exactly alike: brown eyes, bronze skin, eyebrows thick and curved. There are just two differences: one, she's a head shorter than me, and two, she's got a rich, black-velvet stream of hair, and I'm buzzed quarter inch to scalp. Of course, she's the crazy—half the bay's buzzed. Too hard to keep long hair when nothing ever dries.

Just the image of her waiting puts my stomach in my throat. *I can't face her like that. I have to get it done—and fast.*

Three thrusts and I blast through a shattered window. The inside of the home's small, two rooms, and mostly gutted. A moldering green couch in this room, a synthetic mattress melting into the floor in the next, some seagrass growing up through the floorboards, and a bouquet of white glass sponges growing like a chandelier from the bedroom ceiling. I open a door toward the back and there's a bathroom, toilet covered in a dozen purple sea stars and a creature's large translucent eggs in the sink (nesting ground—dangerous). On the bathroom's left side, there's a tub with a plastic curtain covered in orange algae. I yank that back and—*oh god.*

My eyes shut immediately, my chest contracts, my toes curl in the fin. I should go. I should break for the surface. My head spins, bile traveling up my throat. But I have to look, I have to. *Be strong, Jin. Look. If there's nothing, you go.*

I open my eyes, and the body is still there. I swallow several times, trying to hold myself together, push Dad out of my thoughts. It's an old woman by the looks of it, swollen, bloated, skin half-eaten to bits, missing an eyelid. *Did her family leave her here? Did she decide to stay?* I don't know, and I don't have the breath to wonder about it. There's only one thing I need to do. I scan her ears, neckline, hands, wrists. I even remove her tattered shoes, inspecting her toes. No jewelry. *Damn.*

Her naked eye is fixed on something, though, and I follow the eye's gaze to the bathroom's entrance. That's when I see it: a saber, mounted directly above the doorway.

One look and I know it's precious. A commissioned officer's saber, with an aluminum hilt, a pressure-sealed black sheath, probably a stainless-steel blade beneath. Looks about three feet, and it'll sell for several dozen ounces, maybe more if it's an admiral's blade with any decorative gold or silver. Dad never made it high enough as an officer to be granted a weapon like this. He admired them. Used to point them out whenever a senior officer was at the inn. "Lot of valor in those blades," he would say, his reverence lengthening his words.

For a moment, I wonder who it belonged to. *The woman, her child, her spouse?* Did she mount it here herself, so it'd be the last thing she saw as her home flooded?

I rip the blade free from the wall and pull the shower curtain around her again. Least I can do is give her this last bit of dignity. As I blast out of the bathroom, I glance at my watch. Four minutes thirty seconds down, and I can feel the tips of my fingers and toes growing numb. That's my body redirecting oxygen to more vital organs. I need to surface—immediately.

I know I can hold my breath for six minutes, but past that—well, Dad never let me push that far.

We used to train weekly. When I first started, I was awful, but Dad said the key was reducing your heart rate. It falls naturally when you dive, but you can drop it way down if you stay calm.

Just after my eighth birthday, I finally broke through. Dad and I were in the bay. He told me to focus on a Rigveda prayer. "The light in my spirit broadens," he said. His voice had the deepest bass. I dropped below the surface, closed my eyes, and replayed the words, hearing Dad's voice as it reverbed through my head. Dad put two water-wrinkled fingertips to the pulse in my throat, and when I opened my eyes, his whole face was glowing. He raised a hand with three fingers and then made a circle with his thumb touching the others. I knew what it meant: thirty. I'd dropped my heart rate down to thirty beats per minute.

Dad was amazed, but that's not the important part of the memory. Not anymore. The reason I visit that memory is because I can still hear Dad's round voice in it; I can feel his gentle touch; I can see the light sparkling in his dark-brown irises.

For other memories of Dad, I've lost those specifics.

That's one of the horrible mistakes I made in the first year after he died. I tried not to think about him, and he faded.

Now, I stay up late at night, my chest so heavy, eyes shut, playing memories on loop. Sometimes I find a clear one, and I squeeze my eyes down on it, and remind myself.

You don't have to ever let him go.

I fix that memory in my heart and steady my aching lungs as I punch out of the home with several thrusts of the mono-fin. The saber's in my right hand as I ascend. Maybe it's the current pushing things around, but about halfway up, I drive into a wide swath of kelp, not quite a forest, but the makings of one. It's thick, and I'm shoving through it, until my fin catches on something. I thrash, but the fin's not coming free, and that's when I feel it—something snaking up my legs, twisting around them, winding.

I look down and see the head of a massive California moray, easily eight feet long with a mottled yellow-brown body as wide as my thigh. Its eyes are rimmed a bright blue, and my headlamp reflects off rows of spiked teeth as the eel unhinges its jaw. I've seen this kind before. Small, sunken homes make for a perfect cave-like habitat. They're nocturnal hunters, the apex predators in the bay, and while they're not venomous, a moray this size could shred its needle teeth halfway through my arm. That happens, and (given how far I am from a hospital) there's every chance I lose the arm.

I jerk the monofin, but the moray's gripping it tight. I could pry my feet loose, but I'm too deep, too low on air, and without the fin, I'll never surface in time. The moray's already curled two loops around my legs, the head sliding up my backside, veering off at my waist, craning toward my right elbow. I swivel, staring at that elbow, and my eyes travel to my hand— the hand holding the saber. My brain realizes then: the fin's not coming free, only one option. My heart slams beneath the wetsuit as my left hand wraps around the sheath, thumb plunging down on the pressure release. I slide the sheath off as the moray's head hinges into an impossible angle. Skin taut, pulse exploding, I slash down, nicking my thigh, but sweeping the blade clean across the moray.

I sever the neck, and those blue eyes blink out, the head tumbling in slow motion away into the darkness of the deep.

With my free hand, I reach down and seize the moray's body, still coiled tight around my legs. It writhes (nervous system must still be running), and I pull it free. My feet flap several more times with the fin, and finally I burst through the kelp.

Blood leaks out of my right thigh, but I can't pay that any mind. Violent contractions surge through my diaphragm, and my torso twitches from the lack of oxygen. I glance at my watch, which is now at six minutes, twenty seconds. *Good god.* I beat my legs in the fin, no time for a rest, I need to get into positive buoyancy. Good chance I black out, and if I do, I need to make sure I float up. Taim will notice me on the surface. Hopefully.

I unfasten my weight belt and kick my legs as hard as they'll go. My heart's about to burst from effort, adrenaline, and raw terror. Convulsions rip across my chest again. My thoughts fade. Can't feel my hands, feet. Vision blurring, the mental disorientation of hypoxia clamps down. My father's voice—*Push, Jin. Push.* My eyelids flutter. *Where am I pushing to?*

My legs finally give out—something wraps across my body, and my last coherent thought is a question: *Do morays hunt in packs?*

2

Moments later, I emerge into my next life, cold, wet, and gasping for breath. I think of the mother at the inn who couldn't make it to Prescott Hospital. The baby was born right in our parlor, squirming, wet, covered in a white film. The cry that erupted was so shrill—like a lobster being dropped into boiling water. Guess that's the type of cry you have whether emerging into the world or departing from it, and that's the kind that peals out of me as I gag and cough and open my eyes to finally meet the Creator.

No, not the Creator. Taim Mazatlán floats beside me, his hands under my back. He tilts my head to the side, and his words are soft and soothing. "I've got you. Get it all out."

I do, gagging and spitting salt water in his face. Must have been Taim wrapping his arms around me in those final moments below. Morays are solitary hunters. I know that. I was in a hypoxia-induced delirium, thinking otherwise.

I try to lift my head, my mask is off, but it's just more coughing and gagging.

"Take it easy. Slow breaths. I'm holding you."

I can feel Taim's hands beneath me. One on my shoulder blade, one on the small of my back. That makes me think of my own hands. I raise them out of the water and—no saber.

My whole heart sinks, and I'd send my body down with it if Taim weren't keeping me afloat. *No saber.* It would have covered a year's worth of conscription tax, months of Thara's schooling, repairs for the inn. And after all that I just—dropped it.

I close my mouth and try to focus on my breath. Long in through the nose, slow out through the mouth. I calm myself the way Dad taught me. I could dive back down for the saber, but the chances of finding it—not good. I tremble on top of Taim's hands as the realization hits. I'm done for tonight.

I sit up and pull my fin off. Can't even make it to the boat, though. Too exhausted.

Taim wraps my body around his, and I am hugging him, sobbing.

"I was so close," I whisper into his ear. "I found a saber, but there was an eel, and—" My chest shudders as I try to make my way through it.

"Just breathe," he says. "Breathe and let me get you into the boat. Your right leg's bleeding. Not bad, I think, but I need you out of the water. It's a miracle you're alive. Do you know how long you were down there?"

"No," I say, exhaling, dropping my head onto his shoulder. He must be kicking hard to keep us both afloat.

He takes his own ragged breath, and I feel his chest expanding. "Seven minutes, Jin. You were down there for seven minutes."

It's the longest I've ever been under. Different circumstances, Dad might have been proud.

Taim swims us over to the utility boat, and in moments, I'm up and in, and Taim's digging into his dry box, pulling out a medical kit (such a cadet, of course he'd have one). He sits me down on the bench and tells me I need to get the wetsuit off so he can take a proper look at it.

I unzip the back of the wetsuit and hold my arms up for Taim to tug on my neoprene sleeves. He does, and my arms suction out, revealing the top of my navy two-piece. Taim glides the wetsuit down, below my waist, gently over my thighs, past my calves; he pushes it down around my ankles while he's crouched below me.

I step out of the wetsuit as Taim pins the neoprene down, his knuckles grazing off the tops of my feet. Then we both sit back down, and Taim lifts my right foot into his lap. His fingers trace back up my leg, searching for wounds, flecking a trail of goose bumps. I remain perfectly calm, not squeezing my entire lower body at all.

Taim inspects the cut. It's leaking a bit of blood, but it's not bad. No stitches needed. It's just a long, thin red line two inches above my knee. Still, my heart thunders, thinking how lucky I got. Give that saber another inch, the skin would be flayed, and I'd need more than Taim's hands to put the life back inside me.

He takes a bottle of iodine out of the med kit, pouring it over the cut, coloring my leg yellow as I wince. The rain washes it away, and Taim places a pad of gauze over the top, applying pressure, tape, and finally a water-repellant bandage.

When he's finished, he looks up, and that's when I tell him my foot needs attention too. "It's cramped from the fin. Can you press it?"

He doesn't catch my teasing tone. Just drives his thumbs into the sole, and I groan as he says, "How's that?"

"Better," I squeak, and after a few moments, I pull my foot away, standing, my body vibrating with a swirl of emotions: fear, relief, want.

Taim stands as well. He's a good six inches taller than me, and he presses the flats of his palms into his eyes. "I was so scared in the water—when I couldn't find you."

"Me too," I say, fumbling.

He leans down, kissing my forehead, whispering against it. "Thank god you're okay."

My eyes drag up, finding his, and the words just spill out. "Kiss me again."

He startles, and I watch his throat flex, gulping. "I thought you wanted to be broken up?"

"I do." Those two words come out crystal clear. Taim is moving two hundred miles away. He chose the Guard over me. He already did the breaking up with his actions. I just said the words.

Doesn't mean I can't have a last kiss.

"What is this, then?" he asks. "Goodbye?"

I take the slightest step closer, our bodies connecting in about seven different places, as I whisper, "Goodbye."

He cups his hands to my cheeks, tilts his head down, and he pours that last kiss into me like a flood.

An intoxicating swell of desire rushes through me. Wave after wave as his mouth shifts, opening mine, closing it again. His fingers on the back of my neck. Prickles across my skin. Then heat. The rain, boiling. My body, pounding. His tongue is inside me. The flood dams burst, and I'm sinking, sinking, while a terrifying thought takes hold: *Get back to the inn, go upstairs, you can drown in him right now.*

Rain patters on my face. It pulls me back from the deep. Taim's lips still brush mine, and I keep them there as the rational-me claws back to the surface.

Let him go now. You offered him the innkeeper life. He didn't want it.

I drift back, and I can hear the soft smack of our lips parting. I take a hand off his waist, and he glides a finger down my forearm, and then we're no longer touching.

"We should go back," I say.

He looks me over. "Wish we could." And he's not talking about the inn.

I sit down again on the bench, my heart pounding out a slow, heavy beat.

"Where'd it go wrong?" Taim sits beside me.

I fold my arms. "We just—we just want different things."

"*I* want to make it work." Taim's voice is flush with anger and maybe something else—hurt.

"No. *You* want to be in the Guard. You want—power, authority."

"And what do you want?"

A wall of water crashes into the bay in the distance. It's a drainage spout in the cliff face. They open every few minutes, releasing all the rain that collects in reservoir pools below ground. They're grand and loud—like momentary waterfalls. I wait for it to shut, and my chest aches as I respond. "I want to survive. That's why I'm out here tonight. So I can pay the tax, Thara's schools bills, everything."

Taim furrows his brow. "Thara's fourteen, Jin. You can't live your whole life for your sister."

What does he know about it?

"And you need to pay the tax, sure, but if it was just that, you'd sell items from the inn." Taim sighs. "You wanted to be out here. You missed this."

"Missed it? I don't *miss* the thing that killed my father."

Taim reaches down to the deck, grabs his poncho, and pulls it back on. "It's dangerous, and you're damn good at it. Both those things are true. Don't use Thara as an excuse."

I swallow, my heart in a knot, and my eyes scan the desolate landscape. Black sky above, dark waters below, rocky cliffs in the distance, gray deck at my feet. The only color in my view is the white rope light illuminating Taim's indigo poncho. At last, I say, "We made a promise, Taim. Do you remember? One day, we were going to see the sun. What hurts is that you don't care about our promises. *You* care about the Guard and your own damn self."

Taim rolls his eyes. "All that crap you just spewed boils down into two words: you're scared."

"Of what?" I spit back.

Taim doesn't flinch. "Of caring about us as much as you care about your sister." He pauses, and in those still seconds he can see right through me. "And of wanting something," he says. "For yourself."

Thunder cracks in the sky, and it's like the gods confirming Taim's words. Lord Indra punctuating the moment, Dad would say. I decide to add my own punctuation, gathering all the weight of my voice. "You leave tomorrow, so I need to be clear. Do not return for me. Do not return to the inn."

Taim shakes his head, placing a hand on the throttle. "I'll

return when I damn well please," he says. "I'll want to see Thara."

Almost dead silence on the ride back to the Admiral's. Just a fine spray of rain, the flutter of two gulls that keep pace with us overhead, and the churning of our wake as the utility boat cuts a trim line straight across the bay.

There's a lighthouse on the southeastern cliffside. A narrow white spire, it beams a pillar of light straight up at the clouds. I always notice it, because beside that lighthouse is a Navy-run orphanage.

That's where Thara would be if I hadn't emancipated and dropped out of school. Judge let me do it because of the inn—a home *and* a job, not easy to come by both. One thousand kids in the orphanage (five thousand residents in Coconino), and the Navy runs it like a factory. They offer food and shelter in exchange for mandatory service. Starts at sixteen for Navy-supported orphans. At that age, you get assigned to a frigate in the Pacific or the Straits of Southern Africa (where the powers that be are *still* fighting over scraps of land). Gedunk sailors have it the worst: first two years are spent doing underwater hull repair, trying not to drown.

That makes me quiver, and I finally put the wetsuit back on. The idea of Thara in that orphanage is too scary, and this whole ride back with Taim is much too awkward.

The rain blurs our approach as we near the dock, but I stand, readying myself to leap out of the boat. Once we're within ten feet, the blur over the dock fades and a jolt courses through me. There's a tiny sloop moored in our third slip.

"You expecting someone?" Taim asks.

"No." It's the thickest portion of the night. Not a time when guests arrive.

Thara's up there alone. She knows not to let anyone in. Folks can sit on the stoop and shelter from the rain, and there's a door sign that says we're closed midnight to five. Still, my heart's flapping like a fish out of water. I need to get up there.

"I'll come," Taim says.

And in so many ways, yes, I want him to, but even I know he can't. Far too dangerous, getting that close to my bedroom.

"We'll be fine," I say. "Good luck with the Guard." My voice comes out flat, uncaring, and it's terrible. I can't let him leave like this, so I place a hand on each of his shoulders. The physical contact brings the truth of my feelings forward. "Thank you," I say. "Really, thank you. For coming out with me tonight, for diving down after me, for saving my stupid, rusting life." I pause, pull back, and look him square in the eyes. "You're right, you know. There are parts of me that are really messed up." My voice catches, my throat so swollen. "But you—you deserve a great life. Go and have one."

The look he gives me makes my heart splinter. His eyes

start filling then, and I need to break contact or it's never gonna happen. I take two steps backward, twist, grab my dry bag and fin, and leap onto the dock.

"Flick the lights on the sign if you're good," Taim shouts after me. "Turn them off if you're having trouble."

A grated metal staircase zigzags back up the bluff, and I could take those stairs (save us some power), but I decide on the open-air electric lift. Faster.

"Goodbye, Taim." The words come out calm and even as I step into the lift, flick the power on, and I'm rising.

"Goodbye, Jin!" he calls. "I'll write you!"

"Sure," I whisper, but by then he's far below.

I'm on my own.

The lift climbs the three hundred feet straight up the bluff, and I exit at the top, my feet crunching through soggy gravel as I round our ramshackle building. No lights from the top floor windows (that's our residence), nothing in the parlor either, and my breath rushes out of me, relieved. *Thara didn't let them in.*

When I arrive at the stoop, there's a hulky woman seated on the old aluminum bench that Dad pulled from the ruin of Once-Buckeye. She stands, and she has that sea swagger: smirk embedded into a brown pockmarked face, one eye squinting, sizing me up, brow creased, washed-out maroon slicker neck to knees, and five thick salt-and-pepper locs (three back length; two cut short at the shoulder) thumping behind her. "This 'ere your cave for the restless?"

I nod. "Where you sail in from?"

"Last port of call's my own, but these bones need a good dry bed. The sign true? You vacant?"

Being a seaside inn, I've met many of these drifter types: some Navy deserters, some dodging conscription, some who shelter in abandoned coves and ride ashore from time to time to resupply. Dad never liked taking them on—*more problems than their money's worth*. But that was some classist gullshit, and I ask the only thing that really matters. "Do you have coin?"

She lumbers forward, fishing something from her jacket, and she flicks it off the stoop toward me. I snatch it from the rain, turn it over in my hand, and I'm staring down at a thick gold coin stamped on one side with a grizzled-looking parrot. On the other are two embossed words: *Treasure Island*.

I've never seen a coin like that, though it doesn't matter much; an inn sees a lot of coins, and besides, that's one of the perks of living on the gold standard. Markings don't matter for squat. Weight matters. Purity matters. And that Treasure Island coin, well, I'll check the purity inside with vinegar, but I can feel the weight, and my saliva's already flowing. It's a fat two-ounce prize at least.

I unlock the door and usher the woman inside. In seconds,

she's boots-up in our parlor, barking out orders from a reupholstered recliner that Dad pulled from a stone mansion in Once-Scottsdale. "A steamin' cup-a-tea, that's what I need. Double steeped and make sure it's hot as a fresh island; I wanna burn my tongue as I suck it down."

The parlor's made of dark polywood—plastic shaped into lumber—most of it warped and creaking. It's more durable and about a thousand times cheaper than the real stuff (given the difficulty in growing trees).

Fist-size bulbs hang down from the ceiling without ornament. The bay-side wall is near floor-to-ceiling windows. Night's still pitched, but in a few hours, the morning light will seep in—a dull sepia, about as bright as it ever gets.

Dad did the parlor right, though: a massive steel bar, eight stools, shelving behind it dotted with jars of dried teas, matés, spices, and a panoply of pots and mugs all recovered from our wrecking tours.

Furniture across the parlor is all from the wrecks as well. No point keeping it upstairs, when down here it can serve as an attraction for guests and locals who want a taste of the old world and Thara's cooking (mine's crap). Brass end tables, stainless-steel dining chairs, broken metal clocks, ceramic lamps, and the oddest menagerie of formerly water-logged decor.

On the wall opposite the bar is a fireplace, usually fitted

with electric glowing logs. And, on the floor near the windows, lies Dad's showpiece: five strips of artificial turf, almost a hundred square feet, sewn together into *the lawn*.

We found them rolled up, still sealed, in a gardening store in Phoenix-Below five years back. Folks come from all across the bay now to have a maté, kick their boots off, and pretend they're walking on grass.

I saunter behind the bar, tap on one of the electric kettles, fix a mug with a Oaxacan maté, and finally realize I'm still in my damn wetsuit. *Need to get out of this before Thara comes down.*

"Do you have things?" I call to the woman.

She's craning her neck all around the parlor. "A chest in the sloop; you can get it later."

The glamorous life of an innkeeper.

"Okay, well, I need to head upstairs for a moment," I say. "You hungry? I'll fix you some food when I'm back." The breaker box for our rooftop sign is below the bar, so I flick that switch several times, letting Taim know he can leave. The woman's bedraggled, but harmless.

As I pick my head up, I catch her leering at our atmospheric diving suits. They're both mounted on the wall near the fireplace, each with round steel helmets, face shields, white exoskeletons, and red strips of synthetic carbon at the joints. They have biometric locks, connected to my thumb only, but she's staring far too long.

"Nice suits, there."

I try to ignore that. "I said, are you hungry?"

She smiles, wide and wicked, with half-black teeth. "My belly's turnin' over like a fish spanked ashore. Appreciate it if you fix me something now."

I sigh, but it's probably better I keep an eye on her, so I duck into the little galley kitchen behind the bar. Thara keeps a few barley flour pies in our fridge. Barley is our staple grain, as it's shade and salt tolerant, and the mini pies Thara makes are perfect for hiding all kinds of junk-end gobbets of shellfish. I grab one and throw it into the small electric oven on the counter. In minutes, I've poured the maté, pulled the pie, and the brine of baked clams wafts into the air. I return to the parlor, where I find the woman toes-deep in our lawn (I won't mention the condition of her toes). Her forehead's pressed to a rain-streaked window, staring out across the bay, and I place the plate, tea, and a fork down on an aluminum table with a clatter. "My sister makes the best seafood pies."

The woman wheels around, pulls a chair, and plunges into the pie, not bothering with the fork. After sucking half the thing down, she says, "You's about age for conscription, ain't ya?"

My heart skips several beats forward. No one asks about conscription—unless they're coming to make sure you comply.

"Fancy joining the Navy?"

3

Rust take me. Have I misjudged this woman? Is she in the Navy's Selective Service, here to haul me away?

My pulse quickens, my foot tapping, and, to quell the shakes, I widen my stance, my hands on my hips. "What's it to you? We pay our taxes."

"Everybody says they taxes are paid," the woman says through half-slurped bites. "Till someone comes round asking."

I kick a leg of her chair then, and it swivels so she's facing me square. "Who are you? Answer me straight." My eyes shift across the parlor, wondering what I'll do, what I'm capable of if she is with the Service. I can't run. My whole livelihood is in this place. Thara's upstairs. *Is Taim still down by the dock? Why did I flick that breaker?*

"Easy," the woman says, tucking her chair back into the table and picking up her tea. "Don't like the Navy myself.

Perhaps I can help you avoid them." She flips her fork over and starts picking at her fingernails.

And it's not exactly the denial, but more her general manner of behavior (misbehavior) that convinces me. This woman can't be in the Navy. Every recruiter or Selective Service member I've seen had their buttons polished brighter than pearls.

I relax my stance. "Fine, I'll bite. How can you help me avoid conscription?"

From her slicker, the woman pulls a little black purse, and I hear the delicious sound of thick, round coins clacking together. "How's one goldie a month for lodging?"

Clouds above. She must have at least a dozen coins in there.

"How long are you planning to stay?"

"Long enough as I like, may more, depends."

"Okay . . ." I suck on my cheeks as that sweet jangling fades. "We'll put you in our best room. Second from the top floor. It has a great view on a clear day."

"Good enough." The woman flicks bits of fingernail gunk across the parlor. "Ain't no clear days, though."

I smile. "What's your name?"

"Name's no mind."

"All right, but what do we call you?"

"How about the pretty-little-sailor-with-the-purse-a-gold?" She flashes that black smile again, so big.

"Bit of a mouthful," I say.

She spits out a half-chewed bite, kicks her head back, locs thumping the floor, and a sharp cackle erupts, like nails scraping glass. "You's a funny one."

"I is," I say.

She nods. "Very good. Well, I is too. Very funny. So funny, I may just spend *all* this here gold at your inn . . . if you meet my three conditions."

I try not to piss myself. "And those are?"

"Number one: man comes along with a bionic leg, you tell me straightaway . . . else." She pulls a knife off her boot, tosses it in the air, slams her palm against the table, and the black blade lands tip down between her index and middle fingers.

Very unclear if it's a trick or she got lucky.

"And you got all this stuff here wrecking, ain't ya?" She motions to the furniture. "And them your dive suits?" She swivels toward the wall opposite the bar, and I nod. *Who else's suits would they be?*

"Good. Then condition number two—you and me, pair of funnies, we're going wreckin' together."

My face betrays nothing, but it's never happening. Especially not after the disaster tonight. Still, there's only one condition left. "What's the last?" I say.

The woman stabs the knife into her final bite of pie and takes a big whiff. "Bring your sister down. I'd like to know what's in these pies."

That last part makes me nervous. *Why does she need to meet Thara?* Still, the woman seems intent on spending two dozen ounces with us. The tax is two ounces a month. It's an incredible score if we can keep her.

Plus, I need out of this wetsuit.

So I hustle up the inn's center stairwell, polywood whining the whole way, and at the top, I open the door to our residence.

Worst floor in the building, as it's right under the roof, gets all the leaks. The doorway opens into a long, musty hallway, and on my right, it ends in a kitchen-cum-living room with a slip-covered sofa, a formerly white table, two shelves with ancient books, folding chairs, and photos in rusted frames. Lining the hallway, there's a collection of several dozen foggy mirrors that border on the totally creepy. They were Dad's obsession—wrecking prizes. Down the hallway to my left is a cracked tile bathroom and the two bedrooms. And opposite the entrance is an oversize coat closet with drainage for our slickers and rain gear.

I flick a hallway light on and step toward the closet, unzipping my wetsuit, as I see Thara emerge from her bedroom. "Do we have a guest?" she says, face to the floor, yawning.

She hasn't seen me, so I hop into the closet and ease the door closed. Of course, the damn hinges squeak as I do.

"Jin, you there?"

"Yeah, woman showed up in a sloop. I couldn't sleep, so I

let her in. You go back to bed. It's early."

"Where are you?"

Nowhere. Definitely not hiding in this closet.

"Just putting my coat on. I need to fetch the woman's things from the dock. I'll wake you in a few hours."

I want to tell her about the coin, but I can't right now. Need to change.

There's a long pause from Thara. "Okay," she finally says, and I hear several steps on the polywood.

I give it a minute to make sure she's in her room, then I throw the closet door open, ready to hustle into my room (Dad's old room), but I shriek instead because Thara's standing directly in front of me, arms akimbo. She looks me top to bottom, the wetsuit doing all my talking for me. "Are you *serious?*" she shouts.

"I thought you went to your room!" I say, like that's my defense.

"Yeah, I faked it because it seemed pretty weird that you were hiding in our drainage closet!"

God damnit.

"Were you *diving?*" Thara asks, tossing her lank hair over her shoulder. It should smell like a fetid swamp, but she washes and combs it each night, and it smells like this citrus soap we splurged on once. (Can't afford actual citrus, that stuff's for wealthy inlanders.) We use seaweed and supplements for vitamin C, but the soap's special. Hug Thara, and you're transported off the coast to a greenhouse, where you're pressing your nose into the peel of a fat, juicy orange.

"Were you?" Thara screams it this time, as I'm still scrabbling for a response.

"Yes," I finally say. "But not in the suits. I told you we'd never use those again, and we won't. I swear on that."

"You're unbelievable! I *want* to use the suits. You're the one who's too scared to get in them." She lets that gut punch settle. "So instead, you what—freedive?" She gestures at my wetsuit. "It's even more dangerous! Did you go by yourself?"

"No, of course not. Taim took me."

"Taim! I thought you broke up with him."

"I did!"

"Going out in his boat at midnight doesn't sound like breaking up!"

"Oh, shut up, Thara. I don't need relationship advice from you, okay? I went out with him, and I dove into the bay, and I almost got something good too."

"What?"

"An admiral's saber." Not sure if it was an admiral's, but it doesn't hurt to embellish it. "Dropped it on my way up, though." *Don't need to go into all the details.*

Thara shakes her head. "You're a hypocrite and a half. I'm taking a suit out to Phoenix-Below this weekend."

With a freedive, the max depth is about a hundred feet. Occasionally some fools can push a bit farther. With an atmo suit, a diver can descend thousands of feet and enter the sunken cities. More to salvage that way, but also greater chance you never come up. Like Dad.

I fix her with my deadliest glare. "You are *never* to take those suits off the wall. Hear me?"

"I'm not listening to you. Liar."

My heart twists as she says that. It's a fragile trust between us. Breaking it is my biggest fear. Such an impossible task being both her sister and her guardian.

I sigh. *Guess she needs the details.* "I almost died out there tonight," I say, exhaling a long breath. "Got pinned down by a moray. Killed it and broke free, and Taim helped me surface." I pause. "It's dangerous, Thara. Every kind of diving is dangerous. I shouldn't have gone. I'm sorry."

She walks up, placing a hand on my shoulder. "Are you okay? Did you go hypoxic?"

I wipe two hands down my face, reliving it, nodding.

Thara wraps her arms around me, squeezing so tight. Strange, the relationship we have, but sometimes I need *her* to hold *me* up. My eyes focus. Around Thara's neck, there's a thin gold necklace. It holds a medallion imprinted with the Goddess Lakshmi seated in a lotus position. It was our mom's necklace. She died from pneumonia when Thara was a baby, and though we never knew her, that necklace is more precious to Thara than anything in the world.

After a minute or so, she resumes, her words strong and serious. "You don't have to go in. But we should take a suit to Phoenix. I'll go under and get something we can hawk. We need money for the tax this month, and I know you don't want to sell Dad's stuff from the inn. I can do this, Jin. Haldar sisters to the end."

The last bit is something Thara and I started saying to each other in the months after Dad passed. No matter how bad things got, it was us against the world.

"To the end," I say, stepping back, brushing away the wet in my eyes. "And I know you could—but neither of us needs to go. The lodger gave me this." I pull the woman's coin from my pocket, handing it to Thara, and she studies it with awe, reading the words *Treasure Island* and two smaller ones I hadn't seen on the back: *Hotel, Casino.*

As she stares at it, I grab her hands and say the words I so desperately want to believe. "We're gonna be okay, Thara. I promise you—we're gonna be okay."

Days pass into weeks as the woman settles into life at our inn, and we settle into life with her. I start calling her the Pretty One, which she seems to like, and she calls me the Funny One; Thara's the Cook.

As it happens, the Pretty One also cooks (she really *did* want to know what's in Thara's pies), and they spend a fair bit of time together in the kitchen. It makes me nervous how quickly Thara takes to her, but it's a welcome distraction from nights where I close my eyes and Taim dominates my dreams, his smell still clinging to my bed.

We were friends before lovers, but in the wake of Dad's death, Taim was the only friend who listened. Then all that listening became other things. Taim flicking suds across my face while we swabbed the parlor floor. Me snug under his indigo poncho while we waited out a squall. Taim pulling me down on a guest room bed while I changed the sheets. And then changed them again. When Taim graduated I thought he'd move in. We'd live together, work together, be together. *Couldn't have been more wrong.*

As for the Pretty One, she fills Taim's void with two parts crazy, one part kooky. Mornings, she's outdoors: walking the bluff, squinting through a cracked, black spyglass, hurling oaths at the rain. Evenings, she's yelling at the pots and pans, cooking with Thara. She fishes for us sometimes: kicks the fluffy piles of spume on our dock and takes out her sloop. One afternoon, she slams a long slimy barracuda down on the bar, her forearms sheathed in blood, punctures, and slashes, and says, "I had'a wrestle the toothy beast."

She brings up the diving here and there, usually goading

me while I serve meals to guests, spitting out lines like, "I bets you ain't even do a lick past five hundred feet. Probably scared of the dark. When you start diving anyway?"

I tell her I used to dive a lot when I was young, now I don't. I know she doesn't believe me, though (I was in the damn wetsuit when I met her), and one night just before we all settle in, she pushes me over the edge when she says, "You ever think you gonna die down there? Get stuck. All 'lone, no sight, no sound, just the black and that faint quaking of your heart?"

I swallow several times to steady the heartache inside. My mind flashes to the freedive, but I say something else. "That's what happened to my dad. Buried beneath a sunken building. He never came up."

The Pretty One has nothing much to say to that, which was sort of the point of sharing. With a grunt she takes her gourd of maté to the bay windows, leaving Thara and me to clean up the parlor.

"Dad wouldn't like her here," Thara says with a grin, stacking tin plates and cups on a bamboo tray.

"I don't like her here, either," I admit, "but her coin makes up for her . . . shortcomings."

Thara squints, observing as I meticulously scrape food leftovers into her compost pail. She'd have my head if I wasted a scrap that could otherwise nourish her little kitchen garden. "I don't mind her at all," she sings. "The whole place feels more alive since she arrived. I think even Dad would have come around eventually."

I grumble. There will be no "coming around" to the Pretty One.

My feet pivot, heading for the kitchen, but my eyes pass over Dad's recliner, and just like that I'm filled with an image of him, sitting there with his thick red book: *The Holy Vedas*.

I asked Dad once if he considered himself Hindu. Few people adhere to the old religions. Dad said, "I didn't use to, but now that I'm older, I do." I wish I could ask him what changed.

I know Dad didn't follow many rituals, but he did read the Vedas, the Rigveda in particular. I can still see him in the recliner, feet up, legs crossed, reading out loud from Book X, Hymn CXXIX.

It was one of his favorite passages. About Creation, actually, but Dad said it was important for a diver. You could think about what it meant for the world, but you could also think about what it means for *yourself*—when you're alone in the deep, when you're in danger, fearful, floating between life and death. The verse comes to me now:

That One Thing, breathless, breathed by its own nature: apart from it was nothing whatsoever. Darkness there was: at first concealed in darkness this All was indiscriminated chaos. All that existed then was void and form less: by the great power

of Warmth was born that Unit. Thereafter rose Desire . . . the
primal seed and germ of Spirit.

Desire. Dad used to beat that point home to me. Cave-ins
are so common that he feared I'd be caught in one. (The irony.)
He tried to prepare me, teach me to calm myself, recite these
words in my darkest moments. When I was alone in the *Void*,
trapped and *Breathless*. Become *That One Thing*—choose to live.

I remember Dad asking me to recite it once before we
dropped into Phoenix-Below. I screwed it up, I was ten, and
Dad grabbed my shoulders, our viewports up, rain pinging
off our suits. He recited it himself, and then he implored me:
"You must promise me, Jina. If you ever get trapped, you will
think of this. Find your *Desire*. Fight. *You* must fight—and *I*
will come."

My heart aches thinking of that. Dad would want me to
fight. He'd want me and Thara to find a way to live. And I'm
trying. I am. So hard. But we barely pay our bills, and I have no
future beyond the inn, and Dad . . . he's gone.

He can't come for us now.

I step into the kitchen, place the plates in the sink, and run
the water till it steams in the basin, scalding hot. At least the
heat is something I can feel.

Thara comes around behind me and squeezes me in a hug.
"We all have our shortcomings," she says. Then she reaches

over me to turn the cold water tap on just a bit, tempering the water to take out the sting.

With all of the Pretty One's inquiries into my diving, I shouldn't have been surprised to find her waiting for me one crisp morning in November. *The* morning in November.

I step off the last stair into our parlor and see the Pretty One in her maroon slicker, slurping tea, seated at the bar with Thara behind it. Thara's staring down at her Reader. It's a small device issued by her school that has over a hundred thousand books preloaded. It's text, pictures, and audio only, and it's meant for Thara's coursework, but there's also an ocean's worth of random stuff, and Thara consumes all kinds of obscure tutorials, science, and nonfiction. Me, I'm more of a romance and adventure type.

The Pretty One turns to me as I enter. "Cook tells me you two headin' out to Phoenix-Below today."

"We are," I say, trying to keep it brief. Then I squint at Thara, who has her head tucked down in that Reader. Thara's in her bright-orange trench, like a puffin's beak, and I really hope she didn't . . .

"Good. I'll be comin', then." The Pretty One clops her mug down and hot liquid jumps out.

"This isn't an open invitation," I say. "Today is my"—a well forms in my chest, but I find the words—"the anniversary of my dad's death. Thara and I head out to Phoenix-Below once a year to commemorate him."

"Ya celebrate the passing of your daddy?"

"Commemorate, not celebrate." *Why am I explaining myself?*

"How you gettin' there?"

"We're catching a water taxi from Huynh's Market. Not that—"

"I'll take you," she says.

"In your sloop?"

"Aye."

I throw my hands in the air. "What is this, Thara? You told her she could come?"

"She offered a free ride." Thara finally looks me in the eye. "It was nice."

"It's family only," I say.

Thara ducks out from under the bar. "Taim used to come."

"Taim knew Dad! He was there!"

"My sloop has a little outboard," the Pretty One says, standing. "I prefer the sail, but we can be there quicker than you say 'Daddy's kicked the bucket.'"

I really hate this woman.

"We takin' both suits or one?"

"*No suits,*" I say, finally seeing her angle. "We just haul out there, say our wishes, and come back. Still want to take us?"

The Pretty One walks over to the diving suits and swipes

a long finger across a steel helmet. She whips her head back around. "Course I does. Now fill me one of them big, lidded tea tumblers. Need to keep warm on the journey."

Eighty miles due south, and we reach the location where I last saw Dad. It's a bleak seascape: slate sky above, black waters below, drizzly sheets hanging everywhere between. My face is chill and wet from the three-hour ride out here, but I'm hood down now, as the Pretty One cuts the motor and millions of raindrops shatter the ocean's surface around us.

We didn't always rely on sketchy guests for transport. Growing up, we had a rigid-hull inflatable—the *Makara*, Dad called her. I had to sell it a year back, when the electric lift needed repairs. I never thought it'd be a problem since Taim had the utility boat. *Wrong again.*

There are half a dozen wrecking ships spotted around the horizon. I can see the spec of a mail drone flying over-head. Solar-powered mail drones are our primary method of long-distance communication. They carry audio or digitally written messages. Almost nothing else flies above the clouds. No jet fuel production as oil's all required for plastics and poly-wood.

My stomach caves in, looking at the drone. It's a sharp reminder that Taim hasn't written. It's been eleven weeks. *Another empty promise.*

Thara draws a dry bag out from under one of the sloop's benches. She sticks her hand in and removes a mug that reads: *World's Best Dad*. It's a wreck-found souvenir that we pulled from a ranch home in Phoenix-Below. We used to force Dad to drink all his tea from it. He always fussed and complained about how soppy it was, but I know he loved it.

"What'd you bring?" Thara asks.

This is our ritual. Each year we drop a token of Dad's into the deep. Something to keep him company. Something to help our grief, to help us part a little more from him.

Sometimes it's serious. Like last year, I dropped in a small brass idol of Indra, the ancient Vedic god, that Dad loved. I didn't want him to be apart from it—even now.

This year, I have something more lighthearted. I reach into my long yellow coat, and from an inner pocket, I hold up a golden bottle of Mariner's Deep-Sea Gelcoat. It's a wax Dad made me apply to the atmo suits every evening. Literally, *every* evening.

Thara laughs. "Dad is going to be so pissed at you! He wants you using it!"

That's how we talk about him on the anniversary. Present tense.

I lean over the sloop, shouting at the sea. "Hello, Dad! Guess what I have for you?"

He doesn't respond.

"I'm sending down some of your favorite wax. Don't forget to scrub under the arms!"

From age ten on, waxing the suits was one of my chores. Dad would ask me if it was done before bed. Easily half the week I forgot about it, and he'd send me down to the parlor where the suits were mounted. I'm sure he was tired and annoyed, but after a few minutes, he'd always come down himself, and we'd do it together. Eventually that became our routine, and during those minutes I'd ask him about his life: how he met our mother, what she was like, how they migrated to the Archipelago.

I pop the cap on the bottle (haven't used it since he passed), and the paint-like smell pours over me.

In a moment, Dad's beside me in the parlor, his deep voice hushed. "Get all the little crevices, Jina." He squeezes gelcoat onto a washcloth and works it into a suit.

"You go upstairs," I tell him. I'm fourteen. Dad's hands have early arthritis from flexing the metal gloves on the atmo suits. When I was ten, I was happy for him to help, but now I think he shouldn't.

"And miss this?" His brow furrows, two deep lines embed across his forehead like frowns. *I'd forgotten about those lines.* "This is our special time," he says. "One day, you'll be gone, grown-up, and all I'll have are these memories."

Not true, I think, and the thought is like a stab in the gut, wrenching me into the present.

The sloop rocks as I shake my head. But Thara's there, and she puts a hand on my knee. "We can keep it, you know?" Her big round eyes shift to the gelcoat.

I bring the open bottle back to my nose, breathe, and the intensity of that smell is overwhelming. I've been so afraid of losing him, the details, but with this one lacquered whiff, I can see his square frame, the silver hairs in his trim, black beard, the way he'd squat down to lift the suits. "Use good form, Jina. Drive from the legs."

With this one bottle, I could conjure him forever.

My throat swells to nothing, but I push out a response. "You're right. We'll keep it."

Thara's eyes well. "Okay."

The rest of the journey is as it should be. Thara drops the mug, says a silent prayer, and the Pretty One gives us several hard slaps on the back after it's all done. I think she's trying to be consoling. We rip back to Coconino in almost complete silence. Except for the end. As we pull up to our dock, the Pretty One says, "You sure you don't want to dive? May help. I can fetch a suit. Maybe your daddy would like that?"

"He would," I say. "And that's why we'd be damn fools to do it." I shoot a hard look at Thara. "Only two of us left as is. We're not losing another family member to the deep." My eyes land back on the Pretty One. "Understand?"

"Aye."

"Cause if you don't, you can sleep in this sloop. I appreciate the ride and the coin and all. But I'm not diving—*we're* not diving again. Ever."

I spend that evening in a mild freak-out about the Pretty One's influence on Thara, the way she's wormed her way into our inn, our minds, the way she keeps asking about whether we want to dive. I haven't been out again, not with the suits, not on a freedive. I never went back for the saber. We have the gold from the Pretty One. It's enough (for now), and the next day, I make Thara swear to me all over again that there will be no diving.

Thara promises, but she doesn't make me promise in return. Instead, she tells me: *Do what you think is right.* It's a brutal jab, and I know the implication behind her words. *I trust you. But you don't trust me.* And I suppose she's right. Not sure I trust anyone, most especially the Pretty One.

Every night, she makes her way down the bar, downing two drinks per stool. She sits swiveled around so she can ogle the atmo suits. I start waxing those suits again, losing myself in memories of Dad. It's like a drug, opening that bottle, but whenever I pull out of the memories, I turn around and there she is, the Pretty One, watching me.

She's working up the courage for something, though I'm

not sure what—she can't remove the suits without my thumb. *Maybe she'll try to take my thumb.* That thought always chills me, but in truth, the woman regularly drowns herself in ten to fifteen matés, until she's flushed with so much caffeine that her hands are shaking and the boiling liquid sloshes up, scalding her knuckles red and raw.

I'm not sure if she sleeps. Not sure how she *could* sleep. She asks us a few times if we have anything harder. She's referring to alcohol, but that stuff's outlawed. Whole swamping world's dealing with enough depression from our vitamin D deficiency.

Still, with so little sleep and so many matés, it's like I can feel the threads of her unraveling. Some deranged act is coming, and my eyes start tracking her boot knife. *Where is it? How sharp is it? Could it cut through the tiny bones in my hand?* All manner of paranoid thoughts consume me, and every instinct in my bones says the woman's a threat. She's a danger to Thara, me, the inn, and our livelihoods. Problem is, she provides the coin that maintains those livelihoods. So, I keep her on, knowing it's an awful mistake. And finally, the foolishness of that mistake comes home to harbor.

It's a frosty Saturday in February, our casino night. We call it *An Evening at the Admiral's.*

That's when the Pretty One turns my world upside down.

4

We do this one or two times a year: pair up with a local gambler and turn the Admiral into our little casino by the bay. This
time it's with Saanvi Kalpa, a ship's mechanic with the Coast
Guard (Coconino born and raised). Saanvi gets the word out,
we split the rake, Thara cooks up a storm. Everyone wins.

Except, of course, the unfortunate gamblers who lose.

The weather cooperates perfectly. The wind's screaming around the bluff, cutting up and under clothes, nipping
at bones. Rain's pelting down in giant shade-above-freezing
globules that splatter against hoods, heads, leaving us bay folk
two clams short of a concussion by day's end.

No one wants to be anywhere but inside, and—may the sun
shine on Thara forever—she's worked the parlor's fireplace
into a raging glory against the forces that be.

Expensive, replacing our electric logs with a real fire, but
we buy our strips from reclaimers that work Phoenix-Below.

On a night like this, the hot smoky fug will be worth every bit paid for that formerly submerged "re-dried" timber.

By nine at night, the place is packed, and Thara's making the rounds doling out bowls of Dad's famous fish stew: Meen Moilee.

She cooked a good ten gallons of the stuff. It's a richly spiced yellow broth with kelp, chunks of bass, and mussels popped open. Heady, aromatic steam rolls off Thara's ladle as she scoops out the bowls. Each bowl also receives two perfect cilantro leaves. Thara clipped them from the little herb and tea garden she keeps in the kitchen.

The garden consists of three narrow rows of planters beneath a single grow light, the kind the American Archipelago uses in their Rocky Mountain greenhouses. The bulb is swamp-all expensive; Dad traded a wreck-found jewelry box for a pack of six several years back. Each bulb lasts a year and beams down five thousand kelvins twelve hours a day. Thara's immensely proud of the garden, and she should be. It grows ginger, garlic, curry leaves, turmeric, chamomile, the cilantro, and a dozen other plants that keep our food flavorful.

The whole gambling den's sucking Thara's stew down bowls-to-face, but the cilantro's the real highlight, and at least half the gamblers pluck out those leaves first, examine them, and then nibble the edges, like they're tasting the finest of delicacies untouched by salt and sea.

Which, I suppose, they are.

We called over the Huynh girls, Suong and Nhu, from round the bay. They're in school with Thara, just fourteen and twelve, both with pale, pretty, eager faces and black, spiked hair. Suong's got fast fingers on the sitar, and her younger sister can thump our tabla all right. They offer the parlor a nice little background twang to settle the nerves on an off roll.

It's about thirty-five people in all. Most of the young ones are dicing; they seem to like the fast flick of the wrist. Never liked it myself; no strategy in dice.

There's an older wizened set thumbing cards on our hexagonal flattop, which Saanvi moved to the lawn. Saanvi's a thin brown man with an undercut and a tidy side part on top. He's got a thinking, studious sort of look, always scrunching up his face, furrowing his brow. He ran straight to the hexagonal flattop when we were setting up a few hours ago, said it's a turn of the millennium card table, and now it will finally have a chance to serve its purpose.

Okay . . .

A small pocket of folks sit in front of the maps that cover the wall opposite our bar. The maps are both terrifying and genius. A little touch of Dad's that pulls folks back to the inn. Each shows a snapshot of the world. The oldest has seven continents, then Australia goes under, then Europe, most of Africa, and on and on.

The Pretty One's there in front of the maps. She's regaling

a few of the non-dicing youths who sit rapt at her feet (how they can stand to be that close to her bare feet is beyond me).

"Now what you want to hear?" she says. "I's born on a wreckin' ship that haunted the waters of Delhi-Below. Spent most of me youth whalin' in the Sea of India. I been marooned on the atoll of Fuji. Or there's me personal favorite: the time I slayed one of them giant cats that still stalk the Isle of Angola."

With each statement, her finger zips across the current map, the one that's labeled 2532. There are just four shriveled up continents left: the American Archipelago (centered on the Rockies and former Mexico), the Andean Peninsula (running vertically along the western edge of former South America), the Zagros Ridge (stretching across former Iran, Iraq, and Turkey), and the Tibetan Plateau (the Himalayas, Karakoram, western China, and the Mongolian Steppe). Previous generations of Dad's and Mom's families trace back to the Himalayas.

So, I'm working the room, doing my host thing: matés served, fire stoked, condolences to the losers, compliments to the winners. But that's just keeping me busy. The real show's coming, and my eyes keep darting to the door until *finally* Taim walks in.

His entire presence can be summed up in two words: self-assured jackass. Also, Coast Guard cadet. Fine, five words. Taim strides over the threshold, pulls his blue-and-white Guard-issue poncho straight over his head, and all my feelings are confirmed, as the idiot's wearing a red ribbed muscle tank beneath (perfect for the near freezing weather outside). His arms and legs are corded with muscle, like he spends half his days swimming laps in open water, which he probably does now. The exposed top of his broad chest has a faint iridescence, like a starling's plumage (or maybe I'm just staring at his chest too long). And a single springy tendril of hair drips down his face, in that way that's like, *oh, did this just happen to fall here in perfect accent to my beauty?*

Worst.

Well, I did this to myself. I told him not to return, sure, but Taim goes wherever he damn well pleases. Plus, he's sail-to-mast with Saanvi, who's a year older and nearly mentored him through the SEAs, the Standardized Educational Assessments, which most non-dropouts take. The SEAs determine eligibility for the Naval Academy, the Coast Guard, and other prestigious inland occupations that require advanced schooling: logistics, meteorology, robotics, agriculture (what Thara's personally hoping for).

Now Saanvi and Taim are both serving in the Coast Guard's Eleventh, the littoral region that forms a triangle between Phoenix-Below, Angeles-Lost, and Vegas-Drowned. Saanvi's usually assigned to a cutter that patrols Coconino and the surrounding coastline. Easier to police us backwater locals if it's your hometown.

Taim spots me immediately, winks (to which, go shuck an oyster), and then marches right over and says in his rich baritone, "I missed you."

Oh, sure you did.

First of all, we're broken up. Secondly, if he missed me, he could have written. He makes money in the Guard. More than enough to ship a solar powered love note up above the clouds. Instead, he shows up after no word for seven months being all *I missed you?*

Right . . . That's what I'm thinking, anyway.

What I do is gag on the tea I was sipping, so shocked that I spray out the remnants straight onto his red ribbed shirt.

The music stops (stupid Huynh sisters; should have paid for real musicians). And I can feel the slow swivel of thirty-five heads as their glamorous host spews backwash-tea all over the newly arrived Coast Guard cadet.

I glare at Suong, who seems about to let the sitar fall out of her hands. "Keep playing!"

She does, and time resumes.

"Nice to see you too," Taim huffs, snatching a cloth from an end table and wiping himself down.

"Sorry, but don't feed me your lines, okay? I told you not to come back."

"I'm here for Saanvi," he says, "and to see Thara." Taim waves, and I can only presume Thara is waving behind me.

"Though you can boot me into the rain if you like."

I breathe deep, in and out, through my nose. *Rise above.*

"Stay if you want. But don't walk in all swagger, like"—I bow my legs out, thrust my chest forward, drop my voice an octave—"I missed you." I pause for effect. "I don't need that."

He's silent, but he runs his eyes from my toes, up my sexy black-velvet dress.

One point, me.

"Anyway, Saanvi said you're on leave?"

"Yeah," he says. "Short one. First in months."

"How's your aunt? You're staying with her?"

Taim's aunt, Auntie Ximena, is Taim's guardian. *Was,* I guess—before Taim turned eighteen. Both of Taim's moms were conscripted into the Navy. One when Taim was five, the other when he was eight. Both drowned in the Pacific. His moms were powerless against the Archipelago. Taim refuses to be powerless.

"Yeah. Auntie's good," Taim says. "I'm gonna move her to Prescott once I save enough."

Auntie Ximena's a bailiff at the court in Prescott. She's the one who helped me with my emancipation. I owe her a visit, actually.

"That's good," I say. "Get her off the coast. That's a good plan."

An aching silence hangs between us.

Finally, Taim says, "So you gonna ask me what the Guard's like?"

"Just tell me it's awful." I can't bear to hear anything else.

"It's awful."

"Is it really?"

"No, it's—it's incredible. I mean, it's everything I wanted."

My heart plummets into my groin somewhere.

"I wish you were there," Taim says. "You'd be the best diver in my crew. Have you been out?" He says it hopeful, like it'd be a good thing.

"No," I say quickly, and then three more words stutter out: "But—*you're* diving?"

"Yeah. With my experience wrecking, they think I could make it on a salvage crew."

Dicers erupt in applause behind me, like they're cheering on Taim.

"I guess I have your dad to thank," Taim says. "If he hadn't taught me to dive so young . . ."

That's another reason I can't be with him. Because we always come back around to that moment. Taim three thousand feet below with Dad in our atmo suits. Me in the inflatable. Taim comes up, says there's been a cave-in. Dad's not responding on his comm. He's buried beneath a mountain of rubble, under a three-story building that collapsed.

I can barely breathe. I can barely think straight, but I force

Taim out of his suit. His air's almost depleted, but I don't care; I strap on the suit, Taim tethers me with a steel cable, not trusting me to surface when I should, and then I dive.

I spent an hour down there, somehow, huffing dregs of air, tossing chunks of concrete out of the pile, digging for Dad. Eventually, Taim hauled me out on the tether. *Never should have let him do that.* Hours later, we returned with our air tanks refilled and a submersible that helped me lift some of the bigger blocks. I finally found Dad buried at the bottom of the pile. He was long dead from hypoxia, so I engaged the emergency release on his suit, said a prayer, and sent the suit up with the submersible. There was no need to take Dad back. I didn't want Thara seeing his body like that.

Taim sighs, and I'm pulled back into the moment. "I *did* miss you, Jin." Then he cups his hands over my ears, staring at me, willing me to believe him.

All I can think is that Dad used to cup my ears like this. When I was little and had a bad dream, he'd cover my ears with his big, warm hands and whisper, "Don't worry—they can't hear you thinking anymore."

Now he's gone, and Taim—well, Taim's the last person who saw him breathing. I step back, Taim's hands fall away, and I'm hoping the anger will steam off my skin. In the end, it doesn't, and all I want is my interrogation. "Why didn't you tell me?" I say. "Why didn't you tell me you applied for the Guard?"

Taim shrugs. "I wasn't even sure I'd get in."

"Yeah, but then you did, and you said nothing for two months."

"I apologized for that, Jin. Can't you let it go?"

Of course. *I* have to swallow *my* pride. "You told me two weeks before you left, Taim. We had plans: repairs we were gonna make to the inn, trips to Flagstaff. And all of it was just made up."

"I'm sorry, Jin. Are you happy? I apologized again."

My eyebrows furrow. "Tell me why you did it."

"I didn't think you could handle it, okay?" Taim bites his lip. "Your dad was gone. I was about to leave Coconino. I knew you'd freak, and I didn't want our last months spent like that."

"So you lied! For weeks!"

Something shatters in the background. I look past Taim and see Thara with the remnants of a bowl at her feet. She's not picking it up. She's just watching me, along with half a dozen other guests. *Swamp all. Need to keep my tone in check.*

Taim finally speaks. "I wanted *us* to enjoy those weeks. And anyway—I was right. You did freak. So much so that you broke up with me."

"You are so selfish." The words slip out under my breath.

"You know what, Jin? You see all the ways people lie to you, but none of the ways they care."

My mouth goes dry, like he's dumped sand down my throat.

"Look, I'm sorry I said anything," Taim says. "I'll go."

No words, but I swivel my head. *Don't.*

Taim glances around. My throat opens, and I nod to the dicers. "Saanvi's over there."

Taim walks off, and my eyes scan the room, finding Thara sweeping up the shattered bowl. Her eyes meet mine, her lips pursed, head shaking. *Thanks, Thara. Just what I need—your disapproval too.*

It's early in the morning when it happens, maybe three o'clock, I'm not sure.

The entire crowd's cleared out. Half of them gripping when they leave: squeezing their fists so tight, trying to quell the shakes from the caffeine. Saanvi brought a bag of ground coffee, which got folks extra shook. Expensive and highly regulated given the caffeine levels, but the gamblers loved it—slurped it right up as a nightcap after that seventh glass of maté.

We had a good haul. Rake siphoned off about six ounces of gold. Shame no one's spending the night, but it's a locals' event—not expected.

Thara took off too. She spent the latter half of the night dancing in front of Suong while she picked the sitar at a quarter-tempo (Nhu was face-down in the tabla). Then Thara walked out an hour back, saying she'd take Suong and Nhu home and crash at their place.

Please. As if I don't know what's going down.

Suong dedicated a number to Thara around midnight.

Thara melted into a puddle, swaying in place while Suong sang some trash about love being vast like an ocean. So bad. When Thara said bye, I thought, *Would Dad let Thara stay the night with her local musician crush?* Probably not. Whatever, I'm Thara's sister, not her parent, and the girl needs a first kiss. That's the most that'll happen.

Taim and Saanvi just took off as well. Taim tried to pin me down later in the evening, telling me the Pretty One looked sketchy. "Could be a corsair. Be careful." Stupid overprotective crap. Obviously, I'm leery of her. But she also supplies us with two ounces a month. Maybe if Taim had stuck around I'd have two incomes and wouldn't be desperate enough to accept her coin.

Now me and the Pretty One are the only people left, and she just stepped out to escort the last gripper down the bluff. So I'm washing mugs behind the bar, all alone, my legs about to give out from standing up near twenty-four hours—and that's when the pounding comes.

Boom, boom, boom at the door. Strange for someone to be showing up after the party. Still, we're an inn; there are rooms to spare. Maybe one of those grippers decided to crash? I hustle toward the door and throw the latch. Towering before me is a massive, vile man with a polearm, like the undertaker come to drown me himself.

He has a gray complexion, like the blood stopped flowing above his neck, and a long thin white scar running horizontal across his face, as if a saber took him left cheek to right. His eyes are black, baggy, and puckered, and his entire head hairless, except for a braided bit off his chin that hangs in a line, two inches, wrapped with a band.

He's wearing an Inverness cape, the sodden thing dripping puddles at his feet, and as he steps over the threshold I remember the Pretty One's first condition: *man comes along with a bionic leg, you tell me straightaway . . . else.*

I look for a bionic, but it's not there. Just two large normal legs. Still, I'm not exactly put at ease as he says in a gruff voice, "This da Bhargav?"

I nod. The name's on the door. No sense denying it, even to death himself.

"The old lady in?"

I know who he's talking about, but I feign ignorance, telling him my mother's dead.

"Not talkin' *yer* old lady. The old lady; likes her tea, foul mouth, five long locs, thick as the riggin' they is; actually just three of 'ems long, on account'a I cut off the other two." He jostles the polearm, which has a two-hooked spear at the top. They're used for shallow water fishing . . . and apparently also for haircuts.

"She's out," I say, "and we're full up. Sorry!" I attempt to close the door, but the man shoves it in, and I stumble back.

"I wait, then."

5

Ten minutes later, the man's scalding himself on an Andean maté. He's seated, eyes dead on the door, and I'm puttering around, cleaning the parlor, no plan, half-terrified of how this plays, and that's when I hear the Pretty One creeping up the bluff stairs. With the gale outside, I probably wouldn't have heard a thing, but the Pretty One's swept up in one of her sea songs, blasting out her arrival:

On the floor of the sea is a place for me, where the rain ain't touch my soul—
'Tis a watery grave, but I'll surely behave, just as long as I have my gold.

The man smiles at me, a brutal thing, whispering, "That's her all right. Behind the bar with you, and keeps your trap shut, or you'll have this here in your gullet." He lifts the polearm and strides over to the door, hinge-side, just as I hear the Pretty One insert her key. Thara pestered me into giving her a key. *I really shouldn't have given her a key.*

I'm hoping she realizes something is wrong because the door's already unlocked. Doesn't happen, though. She just carols on, carefree as a cloud, until finally the door opens, and the man slams it right back into her. The Pretty One crashes to the ground, the man swings his foot, then it's his boot to her temple, and—*thunk*—she's out cold.

By the time she comes to, the man's lugged her into one of our stainless-steel dining chairs, wrapped her hip to neck in coils of rope, with arms pinned at her sides and her ankles tied together. The black utility knife she keeps sheathed in her boot is resting on the table, and the man's across from her. I'm still behind the bar; clearly no threat at all.

"Where it is, Bhili?"

And as much as I hate this odious man, in this moment, may the sun shine on him in his next life, for after seven long months, I finally know the Pretty One's name: Bhili.

"Where is what?" Bhili says. "And cut me outta this, Pew. Ever it is, let's have a cup-a-tea, settle it civilized."

"You know what is, Bhili Bones."

Bhili Bones! Well, outside of being held hostage in my own inn, this is turning into a swamping good day.

The man, Pew, pulls Bhili's purse from his pocket. He fishes out one of the thick Treasure Island coins. "Where there's some, there's more. Now I want the map, Bhili."

"Ain't no map. Why I make a map, only so the likes a you can steal it. No. Map's in me head; you want it, just come round and cut it out!"

"Well, you know how much I like cuttin' up da hairs on yer head now, Bhili, but you got a map, and you gonna tell me where it is. Otherwise, I'm afraid little miss inn keeper, she's gonna be hook hangin' from her rib cage."

Now this whole time behind the bar, I'm thinking: *Don't be a hero. Thara needs you. No point losing yours over whatever shady past Bhili has dealing with actual corsairs, like this fellow, Pew.*

But when he starts talking about plowing me through with that fishing spear . . . well that's when my eyes start shifting, my head searching for a way to dispatch this intruder. I'm behind the bar, only thing behind me is the kitchen, and no exit from there. And sure, yeah, it's a kitchen, there's knives and such. But Pew has clearly survived a cutlass to the face, so I'm not so sure how well I'm gonna fare with Thara's boning knife.

Bhili says, "All right. Just leave the girl outta it. She ain't know nothin'. There's a map up in me chest. Second from the top floor. Go fetch it, and I'll talk you through the finer points. Ain't no easy haul. Few things you gonna need."

"Yer must tink I'm the stupidest corsair you ever sailed

with. *Go fetch it.* Meanwhile the girl cuts you free? Sorry, Bhili, that's not how it works." Pew turns to me. "Girl, you comin' with me." Then he snatches Bhili's knife off the table, grabs his polearm, and up we go.

We find the chest quick enough. The squat black thing's the size of a sea turtle and near as heavy too. It's sitting in front of the four-poster in Bhili's room, and it has a biometric lock, meaning we're going to need Bhili's thumb to open it.

Pew tosses his polearm on Bhili's bed, and like he's hauling up a trough of lobsters, he lifts the chest up from the brass handles on either end and lumbers toward the spiral staircase that anchors the inn's center.

I spare half a thought for snatching the polearm, but on the swivel of my head Pew barks back to me, "You go down first. Get!" and he motions to the stairs.

So I get.

Anyway, the idea of taking on a man like Pew, twice my size, with an over-size fishhook seems not well considered. I need something more fit to my ship. *Poison his next maté maybe?* A series of stupid thoughts are rattling around my head, the kind you have before you die, I suppose. I'm three or four steps ahead of Pew, and he's tromping down behind me. Must be four hundred pounds he's landing on each stair between him and the chest.

Finally, I round the last landing, scuttling down the

remaining steps, calling back, "I'll get another Andean for you, Pew." Maybe I'll dump a little squid ink in there. Not exactly poison, but squid ink never sits well with me. And I'm wondering, *Will an upset stomach help to get rid of Pew* while also thinking, *You're an idiot; shoulda grabbed the polearm.*

The stairs exit dead center of the parlor on the bar-side wall. I hook left immediately, heading for the bar, and I drop a glance toward Bhili, and as it turns out—there's no Bhili there. Just a pile of ropes cut and sagging on the stainless-steel chair.

My face's gone slack in that scared flummoxed kind of way. I yaw around, scanning the room for Bhili, and then I see her, stiff up against the wall just right of where the staircase dumps off. She's one long-nailed finger to her mouth, shushing me, and in her right hand she flashes a little push dagger: T-shaped polywood handle and a triangle steel blade, three inches base to tip.

Pew's thundering down the last stairs, and his eyes meet mine. He knows something's wrong; probably read it off my gaping, open-mouth face. He drops the chest with a boom, steps over it, into the parlor, and that's when Bhili throws a fist, plunging the knife hilt-deep into his neck.

She rips the blade free and blood sprays six feet forward, like a mini storm cloud erupted red all over the parlor. Pew teeters for a moment, his right arm lunging at Bhili, but she steps back, and then the giant crashes face first onto the parlor floor.

6

Bhili mops up the blood, whistling some merry tune like she didn't just slash a scupper into the neck of an old shipmate. I ask her how she cut the ropes, and all she says is, "Ain't just the boot knife; I got pokey things all over meself."

I kept tracking that boot knife . . . but it's always the one you don't see.

Pew's in a corner, and now that pale skin of his really is bloodless. I've fixed *myself* the Andean maté, no squid ink, though; there's no need. My entire body's shaking, my stomach flipping end over end, my head in my hands, my fingers rattling against my temples. I'm sucking down breaths through my mouth, hoping that the metallic scent from the several pints of blood soaking into the parlor floor doesn't reach my nose. Because when it does, I know what happens. When it does, I hurl this Andean, along with half my insides, all over the bar.

There is no turning back from this. Just the soft quiver of

my jaw and the slow-drip realization that my guest just killed a man. The *deranged act* I long anticipated is here, and that leaves me with two terrible options.

Number one, I head into town and take a water taxi over to the coastal patrol craft that's usually anchored near the bay's inlet. Maybe I can find Taim and Saanvi there? Even if I can't, the Guard will come, take a look at Pew's cutlassed face, know him for a corsair, and that'll be that. Well, that'll be that until word breaks round the bay that corsairs come to murder people at the Admiral Bhargav. Then that'll really be the end of the inn. No more local business. Bhili probably sets sail the minute I tell her I'm reporting the death to the Coast Guard, so I'm out of her coin too. Thara (thank the faint light of day she's at the Huynh's) and I scrape by for a year or so, selling items from the inn, but then—no money, and the Navy conscripts me, and I'm drowning at sea like the rest of my generation.

Then there's hatch number two: sink the body.

Bhili says she'll do it. I'm sure she's sunk hundreds of bodies. Sogging Bhili. Should have kicked her out months ago. Dad's probably roaring from the ocean floor with how much silt I've got myself stuck in.

My eyelids are half-burned now from the steam of the maté, so I finally look up. Billy cuts me a raw smile, far too wide for someone mopping up blood.

"Well, what's it gonna be?"

"Are you sure it'll stay down?" I say.

By *it* I mean Pew.

"Sure as the foam rides the wave."

"How do you get it to sink? Stones in his pockets or something?"

I'm not sure why I need to know this, but I do.

"Yeah, that's it. Stones in the pockets. Sumpin' like that." She wrings the mop out over the bucket, red rain sprinkling down.

My mind flashes to that old woman I found in her bathtub. I suppose Pew's body should stay under once he's into negative buoyancy. "And you'll do it now?" I swallow. "I don't want Thara to see. I don't want her to know about it even."

"Yeah, yeah. All those things. Don't worry too hard. You the Funny One. You stay funny. Me, I'm the Pretty One. You let the Pretty One clean up all these ugly things."

I stare back, but I'm not even thinking about her. I'm thinking about myself, Thara, the inn, our lives. We're taking on water, and if this kind of luck keeps up, we're going down, no way to recover.

"So," Bhili says. "What tis?"

"If he bobs up, I want you gone," I say.

"Ain't gonna bob up."

"And are there more Pews coming?"

"May, may not."

Swamping gripper. "What does that mean, Bhili? If there are more, then you take your chest, your map, that rotten fish-hook that Pew left behind, and you cast off—gone. All the coin in your purse isn't worth these people—"

"Friends," Bhili says, wringing out the mop again.

"These *friends* of yours coming around trying to kill us!"

"How much coin that be worth?" Bhili says.

"Worth what?"

"Worth may gettin' killed over?"

"A lot, Bhili! More than you have. Enough for me and Thara to buy a place inland, away from this sodden Coaster life."

"Fi-hundred a these goldies sound like enough for that?" Bhili fishes one of her gold coins from behind her ear like a magic trick.

"Sure, Bhili, that sounds great. Please deposit five hundred coins on the bar and I'll happily take on any number of corsairs that come banging down the Admiral's door."

"Ain't need you to take them on," Bhili says, chuckling. "Just need you to come fetch it with me. The gold."

"And where would that be?"

"Vegas-Drowned," Bhili says, dark eyes glowing, nodding at the diving suits on the wall. "I'll get you the fi-hundred. But me and you—we need to go for a swim."

* * *

Thara's beaming like the sun herself when she gets home. I'm four matés deep, Bhili clouds know how many, the body's in the bay, the blood mopped, and Thara's hair swishes behind her as she steps into the parlor.

Bhili hoots from the bar. "Oooo, you got the look a someone who just been kissed!"

Thara's face ignites like a fireball, confirming it.

Fantastic. Thara's first kiss. My first murder. What a lovely day.

"What was her lips like? You tell me everything," Bhili says, stalking up.

"It was warm," Thara says. "Really nice."

"Congrats, Thara," I say from near the maps. I walk up to hug her, but her face twists, and I can see right then—she knows something's wrong.

Thara glances around, and before I reach her, she's fifty questions to me and Bhili. "Why so somber, Jin?" and "What is that stain on the floor?" and "Why's the mop out?" and "Did something happen?"

"Bhili and I got into a fight," I say. "I spilled some tea. It's fine. We worked it out." Most curt sentences I've ever spoken to my sister.

"Sure did," Bhili says. "Right as rain."

I always hated that phrase.

Thara puts fingers to her dimpled chin, looking bemused, and says, "So you finally told Jin your name's Bhili?"

73

* * *

Over the next few nights, visions of Pew's body swim to-and-fro in my dreams. First of him in the parlor, neck spewing a thick scarlet stream. Like a gutter in a gale, it rushes forth—frothy, endless. Then of him stiff as a stave right below our diving suits on the parlor floor, bloated, his face lightest gray, like tarpon. Then of him in a tub, on the bay's bottom, missing one eye, while little fish nibble on his chin hairs.

Whatever my dreams, I'm thankful to say Bhili must have sunk him good. No bloated body parts lap against my dock. No visits from the Guard. Including Taim. *Guess he went back to his training.*

The only reminders that the thing even happened are the faint stain on our parlor floor and that eye-hook polearm that Bhili sleeps with, like it's a dangerous, desirable lover.

Truth is, I'm not sure Bhili's slept at all these last few days. She's sucking down cup-a-teas with a steel straw, so wired, she lies down in her room, and from the floor above I can hear her bed, jittering through the night. At one point, Thara grinds up several chamomile flower heads from her garden, trying to medicate Bhili to sleep. No use—it's like the woman's eyelids are taped to her brow.

All the while, Bhili keeps telling me we're going diving "soon, real soon," and then she starts sputtering about the "booty" she knows is buried deep down in Vegas-Drowned, supposedly in a crumbling underwater tower that's the coin's namesake. I don't indulge her.

Thara, of course, knows something is up. I still can't believe she knew Bhili's name before I did. It's the first time I know flat out that Thara lied to me about a guest.

Is that what our relationship is now? Lies and lies and lies?

Suong's around all the time too, always with her arm around Thara. *Stupid kid—go home and practice the sitar.* When she's not, though, Thara's trying to pry the truth out of Bhili. I hear Thara whispering questions while they cook, like secret ingredients tossed into a cauldron. *Where'd the polearm come from, Bhili? And why was your chest in the parlor? And what was the fight about?*

So, I suppose it was inevitable that Thara would pin me down. It's early one morning, and I'm on our fifth-floor balcony, staring out over Coconino. The clouds are tinting into their pearly morning gray. The rain's beady and warm. There's a mold that's growing in the corner of the balcony, and I can smell it. A slight green funk that threatens to roil my stomach. *Gonna have to scrape that off.* Across the bay, several pontoons and a fishing trawler are already out looking for the morning's catch. Then behind me, the sliding glass door sucks open, and Thara's hands are on my shoulders, like she's trying to console me.

"Bhili told me," she says. "Is that why you've been so moody?"

"What did Bhili tell you?"

Thara drapes her arms around me. "That there's treasure in Vegas-Drowned. That we can go get it with her . . . if we're willing to dive."

I don't speak. The rain drones on: *tap, tap, tap* against the polywood railing.

"Are you thinking about going?" Thara asks.

"No."

"Dad would have wanted us to go."

"No. Dad would have wanted to go *himself.*"

"It's the same thing."

"It's not, Thara." I take two steps back from her. "Dad didn't dive so he could get rich and stop one day. He didn't do it for *us.* He did it for *himself.* If Dad ever dug up five hundred coin, he'd just be diving down the next day to find five hundred more."

"How did it feel when you dove into the bay seven months ago?"

Wonderful, terrifying.

"Terrifying," I say.

Thara exhales. "We don't have to be like Dad. We can take the money, move to Flagstaff. Clouds, with that kind of money, we could make our way to Albuquerque or Denver." She draws a long breath through her nose. "You'd never have to smell the salt again."

Which is a delicious thing to imagine, but it's not reality.

"Whole world's an ocean, Thara. There's no running from it."

She scoffs. "Well, I'm going with her. You make your choice."

"Over my dead, bloated body."

"You don't get to decide for me, Jin. It's not just about *you* avoiding conscription. I'll turn eighteen one day too. This may be *my* only chance."

I swipe my hand across the railing, sloshing off the rain. "Thara, we unlock those suits, Bhili's gonna kill us and take them for herself."

"Kill us? You really don't know her at all, do you?"

"I don't know her? Thara, that stain on the parlor floor, the one you noticed from a few days ago . . ."

"Yeah."

"It's the mopped-up blood of a man. Someone Bhili killed; knifed in the neck. He came around looking for the map to her supposed treasure. She gutted him, sunk him to the bottom of the bay, and now he's food for the anthros."

"I know," Thara says. "She told me."

I blink. Twice. "So what are we having this discussion for?!"

"Doesn't change anything, Jin. I trust her."

"You trust her! She's a murderous old gripper two matés away from croaking. And you trust her. Based on what?"

"She's lived with us for seven months, Jin. She could have stolen from us, held us hostage, taken our generator battery, the deed to the inn. She could have forced you to unlock the suits. She could have gone after the treasure herself. She didn't. Instead, she paid us on time, a generous amount, considering she swamping near works here with all the fishing and cooking. And so what—she has a few matés."

"More than a few."

"What Coaster doesn't? She's earned our trust, Jin. Have you stopped to think why you *don't* trust her?"

"Oh, come off it, Thara."

She steps forward, inches from me, looking up. "I'm going to tell you something now, and I need you to hear me—really hear me." She closes her eyes and opens them again. "Dad's dead, Jin. He's gone, but he didn't die as some sick way to betray you. He didn't plan to leave you with the awful burden of me and the inn. It just happened. Same thing with Taim. He wasn't trying to leave you. He just got into the Guard. You should be happy for him."

"Don't bring that up, Thara."

"Clouds above, Jin. He apologized for not telling you sooner. Let it go."

"Shut up, Thara. You don't know a thing about it."

Thara clenches her jaw and her unblinking eyes burn holes into mine. "You think the whole world is out to deceive you, to do you in. It's not. Bad things happen, yeah. But there are also good things, good people. There are people who care about us. But if you don't stop questioning them; if you don't find the courage to trust someone . . . well, you're gonna have a life that's not even worth living."

I squeeze my eyes closed, rain and tears coursing down my face. My teeth are ground together, my fists clenched at my sides, my breath swirling a storm in my chest. *She has no right.* "Go inside, Thara," I say through the smallest crack in my lips. "Go inside before I do something that would make Dad ashamed."

I stand out on the balcony for several minutes after Thara leaves. My boiled blood returns to core temperature. Sogging curse of the rain to have a younger sister like this. I sheltered her too much these last years. She doesn't have a clue what it takes to survive: how careful I've had to be, how ruthless, how calculating.

When our generator battery needed a top up at the Sedona Hydro Plant—who did the journey under cover of night to make sure it wasn't stolen?

When that creepo boat dealer offered coin to pet Thara's hair—who found someone to break his nose and send him sailing?

When I borrowed money off that disgusting loan shark so I could pay Thara's school bills, who got the deed to the inn back the day before the loan came due? We could have lost everything. But I came up with the idea for the first *Evening at the Admiral's,* and I kept Thara in school, and we survived.

We survived . . .

A long, exhausted breath escapes from my mouth, and the rain rattles away on our roof. It pills on my hairline, dripping down my forehead. I crane my head back, letting the rage melt away as I stare up at the dense gray mass of clouds. Five hundred years of oppression beneath those things. Five hundred years.

Like all the world's great mysteries, we have invented stories to explain the clouds. The official story is that the Stitching happened in the mid–twenty-first century, caused by a climatologist, Maxwell Virectensun, when he dropped a billion microscopic sensors into the atmosphere. The idea was to better predict rainfall, flash floods, hurricanes, all weather events. There was something called Climate Change making weather more extreme (kinda laughable now). With the sensors, scientists could isolate weather to the minute, to the exact geo-location. Cloud technology, they called it. Idiots. According to the theory, the sensors caused a chain reaction that fused the clouds together, unleashing the torrent of water torture we still suffer under.

Most Coasters don't believe it. There's countless scientific holes. With the sun blocked, what causes the evaporation that fills the clouds? How have oxygen levels maintained with most soil and forests gone? Why has the world not plunged into a frigid darkness? And where does all the additional water come from?

It's not the science that causes people concern, though. Mariners and Coasters know swamp all about science. Most can't afford school. The reason they doubt the Maxwell Theory is something more base, more instinctual. It's a feeling you get from watching the rain fall, the waters rise; they flood our lands, claim our homes, drown our families. There's too much intent, too much purpose.

There's a relentless nature to the rain. And relentless things are not caused by chance. *Water makes its own plans*, Coasters say. And though they won't speak it, everyone knows those plans. Five hundred years since the Stitching, and there's only one desire the clouds can have.

To drown our world completely.

As those thoughts fade, the clouds plunk a drop directly into my right eye. I blink rapidly until my eye clears, my vision settling back upon the thick fog that coats the bay. The faint yellow light of a trawler pushes through the mist, foghorn blaring again and again. The sound rebounds across my own thoughts, my ears ringing, my head aching, and Thara's words return to me: *This may be* my *only chance.*

Her only chance to avoid conscription, to make a different life, to move inland. And what have I been thinking? About the choices that *I* wanted to make, the promise *I* made myself not to dive again, about what *I* could live with.

Could I even stop her if I wanted to? What would it take? Kick Bhili out, tie Thara to her bedframe for a few weeks? I shouldn't even be thinking it. Even if I had the right, I wouldn't trade our relationship to protect her.

Though I'd trade most everything else.

I step inside and eye the slanted bookshelf above the sofa. We don't have many books. They're frail things in our rain-drenched world, but Dad considered them very special, and he bartered wreck-found souvenirs for a few. That's how he acquired his favorite, and I pull down the dark red binding with an embossed golden lotus flower—*The Holy Vedas*.

"The words are thousands of years old," Dad used to say, like the sheer immensity of that fact could not be overstated. Dad's copy is an English translation, well worn, and I open it now, gently flipping to another favorite Rigveda passage of his: Book X, Hymn IX. This is the prayer I spoke for Dad after he died, when I released his body from the suit and left him in the deep.

O Waters, teem with medicine to keep my body safe from harm,
So that I long may see the Sun. Whatever sin is found in me,
whatever evil I have wrought, If I have lied or falsely sworn,
Waters, remove it far from me. The Waters I this day have
sought, and to their moisture have we come.

My chest swells, reading those words, thinking of Dad, and my eyes pass over that middle line again: *If I have lied or falsely sworn.*

Goosebumps erupt on my skin, because I have done both.

I did that freedive, and I tried to hide it from Thara. I swore to myself that I'd never dive again. But perhaps my falseness is not that I broke my oath . . . but that it never should have been made in the first place.

Waters, remove it far from me.

Dad entered the water almost every day of his life. To go wrecking, yes. He loved the search. And in many ways, it was beyond reckless. Doing something that dangerous, for so many years, when he had two young kids.

It wasn't just the thrill that Dad loved, though. It was the water itself.

When Dad stepped outside the inn, he'd crane his neck and let the rain scatter on his face. When he was out on our inflatable, he'd cup a hand to the sea, raise it high, and let the water dribble off his bald head.

As a kid, I thought him foolish. We're soaked beneath a torrent all day long, why pour more over yourself? But I think that mindset gave Dad a kind of power. Most Coasters curse the clouds and the rain, but Dad did something else. He let the water wash over him, he entered it, he took a thing that most people fear—and he sought it out.

To their moisture have we come.

That made Dad tremendously brave. And maybe I've lost that, maybe I still fear the water. I don't want to dive—I tried, and I almost drowned, and I'm still scared to death of entering it again.

But Thara's not.

Her words come back to me: *I want to use the suits. You're the one who's too scared to put them on.*

And if that's the case, if she has the type of bravery Dad had, well, who am I to deny her? Sister, guardian, it doesn't matter. If Thara really wants to go, then I only have one choice—to go with her. I'll still try to convince her out of it. I don't trust Bhili—I just don't. But if she's determined to go, then I'll be there too. I need to make sure that whatever plans the water has for us, I honor my real oath to Dad. I made the same promise over and over, every time Dad dove, every time he knew he may not come back.

I promised to keep Thara safe.

When I step into the parlor later that morning, Bhili is already there, sitting legs-crossed on the lawn, flipping one of her few remaining coins. She looks up at me, squinting with one eye, takes a big slug from the maté in her other hand, and says, "You're thinkin' about it. I can smell it on you."

I can't help but snipe back. "What I'm thinking is that I should have booted you into the rain long ago."

"But you didn't." She wags her finger. "And now we're in deep." She flicks the coin again, high into the air, catching it on top of a scarred hand. Then she tucks the coin into her shirt pocket and looks me square in the eye. "Ready to go a little further?"

"What's the plan?" I say, finally speaking the words she desires.

Bhili erupts in laughter, and after several moments, slows, spitting into her maté. "For so long you wouldn't hear of it. Now: what's the plan." She cackles and spits again. "Plan is, you get a drone out to that handsome Coasty boyfriend of yours."

"Taim? He's not my boyfriend."

"Whatever you say, but Thara tells me not-your-boyfriend been diving with the Guard."

"Sure, but—"

"So, we need him. And when he comes, that's when I tell you the plan."

7

Four weeks after the sinking of the-man-formerly-known-as-Pew, and that rusted utility boat slinks into our dock carrying Taim and his lackey, Saanvi (never should have cohosted a party with that fool), both in blue-and-white ponchos and Coast Guard fatigues.

I'm ankle deep in spume, the air's misty, and the sky has a black-dappled look with dense pockets of vapor all thick, dark, and wet. March is cloudburst month in Coconino, and every few hours it's—*crack, crack, crack*—thunder erupts from above and rain pours down like a well from the sky.

I sent a drone out to Taim ten days ago, which was super annoying after all *his* talk of writing and lack of actual . . . *Whatever. Over it.* Bhili paid for the drone, and Taim said he was finishing up training on a dive tour. He needed a few days to wrap, but then he had graduation and two weeks leave after. He was excited for us to have some "quality time" to "talk things through."

Mm-hmm.

Anyway, I used the days well. Thara and I mostly made up. In the forty-eight hours after I said I'd hear the plan, Thara hugged me about fifteen times. I haven't processed everything she said, but she's my sister. We're all we have. And besides, she's been cooking every dish I like; the inn's smelled like a pungent spice shop as Thara served up prawns thokku, whole bass Malabar, Amritsari flounder.

I still have no idea what the plan entails. So backward. Thara and Bhili spent each evening poring over crumpled papers from Bhili's chest. Whenever I approached, they hushed up and said all would be revealed shortly. *Who's not the trusting type now, Thara?* Fourteen years of loyal sisterhood thrown away when a gripper promises you riches.

Stars and moon.

Well, I'm standing on our dock as storm clouds crackle above, black waters churn in front of me, and Taim lashes his boat to our cleats. He looks incredible, like he added another ten pounds of raw muscle. In moments, he's leaping onto the dock, and I'm hating him all over as he says, "So you did miss me?"

Arrogant and beautiful. The worst pairing.

Bhili and Thara said not to get into much in the drone. Keep it short and sweet and say that I wanted to see Taim. Smart, given his first instinct on seeing Bhili was, *She's a corsair; be careful.* Still, Bhili and Thara didn't quite understand the implication of the vague "I want to see you" drone, which was essentially: sex, please.

"What's Saanvi doing here?" I say, as if I'm expecting some private romantic encounter. "No offense, Saanvi."

"None taken," Saanvi says. "I'm just dropping off the *lieutenant* here."

"You made lieutenant?" I say, astounded. "You've been training with the Guard for eight months!"

"Lieutenant junior grade, but yeah. They give it to a few of the cadets who graduate with honors." Taim winks.

It's really annoying how well his life is going.

"You look good, Jin," Taim says.

Such a line. Compliments will get him nowhere.

"Is that right?" I say. *"How* do I look good?" *Try to compliment me, best bring some specifics.*

Taim stares at me for a while. It's not some body scan, though; his eyes are just glued to mine. Finally he says, "You look strong. I always liked that. Like you could stand right here and make the bay back down if it tried to rise over you."

Wouldn't that be something.

I hold my arms up and flex. Don't have Taim-level muscles, but I am strong, and it's nice to hear him say that.

He laughs, walking up to me.

"Go on," I say, getting all kinds of reckless. "Feel one."

Taim cups a hand over my right bicep. His fingers are slick

on the yellow sleeve of my coat. He squeezes lightly. "It's good," he says. And there's a pounding deep in my chest that senses the unspoken words between us.

We were good.

"Anyway . . ." Saanvi shouts from the boat. "I'll be taking off now. I'm sure you have a *very* busy afternoon planned."

That jars me back to reality, and I pull myself together. "There's no need," I say. "You can both come up for a tea."

Confusion passes over Taim; three lines crease his brow.

Then a raspy voice calls down from two landings up the dock stairs. "Good idea, Jinny! That boy's a ship's mechanic, yeah? We'll be needin' one a them."

I turn, and of course she would be there: Bhili, slugging down tea in a chipped pastel mug. She pulls the black knife from her boot and jabs it up the bluff toward the inn. "All three of you get up there. Now!"

"All right, talk," Taim says.

We're seated in five chairs around the card table on the lawn. A kettle pours out steam in the middle of us, a jar of loose-leaf green tea beside it. I always hated green loose leaf; millions of tiny flecks end up in your teeth. Thara loves the stuff. *Green tea gives you long-lasting energy*, she says. *It has caffeine, L-theanine, and it absorbs quickly.*

Uh-huh, uh-huh, uh-huh.

Bhili scoops a mound of tea leaves and tucks them between her lip and gumline. *No wonder her mouth is so black.*

When no one says anything, Taim leans forward, puts his hand over mine, and says, "What is it? Are you in trouble?" His eyes shift to Bhili, who's fingering the lump of tea leaves in her mouth.

Finally, Bhili comes to, saying, "Quite the opposite!" She wipes a saliva-wet finger across her tattered blouse. "Me and Thara would like to present you with an opportunity. No doubt you aware I been payin' for my stay at the Bhargav with these pretties." Bhili pulls one of her gold coins from her shirt pocket. "For five years now, I been scoopin' few a these outta Vegas-Drowned. A year back, though, I found myself something special—a big ole vault full of coin. I've been looking for the right team to go back with me and get it. Proud to say, I found them. This right here is the crew."

Taim, Saanvi, and I stare back, and all I can think is: *us?* My fourteen-year-old sister, a gambling addict, my came-here-for-quality-time ex, and me, the swore-on-my-dead-father's-watery-grave-that-I'd-never-dive-again innkeeper?

Thankfully, Taim pipes in. "Okay, I've heard enough. Saanvi, let's cruise. We can hop across the bay and get a few dice rolls in at Agua Fria." Then he stands up, pats the back of my hand twice, and says, "No hard feelings, Jin. Just be direct next time."

No hard feelings? How swamping magnanimous.

I'm looking directly through him in that way that means *suck a puddle.*

Saanvi stands, and Thara elbows Bhili, who harrumphs loudly, little bits of loose leaf spraying out of her mouth as she says, "I ain't done with my proposal."

"Well, we are," Taim says.

"You ain't curious how much is down there?"

Saanvi's whole face scrunches up. It's kinda cute actually. Boyish with his clean-shaven cheeks and side part. I can see him calculating something. It's part of why he likes to gamble: He likes guessing games. Odds. Though his face also betrays every emotion inside him.

"Wait, don't tell me," Saanvi says. "I'm thinking. Hmm, you're paying one coin a month; you've been here eight months or so; Vegas-Drowned; gotta dive; need a crew. Maybe fifty on the low and five hundred coins on the high?"

"This boy's good," Bhili says. "Very good. Fifty is exactly what it is. Fifty *thousand.*"

The room gets very still, just the sound of Bhili sucking on her wad of tea leaves. Saanvi looks like he may be ill. He pulls a chair, sits back down, his face starting to sweat with just the mention of such a large haul.

As for me, well, I was expecting something a bit ludicrous. Bhili said my share alone would be five hundred. Still, fifty thousand? How do you even make sense of a number like that? The inn itself is worth maybe five hundred ounces. Bhili's coins are two ounces each. So that's like two hundred inns? Or twenty really nice inns? A share of *that* is not just enough to dodge conscription. It's enough for a private security team, or better yet, enough to buy a hill in the Rockies where future generations of Haldars can prepare for the end of days when the seas finally swamp these miserable remnants of continents.

Thunder erupts outside, and the entire inn shakes. Rain falls down like barrels, exploding on our roof—three or four cloudbursts in quick succession. I glance out the bay-side windows at the clouds as another thought takes hold.

Maybe that's enough for a trip to see the sun.

"Is a lotta goldies, I know it is," Bhili says in about the most sober statement I've ever heard her make.

"I thought you said our share would be five hundred?" I say.

"Five hundred was just a number I put out so as not to spook you, Jinny. Now, the real pot's fifty thousand. And I'm willing to go even splitsies on it. Fifth, fifth, fifth, fifth, fifth. Ten thousand each."

Taim raps his knuckles against the table. "And we just take your word on it? You know they teach this scam at cadet training? Corsairs run it eight ways to port. Step one is to cozy up to some rose-tinted Coasters in need of hope and adventure.

Promise a big reward, get them out on the open sea. Next thing you know, those pretty little innkeepers are in the hold of a corsair's frigate, and the real reward is ransom being paid to the pirates."

That's true. I've heard tales like that whispered around tea-bars. Still, it doesn't seem the smartest play. Thara and I have no other family that we know. Not sure who'd pay our ransom.

Bhili seems unperturbed. She swallows the lump of tea in her mouth, bares her teeth—which look like they were just brushed with some kind of kelp-paste—and says, "Ain't no need to take my word. Just sit down and take a look at my map."

Thara pulls a packet of large faded blue papers from below the table. *Never should have let her spend so much time with Bhili.* She spreads them open and on the first is a frontal schematic of a giant rectangular building, at least thirty floors, and with the left and right sides of the building angled forward. In the top left of the gridded drawing are these words: *Treasure Island Hotel and Casino, Blueprint and Architectural Designs.*

"I took these out of an archive in Carson City. This here's a gambling den. Big one. Before the drowning, Vegas had a lot of these swindle shops. People came from all across the Archipelago to run their luck, lose their money. Now these places kept a lotta goldies on hand, case they needed to pay out. Required as law and such and such. I read it in several books."

"You can read?" I say in disbelief.

"Don't insult me, Jinny. Now, after the switch to the gold standard, each casino started stamping they own coins, using them as chips, keep the weights uniform, all that. Mostly, they stored 'em in shared underground vaults." Bhili flips several pages forward. "See here, this the foundation, all concrete. Now, I read me histories." Thara places several bound books on the table. "And most of the casino gold got plucked out straight away when Vegas first went under, round about one hundred and fifty years back.

"But Treasure Island was different. You see, Treasure Island's a corsair casino, named after a tale of the most bravest corsairs ever to sail the single sea. And being a corsair casino, they ain't trust nobody, except they own vault. Now many histories say the owners ain't anywhere nearby during the big deluge of 2388, when the east side of Vegas succumbed. So they decide to keep the coin in the vault, untils about a time as they could go fetch it."

Bhili leans in to the card table, speaking almost at a whisper now, and we all lean in with her.

"Rumor has it, the owners, they never fetch the gold. Had enough stashed away elsewhere, they decide to leave it as a gift for future generations of entrepreneur buccaneers, divers of fortune. Well, I say to each of you here. Is high time we take our swipe at the future!" Bhili smashes her open palm down on the card table and every one of us jumps (as do our mugs).

"You really think it's in there?" Saanvi says, near drooling.

"Don't just think it, know it," Bhili says, holding up one of the fat coins she's been paying with. "But you don't have to take my word. Is in all the books." Bhili nods at the stack of blue bindings in front of Thara.

"And you have the lats and longs on the tower?" Saanvi says.

"Aye," Bhili says. "I do."

Devices that can isolate latitude and longitude are one of the great rediscoveries of modern times. The technology was lost when satellites got knocked out during the Stitching. Then, two hundred years ago, the American Archipelago started flying small solar powered drones in circumnavigation routes. They charge above the clouds, but fly mainly below to communicate with ground stations, and they can be pinged by personal geo-location devices (like the ones in my dive watch or our atmo suits).

"Why us?" Taim says.

"Easy enough. This here the crew with the two things we need: pair a dive suits"—Bhili shoots a look my way—"and a Coast Guard passport that gets us through the cordon at Vegas-Drowned." Her gaze shifts to Taim and Saanvi.

Taim looks away, biting his lip. "Let's say we can get through. How do we know for certain—not books, rumors, hearsay—how do we know, for sure, that it's down there?"

Bhili slugs back her tea and clops the mug down, her eyes twinkling as she meets Taim's gaze. "You know because three months before I show up at the Bhargav, I was on a dive with friends in Vegas-Drowned. That's when I found the vault. And it ain't been opened."

Taim spends the better part of the afternoon at our inn poring over the prints, flipping through the books, shooting probing questions at Bhili.

Why didn't you open the vault last time? "Ain't have the right tools for the job. That's why we need your boy Saanvi. Mechanics got access to all kinda pokey things."

Why don't you just go back to Vegas with your other friends? "They're, let's say, a little preoccupied now. Besides, for a haul this big, we need a proper craft, run by a right good Coasty like you who can steer us through the cordon."

What floor is the vault on? "No, no, no. If I tell you the location of the vault, why you need pretty Bhili? No, I'll tell you once we on the dive."

Saanvi hangs around for the afternoon too, though he seems much less interested in the plot. He just keeps ogling the Treasure Island coin, knuckle-rolling it up and over his long, thin fingers.

I pull Thara aside several times, trying to dissuade her of

this thing. I remind her that we swore off diving, that Dad died diving, that I almost died freediving, that we're more than likely going to get nabbed by the Coast Guard (probably what happened to Bhili's friends), and that, even more likely, the gold is just not there.

She's not having a word of it, which I expected, but is no less annoying. Finally, late in the afternoon, Thara leads me back to the blueprints of the casino, trying to talk me through the specifics of the dive, how we're in and out in an hour, blah blah, and all the while something is poking me in my back.

Well, not my back exactly. My shirt's riding up as I'm bent over the table, and a finger is poking me in that pocket of flesh just below my back right waistline . . . where my sun tattoo is. I whip around, and Bhili's smiling wide, her finger outstretched. She says, "Anyone ever tell you the Sun Shines Within, Jinny?"

The Sun Shines Within is a religious group who believe we should stop yearning for the sun, stop trying to figure out how to blow the clouds out of the sky (there's been a lot of attempted "cloud dispersal" over the years—none of it effective). Instead, we need to just focus on the inner warmth and beauty inside us all.

"Please don't tell me you're one of those cult crazies," I say.

Bhili looks aghast, and then she bellows, finally chugging some tea to settle herself. "Me? No, never held with such foolishness. But why do you have a sun tattoo? Only folks I know has them is the cult crazies, as you put it, or people who fancy seeing the sun."

I bite my lip. "It was a dream I had once . . . seeing the sun. I got the tattoo then."

A year ago, when I was in love, when I thought anything was possible.

"Sad that," Bhili says. "Cause with ten thousand goldies, you could make your way up above the clouds, no problem."

"How's that?" I say way too quickly.

"Well, you know I's born near Delhi-Below. Quite a few peaks in the Himalayas that pierce them clouds. I've a friend, she lives in Southern Nevada now, she made the journey. She one of them industrial types. Lots of businesses. Not all of them legal, but one she call sun-tourism. Helps rich folk see the sun."

"What's *tourism*?" Saanvi says, scrunching up his face.

"Is like how rich people travel for pleasure," Bhili says, "not just for stealing and swindling and such. Point is, you want to see the sun, Jinny—my friend could take you . . . if you have ten thousand coin in your pocket."

Saanvi places the Treasure Island coin on the card table, flicks it until it's spinning round like the Earth. He cracks one of his easy smiles. "We're gonna need some bigger pockets."

8

Two days later and we're on the Huynhs' twelve-seater deck
boat, hauling out to Tonto Island. Thara, Taim, Saanvi, and
Bhili are scattered about the boat, along with our red-white
exoskeleton dive suits, air tanks, and two dry bags with spare
clothing and Bhili's maps. Suong's at the conn with Nhu near
the rudder, their hair flattened by the terrible speed we're
cruising at. *I'm telling their mom about this; Suong needs to slow
down.* I'm at the bow, thankful for my quarter-inch buzz, and
Thara's squeezed into the driver's seat with Suong, looking
like a black hurricane took hold of her hair.

The rain's holding at a light mist, which makes the trip
bearable with the top down. It's sixty-five miles out to Tonto,
and the Huynhs make the round trip twice a week to fetch
supplies for their market. Bhili offered them a quarter ounce
for the ride, but Suong refused, saying she'd take Thara anywhere her heart desired.

Kid literally said that. *Rust take me.*

The plan's fairly simple: A pit stop in Tonto where we secure berths on a private vessel that's running up to the Gulf of Nevada. That's a two to three day cruise, depending on the ship. From there we do two nights on Mojave Main, a littoral island eighty miles south of Vegas-Drowned, where Bhili picks up a third diving suit from a friend (she keeps insisting she has friends) and Taim requisitions a local Coast Guard patrol boat from an outpost called Castle Mountain. Then it's a day trip into Vegas-Drowned at dawn, where Bhili, Taim, and I dive down to Treasure Island, haul out this non-existent gold, and then we all get on with our lives.

I'm still rather astounded that Taim went for the plan. Saanvi, sure, the man craves coin like a barnacle sucks hull. But Taim? It's a risk to his newfound position with the Guard. He needs to be doubly sure we don't get caught.

He jumps into the seat next to me as Suong lowers the throttle to take us past a giant float of sargassum, a stringy brown seaweed that mounds and forms rafts in the open water. The stuff reeks of sulfur, like rotted-out gull's eggs, and I pinch my nose.

"Like the view?" Taim asks.

"Better than the aroma." My voice is two octaves higher from the nose clamp.

He leans in to me and breathes deeply. "You're right, you smell horrible."

I shove him back, which he seems very pleased about. "Why are you here?" I say, glancing behind me. Bhili's aft ship, near Nhu. "I know you don't like her. Bhili, I mean. And you don't trust her."

"Right on both accounts."

"Then?"

"The gold, same as you," Taim says. "Gotta get it. Otherwise, you'll stay anchored to that inn till you drown with it." He stares at me beneath those long lashes, and I'm thinking that, if I act fast, I could reach out and rip 'em straight off his eyelids.

It's not funny. It's maybe a little bit true—but it's not funny.

"I'm not here because I want to escape the inn," I say. "That *is* something I'm going to do—one day—but it's not why I'm here."

"Why are *you* here, then?" Taim says.

I sigh. "Once Thara has conviction on a thing, she'll sail inches from the wind to achieve it. If she's going, I'm going."

Taim nods. "It's the same for me, you know."

"What?"

"Can't let someone I care about do this alone," Taim says.

And I hate myself, because for a split second I think, *Me? Does he mean me?*

Then Taim winks (his least attractive facial gesture), and says, "Somebody's gotta look out for Saanvi."

Of course. *Swamping Saanvi.*

I let that sink in for a few moments while we float past the sargassum. Then I cock my head back toward Taim. "Is that really it? The whole reason you're here. I know you. That's not how you work."

He looks away, and his eyes glaze over, like he's peering inside himself. The boat picks up speed, and the wind rustles in my ears.

"You can still talk to me," I say, unsure why he's so hesitant.

After several moments, Taim's eyes focus, the air clears, and his voice is trembling with emotion. "I don't even remember Mommy. I was five when they took her. At some point, I realized all my memories are just stories Auntie told me. I—I guess you know that feeling."

I swallow because Thara and I know that *exact* feeling.

"Mamá was different. I was eight. I remember when she taught me to swim, her arms seemed impossibly long, so powerful, like she could cup her hands and move the entire bay. I remember the way she smelled too—like these dried water poppies that she'd rub behind her ears. I remember this sweet coffee she brewed in a clay pot, café de olla. It was a treat one New Year's with some grated cinnamon. She learned to brew it from her mother in Durango."

Taim pauses, and I don't speak. He never talks about his moms.

"When the Navy came for Mamá, she recorded her voice on

a Reader that I still have. She had the most beautiful voice, so melodic—perfect for storytelling."

He's so lucky to have that.

"In the message she left me, her tone is much firmer. She said there are two kinds of power in this world. Authority— the power to make someone's decisions. And money—the power to buy someone's decisions. She told me to find one. Never leave myself weak."

I shift slightly closer to him, so our legs are touching.

"After this trip," he says, "I'm going to have both."

Music blares from several mounted flagpole speakers as we pull up to Tonto. Thumping bass vibrates through my body like I've entered a Flagstaff disco. Coconino folk call Tonto the Pilgrim's Party Island, and true to name, boats and people of every size, shape, and color swarm the floating wharf. Pontoons, sailboats, multi-hulls, sportfishers, trawlers, yachts, whalers . . . there are several dozen craft, all coated in lurid shades like aquamarine, and most with wealthy boaters dancing on deck in bikinis and tight trunks.

Suong pulls our outboard up as we ease into the marina. The smell of grilled seafood wafts over us, and twisting veins of smoke rise from corrugated metal stalls that line the island just beyond the wharf. Past the market, the terrain climbs through a densely packed town that stretches along the shoreline. In the distance, the island plateaus, and there I can just make out the tip of the giant glass pyramid that makes Tonto such an alluring destination for the rich and superstitious.

Bhili marches up to the bow. "First trip to the Pilgrim's Pyramid?" she says to me.

"No, I've been a few times."

"Ever touched one of them beads?"

The pyramid is filled with little glass beads that supposedly fell out of the sky when the Navy attempted a cloud dispersal fifty years ago.

I wrinkle my nose. "That bilge? No, Dad and I used to come hawk some of our wreck-found goods."

"Aye, well then—you ain't truly been," Bhili says. "I prayed to them beads once. Round about twenty years ago, I laid down before it and asked the great pyramid for a long, dry life."

Saanvi shuffles over from down the bench. "How'd it respond?" he asks earnestly.

Gamblers are always the superstitious type.

Bhili throws an arm around Saanvi's neck and knuckles his side part until it's a shiny black mess. "Pyramid responded by saying—nothin'. Because it's a cuttlefish con run by them lousy locals."

I nod, for once agreeing with her. "I was not expecting you to say that."

"Course I would," Bhili says, releasing Saanvi from his

headlock. "They charged me an eighth ounce just to kneel down there. Coulda gotten myself well shook on matés for that."

Suong eases us into a slip, and then we're up against the bumper. Bhili's out first, and then the rest of us hop onto wobbling planks as a group of urchin kids run up, shouting:

"Tour? Want a tour?"

"You come to pray? I'll give you a special rate."

"Low price. Best price. All prayers answered. We guarantee!"

Bhili swats at them. "Shoo, shoo—we ain't prayin', ya little demons."

One of the kids kicks Bhili in the shins, and then they all run off. Bhili's about to run after them too, until Taim snatches her forearm.

"Let them go," Taim says, pure command.

"Lousy, good for nothin' child swindlers," Bhili mutters, then she sticks her nose into the air, sniffing. "That grilled squid? Who's coming with me for some squid?"

Taim steps onto a crate next to us, rolling his eyes. "Right. So, while Bhili's eating squid, the rest of us need to find five berths, beds if we can get 'em, seats if we must. How much coin can we offer, Bhili?"

"Well, I has eight ounces . . . though gonna need a few bits for the squid, so—"

"Okay, so eight at the most," Taim says. "Start at two, and we'll leave the suits here. Folks see those, and they'll charge us triple."

"I'm not leaving our suits," I say. "They're the most valuable things we own."

"We can leave them with Suong," Thara says.

I swivel toward Thara. "Not happening. And it's time for Suong and her sister to leave."

Thara shoves me in the shoulder. "Don't be an ass, Jin." Then she turns, plants a big kiss on Suong, who goes crawfish red. "Thank you again for dropping us off. Time for you to leave, though."

"You sure?" Suong pleads.

Thara smiles. "I'll be back in a few days."

"I'm going to finish the lyrics," Suong says. "For the one about you."

"That sounds nice," Thara replies, as if she has dozens of people writing music for her.

Suong and Nhu step back into their boat, and Suong's eyes stay locked on Thara.

My eyes find Bhili's, and we exchange this weird parental look, like, *Our little Thara. How many broken hearts will she leave in her wake?*

"As I was saying," Taim continues, still on his crate-perch. "We need to find berths, and—"

"Good planning, Lieutenant." Bhili salutes Taim. "You and the gambler do that. Jinny, Thara—let's go get us some squid."

We're standing beneath a row of umbrella carts, squid grill behind us, calamari skewers in our hands, dozens of people streaming down the main road between us and the wharf. Saanvi and Taim are working the wharf, quay by quay, trying to find passage, but Bhili had the right idea here because the squid's delicious and we're lounging, sheltered from the rain, with our dry bags and the atmo suits broken down and piled in a pair of handbarrows we borrowed from the wharf.

Atmo suits are swamp-all heavy. Normal scuba suits are light: just neoprene, the air tank, BCD, regulator, mask, fins—fifty pounds at the most. The hard-shell exoskeleton of an atmo suit, however, lets you dive thousands of feet to the ocean bottom. It maintains interior pressure at one atmosphere, but it also weighs one hundred and fifty pounds fully loaded (hence the handbarrows).

"Eight oktas today," the grillman says. He's pale, bald, with blond eyebrows, an oil-smeared apron, and a dense frame.

Bhili nods, chomping on her calamari. "Seen any bionics pass through?"

The man lifts his pant leg, flashing a silver foot.

Bhili claps him across the back. "How you lose it?"

"Colossal squid ripped it off when I was doing a tour with

the Navy. Now I cook up their cousins."

Bhili laughs. "You's a sly old grillman."

"Stupid squids are too smart for they own good," the grillman says. "Probably build they own civilizations when we all dead and gone."

"Ain't that the truth," Bhili says, slurping a tentacle down. "Well, you know what I always say: revenge the best healer, two wrongs make a right, and them that needs gettin' gonna get theirs soon."

"Couldn't of said it better myself," the man says, then he kicks out and swipes Bhili's legs out from under her. She lands with a crack, and the man throws an elbow into my face, sending me toppling over as well. I hit the ground, shoulder first, then head. Black spots in my vision, the right side of my face pulsing, and I'm blinking, blinking, until finally, my sight returns, my mind with it—*rust take me, what just happened?*

I glance up to see the man hurtling down the lane with his fingers gripping a handbarrow, *our* handbarrow, which contains . . . one of our two atmo suits!

That swamping thief!

Thara's already after him, ten paces behind. I shoot up, pounding the craggy pavement, winding through sailors, pilgrims, carts, and tuk-tuks. The grillman's quick as a sailfish, near leaping off that bionic foot, and after a few seconds of frantic running, I catch up to Thara only to realize we're losing ground on the grillman.

Really, he's a fool for attempting this. He'll only get a quarter value on the suit, as he'll pay out the rest getting the biometric lock picked. Still, I'll be facedown in a puddle before I let my legs quit the chase.

He swerves into an alley, heading inland. I glance back, no sign of Bhili, and then Thara and I cut in behind him. The alley floor's grated with troughs that lead out to the sea. It's a narrow thing, a little over an arm span in width, and the buildings on either side are well maintained, two stories high, with balconies covered in artificial plants. Nice . . . though they'll all be underwater in ten years.

If the man lives in one of these, we're screwed, because he's an entire block ahead of us. He'll dive into his apartment, lock the door, and then by the time we track down Taim, Saanvi, or a local authority, he'll be long gone.

He doesn't dive through a door, though; he keeps running straight ahead, and I can see an opening at the end of the alley. There's only one town on Tonto, the one that runs the length of the wharf, and it's perched up this bank before reaching the inland plateau that has the pyramid. The town's only five or six blocks deep, which means the man is going to be in the raised center of the island shortly, and then—

Mid-stride, I turn to Thara. "He's going to try and lose us in the pyramid crowd."

Thara nods. She knows. Middle of the day like this, there will be a throng of people, hundreds, surrounding the glass pyramid, and he's so far ahead, all he has to do is stay low and we won't be able to track him.

"Could we get up on a roof to spot him?" she says through panted breaths. The man's almost at the opening.

"You try," I say. "I'll keep on him."

Thara peels off; I'm still racing up the steep alley ahead. There's a trickle of folks, pyramid pilgrims I think, walking downhill toward me. Their backs flatten against a building as the man blows past them. He's through the alley now, onto the plateau. Farther ahead, I can see the tip of the glass pyramid rising; there's a large crowd in front of it. The man will be lost in moments.

I pass two pyramid pilgrims. One scowls at me, exposing a yellowed fang; her complexion's cloud white, and she's in an orange jumpsuit with a green beanie. She yells as I run past, "That thing he got yours?"

"Yeah!"

Then she lifts a black whistle and rips two piercing blasts on it, like an albatross scream. She points at the grillman, and I turn forward as a massive fishing hand, black matted beard, gray prawn bib, extends his arm and clips the grillman right across the ribs. He soars over the handbarrow, skidding on the pockmarked terrain, which is rocky and half-filled in with concrete (a common practice because the topsoil washed away).

I pull up alongside the handbarrow, the packed crowd massing just five paces in front of me, as the fishing hand stomps a foot down next to the grillman's head. "Run!" he commands, and the grillman does, leaving the handbarrow and my suit behind.

"Thank you," I say, my hands on my knees, my mouth sucking up air and rain. "I—what's your name?"

"Renato," the man says.

I look up and see the tip of the glass pyramid, wet and sparkling. The whole thing's maybe ten by ten by twenty feet high. The outer shell is glass and then the locals fill the inside with the little glass balls. The crowd's humming some chant, which is all part of the performance. They'll pass a pot around for collections shortly. Swamping scammers.

"You're welcome!" a woman calls from behind me, the one in the orange jumpsuit and green beanie who blew the whistle. She walks up, yelling at us, "I'm Luz. That your dive suit?"

"Yes," I say, still panting as Thara runs up.

"Good." She smiles with those yellowed fangs exposed. "I got a job for you, then. Ever been to Phoenix-Below?"

"We're not heading to Phoenix-Below," I say. "I'm never diving there again—ever." Maybe that last part comes off a little charged.

"Okay . . . ," Luz says. "Where you heading?"

"Doesn't matter."

Thara steps in front of me. "Vegas-Drowned. And we need passage."

What the— "Quiet, Thara." I pull her back by the shoulder.

"*You* be quiet, Jin. That's the whole reason we're here."

Luz adjusts her green beanie. "Dangerous place, Vegas. There's rumors about the creatures that live there." She twists her lips. "You sure you're going there? They cordoned it for a reason."

Thara wrings out her hair. "We're sure."

"Tell you what, then," Luz says. "I captain a fishing trawler. You do my job, and I'll drop you on Mojave Main just south of Vegas."

I shake my head. "No chance."

"Done," Thara says with her arm extended.

I'm so shocked by Thara's audacity that I can't find words.

Luz shakes Thara's hand. "What's your name?"

"Thara. And that's my sister, Jin."

Luz side-eyes me. "She one of them older, think-she-in-charge types?"

"Yeah," Thara says.

"Have one myself. Annoying as hell."

Am I even here?

Luz throws an arm across Thara's shoulders. "Well, it's good to make your acquaintance, Thara. Let's go get our journey blessed by the pyramid."

The hulking man Renato fills me in while we wait. Their boat, the *Saquear el Desierto*, is a high seas fishing trawler that docks in Baja California but drags the Sonoran Sea, mostly for prawns, but also some bottom-feeders: flounder, sole, and the like. Twenty-five hands in total, they're moored out on Tonto Island for a two-day respite. Luz's a pyramid worshipper, so periodically they come here to get blessed.

At last, Thara and Luz return, and we start walking toward the wharf. I'm pushing the handbarrow down a steep alley while rain pings off it and the dive suit. Renato offers to help, and he seems nice, but I'm not taking any more chances. Instead, I walk extra slow, until I'm a good thirty feet behind Luz and Renato. I hiss at Thara to get back here with me, and then I begin a very productive conversation with her.

"There is zero possibility of me diving in Phoenix-Below."

"Don't care," Thara says.

"Don't—what? Who do you think you are? You don't make these decisions."

"No, *you* don't get to make *every* decision for our *family*. I'm fourteen, Jin. I don't need your approval for every boat I get on."

"Will you stop? This is serious, Thara. Dad died in Phoenix. We don't have time for your teenage rebellion gullshit."

"Fuck you, Jin."

The words land like a slap, and the rest of the walk's done in silence. By the time we're back at the wharf, I'm fuming all over . . . which is only set off further when I see Bhili's holding a cup-a-tea and still nibbling her squid skewer.

"You could have helped!" I yell. Though the other hand-barrow is beside her.

"Bah, knew you'd catch him."

Rusting gripper.

Saanvi and Taim stalk up then, and Saanvi throws his hands in the air. "Everyone's saying ten ounces for passage. Ridiculous."

"Well, you ride with me and it's free," Luz says. Renato's beside her and he's a full head taller than everyone else.

"Who are you?" Taim asks, rolling his shoulders back, trying to stand taller himself.

Men . . .

"Name's Luz, and your girl Thara just organized passage on my ship. You do a wrecking job for me in Phoenix-Below, and I drop you on Mojave Main."

"Perfect!" Bhili says, slapping Thara on the back. "Good work, Cook!"

"I am not diving in Phoenix-Below!" I belt it out loud enough for the entire wharf to hear.

Renato claps hands over his ears.

Bhili shrugs and holds out her squid skewer. Maybe to ease the tension? Who knows, but Luz plucks a ring right off.

"I'll dive, then," Thara says.

"No, you won't. I told you I'd come on this trip, but you *do not* dive without me. That's our agreement. Break that, and I'll drag you by your toes straight back to Coconino. I'm your sister, but I'm also your guardian. I *will* have my way."

Nothing pisses Thara off more than when I pull the G-card.

"All right, all right." Bhili waves her teacup. "Jinny, I take it you're okay diving, but you don't want to do it in Phoenix where ya Daddy died. That right?"

I grunt.

"How about this? I know a sunken gem shop in Once-Havasu, small township 'bout halfway between here and Vegas-Drowned. Jin and Thara, you *both* dive down. Jinny, you'll be there to keep her safe, but one suit is Thara's, and she got a right to use it. As for our new captain, any gems we recover will be yours."

Wow. Did Bhili just broker a reasonable solution?

"Good plan," Taim says. Most complimentary thing he's ever said of Bhili.

Luz squints. "And if there aren't any gems?"

"Don't you worry about that." Bhili tears the last squid ring off with her black teeth. "Me plans don't never go wrong."

9

It's the next morning, and I'm in the middle of the Sonoran Sea, standing on the trawl deck of the two-hundred-foot, high seas fishing trawler *Saquear el Desierto*. My hands are cinched around the portside gunwale, sea spray blasts my face, the rain's coming in sideways, and the fetid stink of shellfish permeates the air in a way that I may never be rid of.

The *Desierto* is a pretty ship by fish boat standards, I'll give it that. There's a whitewashed deck, a red-painted hull, a big silver gantry with two cranes, a long trawl deck, and a tidy-looking forward wheelhouse from which the officers set course. Below the trawl deck there's a factory compartment where everything gets processed. The trawl deck itself, though—that's where the prettiness stops. Thing's as ugly as a whale's insides. The whole deck is littered in fish blood, guts, scales, eyeballs, and the detritus of the thousands of sea creatures that this boat scrapes up from the sea floor on a daily basis.

They seem good at it, at least. The ship's orderly, fifteen hands working the deck right now, plus Luz in her orange jumpsuit, green neoprene beanie, cursing out oaths and orders, stalking the deck like she's anchored to it, and the rollers hitting the bilge aren't enough to waste a wobble on.

Doesn't change the sheer stupidity of this Once-Havasu dive. Every Arizona Coaster knows Once-Havasu's dangerous—much too close to the Sonoran Vent Well. Of course, Bhili says that's what makes it so good. "Ain't been picked over, so it's ripe for the plundering." Apparently, Bhili went wrecking in Once-Havasu eight years back and found a gem shop stocked full. Perfect score, until the whole thing collapsed on top of her dive partner. Bhili's suit got damaged, she had to surface, but the gems (and her partner) are still there.

My takeaway: people who wreck with Bhili end up dead.

According to Bhili, however, all we need to do is peel through the rubble, snatch the gems, and if we find her old partner, we'll have a third suit for the Treasure Island dive.

Perfect, I think. Just the way for me to ease back into wrecking. Digging through rubble for a dead diver. Nothing triggering about that at all. . . .

I draw in a long breath of prawny air as Thara walks up on my right.

"You ready?" she says. "We'll be at Once-Havasu in ten minutes. Luz told me we can use the skiff that hangs off the poop deck. She'll drop anchor and give us three hours below."

"You should let Taim dive," I say. "It's safer."

"Will you give it up, Jin? I'm coming."

I stare off across the empty water while the ship rocks below me.

"Besides," Thara says, "Luz gave me a lucky charm."

I turn back to her, and she's pinching a tiny glass ball between thumb and forefinger. "Please don't tell me you bought that on Tonto."

"No, those folks are crooks. They charge fifteen ounces for a bead. Ridiculous. No, Luz *gave* me this one. Can you believe it? Here."

Thara hands the bead over, and it's small, like a marble, but also light as the air itself. I try to squeeze it, but it's hard, no give. Maybe some coastal fraudsters sell fake miracles, but swamp all if they don't make a damn fine glass bead. "You really think this thing's going to bring you luck?" I say, handing it back.

"Saanvi thinks it will."

"Oh, please. Saanvi'd rub the spines on an urchin if he believed it could grant him favor."

Thara shrugs. "Luz bought a whole bag of them off a local in Guadalajara ten years back. She says you can find them all over. Apparently they bring her good trawl luck, and she wants me to have one for the dive."

I try really hard not to roll my eyes. "That's great, Thara. Really great."

* * *

By the time the skiff's in the water, we've blown ourselves straight into a squall. The wind is whipping in from eight different directions, lightning splinters the horizon, thunder pounds in our ears, and ten-foot swells crash over us, threatening to sink the skiff straight down to the sunken streets of Once-Havasu.

The *Desierto*'s about a quarter mile away, but I can still make out Luz in her emergency orange, like a lit buoy on the midship platform. Before we left, I protested plenty—not exactly the best idea to go wrecking in the middle of a tempest. Luz snarled something wretched, though, pulled me in close, and said, "Ain't gonna pass. We're near the Sonoran Vent Well now. Weather'll be swirling a fury before we swing round it."

Vent wells are shafts of steaming water that shoot up from the ocean bottom. They form around hydrothermal vents in the ocean floor, and the proliferation of such vents is one of the explanations scientists have for why water keeps evaporating, filling up the clouds.

"You be fine," Luz said, yanking me free of the rigging. "The skiff's heavy-duty, and once you're under you won't feel a thing. Now, get on!" Then she hurled me a good fifteen feet toward the starboard ladder. I stumbled, slip-sliding twelve of those feet, then staggered down the ladder only to find Bhili, who winked, saying, "Just a little biter. Let's go."

Now I'm on that twelve-foot skiff in the middle of this

"biter" with our whole crew: Taim, Bhili, Saanvi, and of course, my death-wish sister, Thara. I'm not sure why everyone came. I mean, they all have excuses. Bhili says she wants to make sure we land on the exact lats and longs. Taim says he wants to double-check our dive gear. Saanvi's here for suit repairs.

Still, I get the feeling that they all just think I'm going to freak out and blow a tank down there. First time in a suit in three years, going down with my younger sister who I'm not the slightest bit overprotective of, pissed off about this whole plan to begin with. Yeah, I'm in the exact wrong headspace for this job. Everyone knows it, and that's why we're packed in here like prawns in a dragnet.

As that thought passes, I turn and see Thara puking over the side of the skiff. Bhili's holding her hair, Saanvi's at her side, Taim's at the conn, and I'm doing nothing since I'm an awful, stifling sister-guardian.

"You okay?" I shout as the whole skiff pitches beneath a wave.

Thara glances over her shoulder, nods, and wipes her mouth. Clearly she plans to show zero weakness around me. She sits back on a bench, and Saanvi offers her something while screaming against the wind.

"It's taffy!" he says. "My mom makes them from coconut and agar-agar. Been in the Guard two years, but we all get sick. Taffy gets rid of the taste, and for the nausea, Mom adds some grated—"

"Ginger?" Thara says.

"Exactly!"

"Make him give you two!" Taim shouts. "He's got at least five more in his pockets."

Saanvi smiles—that big easy smile.

Meanwhile, I'm *still* on the bench, getting whipped by the rain. Clouds above. I've been kinda hating Saanvi because he basically got Taim into the Guard. But that there with the candy? That was just plain nice.

Thara unwraps the taffy and drops it into her mouth, while Bhili glances down at the positioning device Luz loaned us. "Stop here! We're on top of it!"

Taim cuts the engine, and we bob in the waves. "Give them the lats and longs," he says.

"Yeah, yeah, I'm getting to it," Bhili says. "All right, Jinny, Thara—the shop's called Jahan Diamond Imports. We gonna drop you right down on it, but if you get turned around, just find the bridge, exit on the north side, and look for a big ole sign with the name. Building's crumbled, but the sign should be there. As for the lats and longs, you ready?"

First part of dive training is remembering lats and longs. It's a must for returning to your point of entry, and most divers use a system of memory rooms in an imagined home. Each room's assigned a number, and then the diver remembers a short, made-up story about their day, like: I cooked in the kitchen (3), ate breakfast in the parlor (6), before heading down to our dock (8), and so on. When I use the technique, I create a morning story to cover latitude, and I transition to an afternoon story for longitude.

I nod, Thara does as well, and then Bhili calls out the numbers. "Three, four, dot, four, seven, four, two, four, five North by one, one, four, dot, three, four, eight, one, nine, nine West." Bhili repeats the sequence twice, and then I start mumbling to myself until I have it. A minute later, Thara confirms the coordinates as well. Our suits will only be able to find latitude and longitude within five hundred feet of the surface, but if we get off course, we can always surface and sink again.

From there, we step down to Taim, who has the lower half of our suits assembled and ready. Stepping into the suit is terrifying. In part because the wind's cracking so hard, I feel like I'm gonna tumble into the water with half a suit on. But in larger part because the last time I put a suit on, Dad died.

Now I'm going down with Thara . . .

The suits themselves are high quality. White exoskeleton made of aluminum alloy, red synthetic carbon bindings at the joints, thruster stubs at the feet and off the arms, steel helmet with a two hundred seventy–degree viewport. The colors are faded and worn from use, but functionally the suits are in perfect condition. *(I think. Guess I'll find out shortly.)* Thara's getting into the suit Dad used to wear. The arms can retract slightly so she can reach the in-glove controls. I asked her earlier if she wanted to switch suits, and her response was, "Honestly, Jin, I think I'll have an easier time in Dad's suit than you will."

That hurts, but it's probably true. My eyes sting with tears. No one notices in the gale.

Everyone, even my own sister, thinks I'm so damaged. Obviously, I *am* damaged. Grieving Dad. Almost forfeiting the inn multiple times. Straining my relationship with Thara over the guardianship. Losing Taim to the Coast Guard.

It's all taken a toll. Still, I like to think that I'm less damaged than other people would be. Than others *think* I should be.

Taim lifts the chest plate over my head, and I swallow as he clamps it in at the waist. I'm not even underwater and I feel like I can't breathe. The front of the chest plate has a row of subaqueous lights. Those will let me see about fifty feet in any direction I'm facing.

I glance over at Thara, who looks as carefree as a clam. The storm's settled some, but it's still incredibly loud with the wind howling and the rain pinging off the dive suits. Bhili helps Thara, fitting her hands into thick metal gloves. They'll be safe and pressurized but with about a fifth of the dexterity of a normal hand.

Taim lowers my helmet down, screwing it in at the neck, but leaving the viewport open. "You sure you can handle this?" he says. "I can go. I'll look after Thara."

"Taim, I don't know how to say this without being hurtful,

but I need to tell you. I need you to understand where I am here."

"You can tell me," he says.

"The last time you were in a suit with one of my family members—they died."

He stares back at me with the saddest eyes.

"So I appreciate the thought, and I know you mean well. But, please, just don't. I will keep Thara safe. I'm the only person who can."

Taim draws a long breath. "We should call this off," he shouts over at the others. "Her head's not right. I don't want her going down there."

Thara swivels, staring at me through the viewport. "Jin?"

"No. I'm ready." I slam my viewport down and form a circle with my thumb and forefinger. It's the diver hand signal for *okay*.

Thara throws her viewport down as well. "Comm check, check."

Her voice comes through the helmet. "Loud and clear," I answer.

"What was that about?" Thara says.

"Just Taim being Taim. Thinking my head's too messed up to dive."

"Is it?"

"Is it messed up—yeah. Too messed up to dive—no."

"That's reassuring," Thara says.

"Look, you wanted to do this. I'm here for you," I say. "Let's go. Haldar sisters to the end."

"To the end," Thara says.

We flick the viewports back up, and Thara shouts over the wind. "We're ready. Hook the air tanks on."

Bhili and Saanvi carry them forward. We'll each have two tanks on our back, and the minute they're attached, I feel that heady mix of tanked air flood into the helmet. The metallic smell is like this rush of nostalgia, taking me back to a time when life was different. When I felt safe.

Diving is not safe. I *felt* safer, though. I miss that feeling.

I miss Dad.

Taim's shaking his head the entire time. "Thara, I really don't think—"

"Taim," Thara says. "We're going."

At last, he pulls cables off two winches that are bolted into the skiff. "Turn around." Taim clips them into rings on the lower backs of our suits. "You'll go down tethered. It's safest. If there's trouble—"

"No," I say. "I don't want someone else in control of when I surface."

Taim's eyes lock onto mine. "If the storm gets worse. If Luz needs us out, I need to be able to pull you up."

"No," I say.

"If you want to play it like that, I don't need to be involved in this. You four can do Once-Havasu *and* Treasure Island on your own."

"Perfect," I say.

"Stop!" Thara yells over the wind. "We *need* Taim."

That hits me, and I realize that of everyone on this crew, I'm the only one who isn't needed.

Coast Guard credentials, essential.

Map, clearly critical.

Mechanic, essential.

Fourth diver?

I'm superfluous. Redundant. Which means none of them are going to listen to shit from me. Why didn't I figure this out before? "A tether is the right way to do this," Thara says. "We're not going into buildings, so it won't be a problem."

I stare at them all but say nothing. Might as well save my breath.

"Boy knows what he's doing," Bhili says. Her tone is consoling, like she understands what I'm thinking. "Now get on. We got a lull in the vent storm, and I don't fancy getting splintered to bits when it comes back."

I tap a switch in my glove to turn my pressure on. Thara does the same. I can feel the air stiffen, the suit securing me at one atmosphere. Then I speak through the comm, "Ready?"

In response, Thara pivots on her left foot and swings back

around until she's facing the water. I do the same, and then I hold out my right hand, which she bumps with her left. The suit's haptics tingle in my glove, and we each shift our fists over our hearts. Dad taught us this. It's a diver hand signal he made up, and we used to do it before every dive. It means *I love you.*

I hold Thara in my gaze, locking her in place, willing her to understand—everything. But she breaks eye contact first, steps off the gunwale, and leaps in, the force of her jump rocking the skiff. I forgot just how strong you are in a suit—about five times typical body strength, though dexterity and out-of-water mobility are severely limited.

I let Thara sink for several seconds. Then, without a glance back at Taim, I leap in myself.

My feet enter first, my body plunging straight down, and in moments, the world fades to black. Comm range is fifty feet, so I won't be in touch with Thara until we're on the ocean bottom. Neither of us will be able to communicate with Taim, Bhili, and Saanvi. Diving is a lonely business, and no matter how many people you dive with, your survival depends almost entirely on yourself.

Is my mind right? I hope it is.

There's an instrument panel inlaid into my right glove, which controls most functions in the suit: thrusters, lights, comms, pressure, viewport dashboard. I flick on the viewport, and a series of digital readouts print across the shield. The viewport displays latitude, longitude, depth (feet below sea level), speed (feet per second), air remaining (hours and minutes left), pressure (percentage), battery level (percentage), date, time, and compass.

I set the display in a resting mode, so it's out of my field of vision, but the suit has me descending five feet per second, which is a bit fast.

The suit's withstanding dozens of atmospheres of pressure on the outside. I burst the foot thrusters a few times to slow myself. Best to ease the suit down. It's been several years since it's seen work, and if the stress is too great, I want to know *before* I'm several thousand feet under.

After a few minutes, I'm approaching the five-hundred-foot barrier where latitude and longitude will stop working. I've kept myself right on the coordinates. Fairly straightforward with a tethered descent, but there are currents, and you can get pushed around if you're not careful. *Start on course, end on course*, as Dad used to say.

From there, I increase the speed of my dive and center myself, maintaining calm, breathing evenly, and reducing my heart rate to conserve air. This job should be two hours at the most, and we have two full tanks—that's eight hours of air. Still, there are certain best practices you follow no matter how wide the margin for error. When wreckers die, eight out of ten times it's due to oxygen deprivation. The root cause is often immobility, but in the end, you die because you can't breathe.

After about fifteen minutes, my depth reads 3,400 feet. Pressure's still at 100 percent, so the suit's fine. I'll be landing on the floor in moments, so I glance down and the view steals an entire lungful of that precious breath.

The sunken city of Once-Havasu is quite literally glowing blue beneath me. There must be millions, maybe billions, of bioluminescent phytoplankton lining the roads, buildings, cars, streetlamps, every surface in sight. It's absolutely stunning, and I've never seen anything like it. I've had run-ins with bioluminescent creatures: water jellies, kitefin sharks, anglerfish, bobtail squid. But this—the closest thing I can liken it to are some ancient pictures of nighttime Earth illuminated by artificial lights. Thara showed me some on her Reader. Apparently, people used to take them from space.

When I was a little kid, I didn't even believe in space. Just thought there were clouds and that was it. Clouds were light gray by day and black at night. Why would there be anything else? Eventually, I learned otherwise. . . .

This must be what space felt like for those early humans. Floating in an abyss, gazing down, seeing strange lights scattered across a vast area, spread in lines and shapes that are utterly unnatural, that show very clearly—mankind lived here.

Once.

I swallow as I descend into a school of blue lanternfish. It's an eerie sight. The creatures are small, half a foot long at the most, but they have blue, glowing photophores along their spines and giant eyeballs that take up the entire side of their head. The haptics in my suit set off faint vibrations as I pass through the school, but when I emerge beneath them, my whole body warms at the sight of Thara—a bright white dot, standing on a sunken bridge that's outlined in blue. She veered slightly, but it's fine. I thrust to her, land, and her voice comes through the comm.

"I forgot how beautiful it can be down here." Her face is pure awe, illuminated by the helmet's interior lights.

As I stare down the bridge, I see that the bioluminescence is not in fact from phytoplankton, but from fungi that seem to have spread across most of Once-Havasu. I crouch down and pluck one of the mushrooms from the floor, examining the umbrella head.

Thara steps closer to me. "I read once that the fungus covering Lagos-Lost is the largest living organism on the planet. It occupies four hundred square miles."

She reads too many of those science journals. "This one's big enough for me," I say.

"Amazing, isn't it?"

"Mushrooms?"

"Life. When it's able to thrive."

Thara told me the word for what she wants to be one day. It's called a botanist. A person who studies plants. Watching her as she observes everything around us, my heart yearns to make her dreams come true. It takes me a minute to respond, but finally I say, "If we find coin in Treasure Island, we'll get you a private tutor. You can go to college at one of those fancy, inland agricultural schools."

"So you *do* think there's money in Treasure Island?"

She's teasing me, but I'm not giving her an inch. "I said *if.*"

Thara plucks the mushroom out of my hand, studies it. "Agriculture school would be amazing. But you know what I'm really planning to do if we find the gold?"

"What's that?"

Thara drops the mushroom and steps in front of me; she places two metal hands on my shoulders. "First, I'm gonna see the sun with you. We'll sail around the world, climb through the clouds, bask in those rays. Then, I'm going to study the things that grow up there. And with whatever coin we have left, I'm going to build us a greenhouse the size of the freaking Bhargav!"

Clouds above, she knows how to dream.

"I know you wanted to go with Taim, but—"

"No buts," I say. "I should have asked you first. Of course I should have asked *you* before *him.*"

Thara's eyes are so big. "Imagine it, Jin. Maybe we'll even

find some long-lost family while we're in the Himalayas."

I know Thara's always hoped for that—finding more of our family.

"But even if we don't," Thara continues, "that's okay. Maybe that's how it's meant to be. Me and you, Jin. We'll come back to the Archipelago; we'll purchase a plot of land in the Rockies. We'll live out our days dry and happy, feasting on our greenhouse bounty. They'll tell stories about us one day. Jin and Thara, bravest of sisters. They descended to the deepest, darkest places in the sea. They climbed to the highest, brightest places on Earth. They were adventurers and scientists and landowners, and they knew how to live! Haldar sisters to the end."

"To the end," I say, throwing my arm around her.

She blasts her thrusters and we float off just above the bridge and over the mushrooms. My heart swells with a feeling that I realize after a moment is relief. God, it's good to have her back. I always thought she'd hate me at some point. That she'd just have enough of all my protecting and controlling and walk away.

It's a raw fear I have—the fear of losing her.

Because—if I did lose her—who would I be?

We exit the bridge and there's a small collection of buildings ahead. The visibility down here is tremendous. Normally, I can't see more than fifty feet in front of me, but with the mushrooms, I can see several hundred in every direction.

On our left is the strangest sight, a group of glowing sail-boats, suspended at odd angles in the water, many connected by a tether down to the ocean floor.

"Must have been a marina," Thara says. "This place, Once-Havasu, the original name was Lake Havasu City."

"But why leave your boat behind?" I say. "The cars I get." Dozens of abandoned, sunken cars line the streets in front of us. "But when the flood came, you'd think these people would realize that their boats are the most important things they own. Boats are how they stay above water."

Thara shrugs. "Who knows. Maybe they thought the rain would stop?"

I land on a cobblestone street just past the sunken marina. Now that I'm off the bridge, I can see that it's not just the mushrooms that cover Once-Havasu, but an entire deep-sea reef has settled here. Hundreds of corals and sponges of every size, shape, and color. Sea fans, crabs, translucent shrimp, spiny urchins, piglet squid. The place is teeming with life, as if the sunken city has been repopulated.

I'm not some wide-eyed future botanist like Thara. I'm a bitter innkeeper. Still, it's enough to make my jaw fall open— the dazzling, unexpected persistence of life.

A light flashes on my viewport then, alerting me that my air's down to 90 percent. Plenty left, but I've gotten a little distracted. We came down here for a job. Get the gems, get the suit, and try not to die.

I peer to my right and notice Thara examining a brittle star on the ocean floor. "Let's get moving. You see the sign for Jahan Diamond Imports?" I ask.

"It's just down there," Thara points farther to the left. "I saw it when I dropped in."

"Let's go, then. If we find the gems and the suit quickly, you can have some extra time in the reef when we're done."

I can hear it in my voice. *Control, control, control.* Can't help it, though. Control is how you survive. Goofing off, ogling fungi and coral—that's how you get yourself into trouble.

I thrust over to Thara, grab her hand, and lead her in the direction she pointed. She doesn't push back, which I'm thankful for. I don't want to get in another fight.

We first pass a building with giant letters hanging at odd angles and a mermaid logo etched into the window. I recognize the name. "Thara, check this—Starbuck—like the mate in that old story about the white whale."

She grunts an acknowledgment, but I know she doesn't get it. She reads to learn, not for fun. "Thara," I call.

"Up here."

I zoom ahead and find her in front of a giant sign that must rise some twenty feet off the ocean floor. I shift my white chest lights onto the sign, brightening the words *Jahan*

Diamond Imports. "This is the spot."

We thrust down, landing next to a huge pile of rubble. The building must have been at least two stories, and maybe fifty feet wide and deep when it was still standing. This is why wrecking is so dangerous. If a building this small can collapse and kill a diver, then our plan to enter the thirty-six floor Treasure Island Hotel and Casino is fully absurd.

But why didn't Bhili come after her partner? She said her suit was damaged, but how? From what?

With the strength from our suits, Thara and I start tossing chunks of concrete and rebar. How we're going to find a diamond or a ruby in this mess is beyond me. At least working together, we should be able to clear it in an hour.

"I'll be right back," Thara says. "I want to have a peek at those red tree corals." She nods left, and I sigh.

"Don't stray far."

Sweat drips off my forehead, and my heart hammers as I hurl block after block behind me. This is how it was digging for Dad. Just a few differences. Rubble pile about four times this size, massive stone slabs, no coral reef, so it was pitch black except for my suit lights. The most disturbing part was this crackle on the comm, like Dad was talking to me. I'm still not sure if it was real or not. When we pulled the suit out, the comm was working fine. Maybe it was in my head. But for weeks after, that crackle stayed with me. I'd have these midday whiteouts where static would blare in my ears. Minutes later, I'd pull out of it to the sound of Dad's deep voice screaming, *"Jina!"*

He never screamed that.

At least, I don't think he did.

Those episodes terrified Thara. She forbade me to go down the bluff stairs alone. Afraid I'd have an attack and tumble right off.

My chest constricts, and I close my eyes, sitting, sipping water off the hose in my helmet. Shallow breaths flutter in and out of my nose. *Dad was alive in there.* That's why I heard the crackle. That was my brain telling me—*don't stop, don't stop, find him.* But I didn't—because of Taim. He pulled me up too soon, and—

No. That's not right. The suit comm wasn't damaged. The crackle was made up. That was delirium, the hypoxia setting in. That's what Taim thought.

I shake my head, lengthen my breaths, try to arrest my spinning mind. *Taim was right to be nervous. I could hallucinate again down here. I'm a danger to myself. And Thara* . . .

I open my eyes, glancing around. *Where is Thara?* I bark into the comm, "Thara!"

No answer.

I thrust over to the red tree corals. "Thara!"

Nothing.

My pulse races forward. If the suit could detect heart rate, I'd have an emergency alarm sounding. "Thara!"

I whip my head around, and finally I see a faint light coming from the far side of the Starbuck building. Different from all the bioluminescence, more white than blue.

It must be her. She's just beyond reach of comms.

She's okay. Don't freak, Jin. Don't scream at her. Stay calm. You can—

My stomach clenches as I'm jerked backward. Water rushes around me. The tether's gone taut. My body spins. The blue-glow city of Once-Havasu shrinks below me. And I finally realize what's happening. They're pulling me up. Far too fast. Must be dozens of feet per second. "Thara! Thara!" I call.

My heart pounds, my head shoved into the right side of the helmet from the spin, but I need to focus. She's down there. Somewhere. And I need to find her. I *won't* be taken from her. My brain sends a sharp, piercing message. *Unclip the tether. He's done this to you before. Unclip!* I hurl an arm around my back. My hand slaps into the clip. But I can't. I know I can't—there's too little dexterity in my fingers. "Thara!" I scream into the abyss, but she's hundreds of feet from me now. Once-Havasu just a speck of blue below me.

Why did I let Taim clip me into a tether?

How did I not learn?

I blast my thrusters, trying to arrest my spin, but it's been too long since I've executed a difficult maneuver like this, and—

Ping. My directional readings come back. *Thank god.* I'm approaching the surface. Once I'm up I can release the cable. Go back for Thara.

The water brightens, further, further, and then I break through the surface, back into our dull gray world.

Oh no.

I'm skimming the surface of the water. Pulled along like loose cargo. They're driving the skiff somewhere while they reel me in.

What is Taim thinking? Our tethers could get twisted, and it'll take me twice as long to get back to Thara.

In time with that thought, I'm reeled toward the boat. I can see Taim, Bhili, and Saanvi. We're pulling up to something massive: the *Desierto*, I realize.

The skiff stops, and I thrust to a halt as well. Then I fling my viewport up, screaming. "Have you lost your mind, Taim? Where is she? Where is my sister?"

At that moment, Thara pops up near the skiff's bow. She lifts her viewport. "What happened?"

"Are you okay?" I yell. "Are you hurt?"

"I'm fine," Thara says, calm as ever. "What happened? Why'd we get pulled out?"

Because Taim is a lying, treacherous backstabber who thinks only of himself.

I manage not to say that.

Instead, I hear Luz's voice screeching through a speaker on the skiff. "Back aboard the *Desierto* now!"

Taim points behind us at something on the horizon. It's large, black—a ship. *Maybe a cutter? Though they're not typically black.* Then I hear Taim utter one word. "Corsairs."

10

By the time I gather my wits, Thara's already climbing into the skiff. The wind's still whipping the rain left, right, and sideways, but the waves have calmed down at least.

"Get in, Jinny!" Bhili calls. "I know that ship, and they don't play nice."

I thrust over and Taim and Saanvi haul me up. "What do you mean you *know* them?"

"I mean what I said, just get in." Thara's already out of her suit, and Taim pulls the skiff up alongside the *Desierto*'s hull. I stand up on the skiff, and with a metal hand, I fling Taim around. "Why didn't you pull Thara up first?"

"Jin, this isn't the time. Those are pirates, and they're heading directly for us."

"Answer my question." I poke him in the chest.

"I pulled you up at the same time. You thrusted, so you came up first. Now will you get out of your suit and back on the trawler? We may still be able to outrun them."

Did I thrust up? Maybe at the end? I was spinning, but I also wanted to surface so I could go back for Thara.

"We ain't gonna outrun them," Bhili says.

"And how do you know?" Taim shouts while helping me out of the suit.

"Because I been in the brig of that ship for nigh six months. I know it, and I know the captain, and I ain't never seen him lose a chase. Especially not to a trawler."

She knows the captain?

Luz's voice comes through a portside speaker. "Leave the skiff! No time to haul it. If we need to make a stand, I want to do it closer to the vent well. Higher the wind, tougher it'll be to board."

"That's smart," Taim whispers.

Saanvi nods. "Very."

Renato throws over two lengths of rope and a stretch of netting. The ends smack the skiff, and his deep voice rumbles through the speaker. "Tie the suits off. Rest of you up, like the captain ordered. Go!" Luz disappears then with the comm. I can only presume she's run off to direct her hands.

"I'll handle the suits," Bhili says. "Rest of you start."

Thara is the first to leap onto the netting. She's quick and bold and my heart's already in a knot thinking about how I'm going to keep her safe through this.

Taim grabs my hand. "We'll be all right. I have—"

"I'm sorry about yelling at you," I blurt out. "I just—I was scared."

"Don't waste a word on it," Taim says, boosting me onto the netting.

Saanvi's right below Thara, and Taim and I follow below them. It's at least a thirty-foot climb, and the wind pummels us into the hull. I glance down at Bhili, who's tied off both suits. She's kept them whole and tied the ropes to the tether rings.

I look up again and see Thara and Saanvi disappear over the gunwale and onto the deck. The wind batters the netting, and my fingers dig into the fibers. I glance over my shoulder and the corsair cutter has closed half the distance. *Good god.* We're not moving fast enough. Taim shoves my left foot. "Go, go, go."

At last, I'm over the gunwale too. I pull Taim up and over, and see that Renato's already lugged the suits up. Just one person left, and I glance back over the side, down at the skiff, and I see that Bhili's not even on the netting.

Why is she still in the skiff?

Thara comes up on my left, Taim on my right, the suits on the *Desierto* behind me. "Let's go, Bhili!" I call, and she mouths something in return, but I can't hear her with the wind howling. I wave her up again.

Thara shouts next to me. "Bhili! Come on!"

Bhili just shakes her head and walks down the skiff to the outboard. That's when it hits me. *She's abandoning us.*

"Traitor!" I scream.

Thara swivels her head at me, confused, but a heavy lump sinks into my gut, because I knew it. This entire time, I knew it was a setup. My body's tense with rage because of what she's done. Leaving us here, in the middle of the Sonoran Sea, to be boarded by corsairs. I'm disgusted with myself for letting it get this far, for giving her even a sliver of my trust.

I let the smallest part of me start to hope, believe, that we could plot a new course, change our lives, escape the salt and the sea and our soon-to-be drowned Coaster existence.

Such a fool I am.

The skiff veers off the side of the *Desierto*, and finally Thara starts screaming too, "Wait, Bhili! Come back! Come back!" I lean forward, looking at Thara. She's distraught. Her face sagging off her bones, her hands in fists, she swallows several times, and then finally screams the words I refuse to say. "Why?! Why leave now? After all this?!"

Bhili seems to hear, at least her mouth is moving, but she's leeward from us, and the wind's vicious and pulling her words away. Finally, Bhili turns the skiff, breaks eye contact with us, and I watch as she rides straight out toward the cutter. For a moment, a part of me wonders if she's going to join the corsairs. But the skiff veers out to the right, and I throw an arm around my sister. "Sorry, Thara. I know you believed in her, but . . . it was always too good to—"

"Oh, screw you, Jin."

"What?"

"You heard me. Rust take you. You're happy she's gone."

Don't react. Keep it together.

"You think I'm happy that we're here—about to be boarded by corsairs?"

"Just don't patronize me with your fake consoling gullshit."

My cheeks flame with anger. "*My* gullshit. Are you kidding? You spent the last eight months eating up Bhili's. Ate so much of it that you started spouting it to me. *There are good people, Jin. People who care.* You know what people care about, Thara? Their rusting selves."

"Are you two done?!" Taim shouts, silencing both of us. "We're going to be boarded in ten minutes, maybe less. We need a plan."

Luz comes up behind us. "There is a plan. You two are in the Guard, yeah? I've got some anti-destroyer weaponry in the rudder room. Can you handle a shoulder assault weapon?"

Anti-destroyer weaponry? Is she serious?

"Of course we can't!" I say.

"We can," Saanvi says. "We've trained with them, at least."

Holy shit. They have?

"Good. Then go with Renato. He'll help you get the weapons, and we'll try and put a few holes in their hull. If we can, maybe they won't trail us over the vent well."

"I'm sorry," I say. "What do you mean by *over* the vent well?"

"I've done it before, outrunning corsairs," Luz says. "We can do it again. Now go."

Luz jogs off down the trawl deck, yelling back at us. "And one more thing. You ever see your friend again, you tell her. I'm gonna scale her toes to nose if I find her. She'll be begging me to let her drown by the time I'm done."

Clouds above.

She turns and continues running across the trawl deck as hands cry out behind us:

"Dragnets aboard!"

"Brace for speed!"

My heart's bruising the ribs in my chest as I start to follow Taim, Saanvi, and Renato, but I glance back at Thara. Tears streak her face as she stares out starboard.

I walk up and place my arms around her. She buries her head in my chest, clinging to me, eyes wide, and a trench opens in my stomach as I follow her gaze. The cutter is huge, at least a hundred and fifty feet, and it's close enough now that I see the giant mounted turret gun raised on the bow. The barrel's maybe twenty feet long, and it's trained directly on us. I hold my sister tighter than I ever have, and I hear a faint whistle, a deep pop, and then a massive chunk of the ocean is blown apart, while a voice behind me bellows, "Under siege! Shots fired!"

11

Bullets shred the waves to our starboard, rain hails down from above, sea water sprays up from below. And behind us, trawl hands scream out in terror while giant plumes of smoke billow into the air near the cutter's turret.

I grab Thara's hand and shuffle toward a starboard ladder, while the sound of that turret gun booms in the distance. Taim and Saanvi slide up at our side, crouched, and my heart's thumping in my chest like an overworked sump pump.

"Go get the weapons!" I yell.

Taim pulls Thara and me close to him. "I will, but have you noticed? They haven't hit the ship yet."

What?

"They're well within range," Taim says. "They don't want to sink us. The trawler's too valuable. Typical situation like this, corsairs will try to scare the crew into submission. If no one resists, it's easier to board. Then they sell the ship later."

Saanvi points starboard, out at the cutter. "Taim, you see who it is?"

I risk a glance, and the ship's much larger than I thought. Maybe two hundred and fifty feet. It's a medium endurance craft, painted all black, with a large bridge, a stern loading ramp, the turret, and what looks like a drone landing pad aftship. Where the words *AA Coast Guard* are normally in large print along the hull, there's just a giant symbol, three shapes, each outlined in white—a circle inside a diamond inside a rectangle.

"The Brazilian," Taim whispers.

Saanvi nods. "We need to go—now."

"Who is—" Thara's voice is trembling. "Who is the Brazilian?"

"Guard's been after him for years," Saanvi says. "He's from a drowned country in the southern Atlantic. Stole an extremely expensive cutter, and—he's a wrecker."

A wrecker? And Bhili knows him. . . .

Taim grabs my shoulders. "I want you and Thara to hide out below the main deck in the factory. Saanvi and I are going to help with the anti-destroyer weapons. We'll also stash the dive suits."

"I'm coming with you," I say. "You'll need help."

Taim swipes a thumb across my eyebrow. "Saanvi and I

barely know how to use those weapons. We won't have time to explain it."

"What if we get boarded?"

"Then we have these," Saanvi says, drawing a pistol out of his back pocket. Rain drips off the silver metal, and Taim pulls out an identical one. Guard issue maybe? The sight of them turns my stomach upside down.

Taim cups hands to my cheeks. "We'll find you, Jin. You and Thara just get to the factory."

"No," I shove Taim aside, but he yanks my yellow poncho as I pass.

"Are you really that unable to follow my lead?"

My pulse is racing. "It's not that, it's—"

"What?"

Damnit! I don't want Taim going out there any more than I want Thara left behind. I can't lose either one of them. Not like this.

"Listen," Taim says. "There's a protocol for this. Once they board, we hide out, then we get away on a skiff later—just like Bhili did."

Bhili. Swamping traitor.

"Jin." Saanvi's hand is on my shoulder now, that easy, knowing smile plastered across his face. "I'll look after Taim, okay? You look after your sister."

I swallow. "Fine."

"Now listen," Saanvi says. "The Guard, they teach us how to handle these situations." His eyes shift to the ladder. "When you're boarded on a trawl ship . . . there's a specific place in the factory where the Guard *recommends* you hide. You're not gonna like it, though."

Ten minutes later, I'm neck deep in a twenty-foot, round steel tub of prawns, and the worst part: they are moving. Thousands and thousands of squirming, silvery bodies—in my boots, down my poncho, up my sleeves, and on my chest. A tail flaps against my throat, and I shudder with Thara beside me. *Stupid Coast Guard.* The only upside of the prawns is they're distracting me from the thought of Taim or Saanvi torn in half by a large caliber bullet.

At first, all we heard was gunfire and explosions, but then a few minutes ago there were several loud thuds and heavy footfalls. Now, the sounds have shifted to pistol fire and screaming, and my ears ring each time with the only possible conclusion—*we've been boarded.*

At least we haven't been sunk. The whole factory is open and intact. There are a few sinks, drains, a conveyor belt across the length, and a tool compartment in one corner. I keep tipping my head over the edge of our prawn vat to peer across the deck. There are many spaces to hide in the factory, and if I was a murderous corsair hunting stowaways,

I would check the frozen holds, the lockers next to the aft ramp room. I would totally not be checking one of the fresh prawn vats; who would even consider climbing in there? Risking death by prawn carcass suffocation.

Thara doesn't seem too disturbed by any of this. "You know what I realized?" she says next to me.

Her poor hair. Do prawns lay eggs? I really hope prawns don't lay eggs.

"That even if I survive this, I'll be forever tortured by hallucinations of prawns crawling across my skin."

"Oh, they're not even biting," Thara says.

Yet.

"What did you realize, then?"

"I realized that Bhili wasn't abandoning us. She was trying to lead them off."

"Thara, you need to get it together. This entire thing is a setup. Bhili's likely half a league out, waiting to regroup with her old crew and take her share of the *booty*—in other words, our dive suits. Clouds above, she was probably in cahoots with that grillman too. She sat on our dock, laid the bait, dangled those shiny gold coins like a lure until we finally got delirious enough to bite, and we did: hook, line, sinker."

"You really just hate everything about her, don't you?"

"Thara, she conned us. Sure as the calm follows the storm, she conned us, and we'll be lucky to—"

Footsteps clop down the starboard passage just outside the factory. Thara and I go still, and then Thara jabs a finger down and sinks herself chin deep into the prawns.

The factory door flings open; it creaks and thumps as someone secures it behind them. I can't see over the lip of the prawn tub, but a pair of footsteps echo across the deck as a prawn snakes its way up my cheek. And yes, those footsteps *could* be Taim and Saanvi.

But I know they're not. I don't need to see Taim to know the cadence of his walk, the lightness of his steps. If he paused, if he was waiting, listening, I'd know. I've heard him in the dark too many times. This is the opposite of Taim: staggered, lumbering footsteps, metallic tings and pings from one of them, and breath that's too soft . . . as if they're trying to conceal themselves.

A hushed murmur slips between two people, and then they shuffle forward. It can only mean one thing: they know we're here.

My eyes slide to Thara and hers to mine, and in that moment, there passes between us a certainty of what must be done. She looks down, as do I, and she finds my hand beneath the prawns, squeezes, and we both draw long quiet breaths up through our nostrils. Then, like the great wrecking sisters we are, we drift below the surface.

However much the smell of the prawns and the feeling of the prawns and the thoughts of the prawns consumed me in the moments prior, I do not spare them a moment's notice now. The prawns are like water to me, just a thing keeping a spent diver from air.

My entire focus is on my body, remaining calm, requiring as little oxygen as possible, just as Dad taught me: *When you're on empty, still yourself, still your panic, drop your heart rate, and find the extra few seconds, minutes, you need to live.*

I know I have enough air to outlast the corsairs. I've done seven minutes below the surface. But Thara? Not sure what her last count was. Maybe five? How long can these corsairs spend in here searching?

Their footsteps are soft, muted reverberations beneath the prawns, but they're growing louder, coming closer, closer, and then they stop.

My focus ebbs; my thoughts shift to the people who must be right above us, staring down into this giant drum—our squirming shield of safety.

Something presses down on the pile above me, then a loud crunch and the smacking of lips.

"How are they?" a nasally woman's voice says.

"Fresh as they get," a harsh voice returns.

The woman snorts. "Toss me a strand of that black sea-weed."

The pile shifts again. My toes curl, and Thara squeezes the blood out of my fingers.

"What—" The harsh voice pauses. "That ain't seaweed!"

Prawns swirl above me as two beefy hands grab hold of my shoulders. My grip slips from Thara's, and I'm pulled clear of the vat, gasping for air, shaking prawns from my face. I stare at a pair of the most venomous looking seadogs. Both have bloody, broken noses. Gobbets of raw prawn slosh inside the man's mouth. And my whole body tenses, fear lashing up my spine as he says, "Look here, Izzy—we found ourselves some stowaways."

In minutes, Thara and I are dragged from the factory, and the woman, Izzy, throws open a topside hatch, motioning for Thara and me to climb. She has a collection of braided black hair patterned into a swirl atop her head. A dozen silver rings are strung across her brown face, ear to cheek to upper lip to cheek to other ear. The effect is like a gleaming second smile.

"Up!" the man yells. He's an equally villainous fellow with no eyebrows, a busted lip, and a black tattoo covering three quarters of his ruddy face, like a poorly drawn picture of a conch. He jabs Thara and me up the ladder (the same one we came down after leaving Taim), and then my mind is swirling with images of Taim: his dark eyes, his long lashes, and that one tendril of hair that always escapes his topknot in that way I can't stand.

Taim—where are you?

We emerge topside, and the deck is a blood bath. Most of

the hands are sprawled out at unnatural angles, blood pooling on the polywood, limbs contorted and broken.

Izzy kicks one of the dead bodies ahead of me. "Out of the way, ya seal-skinned oaf."

I grip Thara's hand, and she walks forward with several prawns in her hair and raw terror in her eyes. This was a big, glittering adventure, with a pile of hope buried in an underwater tower.

Now, it's something else. A nightmare.

After several steps, Thara staggers, nearly tripping on a body that's curled in a cocoon around its own entrails. On my right, there's a pair of long pink trawl gloves, just the gloves, and the bloody stumps of forearms oozing out the other side with cores of white bone. Thara stumbles four more paces and then her hands are on her knees and she's sick with everything in her stomach, her back heaving as I wrap an arm beneath her, keeping her from tumbling into her own vomit.

"Wonder how many prawns she had?" the man says.

When Thara's finished, we walk under the gantry, over the trawl deck, and by the look of the ship, you'd think we were dredging up humans, slicing their bodies to pieces, and dumping *them* into the vats below. Strange to think, but it's one of those rare moments I'm happy for the rain. Without judgment, the rain washes away all sins, and this grisly trawl deck will soon be clean again.

On our starboard, the cutter's anchored. Overhead, the storm's ebbed. Rain pours down by the bucket still, but the wind's settled, and the thunder stopped.

The corsairs must have steered us away from the vent well.

Between the cutter and the trawler, a few corsairs shuffle back and forth across horizontal black beams that they clearly used to board. With pistols at their waists and cutlasses swinging from their sides, they lug cargo and all manner of supplies.

Farther ahead, on the *Desierto*, there's a group of corsairs and a few of the trawler's remaining hands, including Luz and Renato, just in front of the midship platform. No Taim or Saanvi, though.

Please let them be okay.

On the midship platform itself is a tall corsair, a man with olive skin, a thick white mustache, chops, a black mariner's hat pulled low, and a long black vinyl raincoat, reflecting the gray horizon. Below the jacket, he has straight gray pants, dappled with water. On the left leg, the pants extend to his boot, but on the right, the cuff is rolled up to the knee, revealing a carbon-framed bionic: thick at the calf and a slender rod, straight down, curving at the ankle and swooping into a wide flat silver foot with the toes squared off and lined with a black rubber sole.

Before this man even speaks, I know he can only be the captain Bhili knows. The one she's been looking for ever since

Coconino. The one she must have consorted with to sell our souls for the suits.

"Well done, Izzy. Well done, Jobs. You've found our two thumbs, have you?" The captain claps, and I realize that's what we are now. Thumbs to unlock the suits. And after they've used us to swap out the locking systems, even our thumbs won't be worth a thing, and we'll be floating ball-and-chain on the ocean bottom, our bodies waiting for the trawlers to come drag us up.

"Found them in a big box of prawns," Izzy says, licking her lips. "Decent hiding place, but we sniffed them out."

"Very good," the captain says, in a hard drawl. "Now, are these yours?" He motions to a corsair who shifts two portside barrels, revealing our atmospheric diving suits with their white exoskeletons and red carbon joint bindings; the steel helmets are squat on the ground next to each.

So Taim and Saanvi weren't able to hide them. Does that mean . . .

I nod.

"You can speak, girl. The name's Captain João Silva."

"They're ours," I say.

"Glad to hear it," says Silva. "Come along, then, press your thumbs to the edges and unlock them."

My body goes taut; my eyes dart to Thara, who's biting her lower lip. This is the one thing we have. A thing he wants. Technically, only my thumb unlocks the suits, but that piece of information I'm definitely not sharing. Otherwise, Thara's even more disposable. My fingers itch at my sides, and I swipe the rain off my brow.

"Get on, then, girl," Silva says. "Jobs, put her in front of them."

The beefy Jobs, who pulled me from the prawn vat, steps forward. My eyes shift across the ship, searching for Taim, an escape, something. I know I can't unlock the suits. Every prickling hair on my scalp is telling me not to. What use are we if he has the suits?

My eyes finally land on Luz. She swivels her head once hard to the left, the green beanie atop her twisting, her upper lip tucking higher on the left side revealing one yellowed fang. It's as clear a message as she can give without shouting it out: *Don't unlock those suits.*

I stop, whirling to face Silva, somehow emboldened by the hardened captain of our trawler. She's had run-ins with corsairs before; she knows those suits are one of the few nego-tiating chips we have. "No!" I say, shouting to mask the tremor in my voice. "I'm not unlocking them until I have . . . have . . . some reassurances."

(Ugh. That *almost* came out confident.)

Silva stares at me, his lips pinched, his eyes mid-roll. He shakes his head in a tight little turn. "Why'd you have to do that, Captain?" Then he rips his pistol out of his long vinyl coat, turns, and fires a single shot directly at Luz.

The entire thing happens in slow motion. Like watching a drop of rain squirm out of a hole in a gutter. It's not really falling slower than any of the others, but somehow, it comes to your attention and you see it more clearly.

Silva's on the midship platform, five feet above the trawl deck. Luz's below, near the portside gunwale, along with the remnants of her crew. She's out in front of the six or seven hands left, and the bullet plows straight into her right temple. Her head kicks, blood streams a river down her cheek, pooling onto her emergency-orange jumpsuit, and then she keels over, thumping down on the deck, faceup with one fang exposed.

A few of the remaining hands leap forward, but Silva fires two shots over their heads, and they go still. "Easy now," he says. "Don't want to put everyone down. Few of you would serve well on the *Bandeira*, I can see that." Silva turns back to me. "Now, then—carry on. Let's unlock those suits."

Did he think shooting Luz was going to make me more malleable to his demands?

"I'll unlock them," I say. "Just take us to shore, and I'll do it once my sister's free."

Silva wags the pistol at Jobs. "Bring the little girl to me." He says it flat and low, and the minute he does, my heart pounds against my ribs.

"Leave her be!" I grab Thara's arm, but Jobs is twice my size and he shoves me to the deck, breaking my hold on Thara. I jump up in an instant, but Izzy steps into my way, holding the tip of a knife to my throat.

"Stay put," Izzy whispers, and Jobs leads Thara slowly up to Silva on the midship platform, while I hate myself. *So stupid. Why did I say she's my sister?*

On her walk, Thara keeps glancing back, and I try to be stoic, meeting her eyes, giving her confidence, but beneath the hood of her orange trench, I can see her entire jaw trembling. She arrives in front of Silva, and he lifts her hood off gently. Then he takes a long look at her.

I do not like that look. Far too many men have entered our inn and given Thara that same look.

My breath becomes very shallow, very purposeful, and I stare up at Silva, imagining my hands at his throat. Unfortunately, there's an actual knife at *my* throat. I couldn't move if I tried.

At last, Silva pulls his eyes off Thara, and he shouts down to me. "We're not taking anyone to shore." He lifts Thara's hood back over her head, and while that should be good (keep the rain off her), all I can think is: *Don't you fucking touch her.*

I don't say that, though. I don't move, until finally Silva growls down at me. "Final time I'm asking. Otherwise, I'll direct my questions to your sister. We can go have a conversation in the wheelhouse there." He nods behind him. "I'm sure she'll be more amenable."

Sun be saved.

Thara glances over her shoulder, and I can't even meet her eyes. All I see are her cheeks, and the water streaming down that I know is not rain.

"Go on now," Izzy whispers, lowering her knife. "Unlock them. Do it fast."

With that, I peel my eyes off Thara, and my feet start moving: one step toward the suits, another, another. When I'm in front of them, I call back to Silva. "You'll let us go if I unlock them?"

Silva smiles, slow and predatory. "I think you'll find you're better off staying with me."

Staying with him? What does that—

The next thought comes quickly. *Don't be naive, Jin. You know what that means.*

Silva pauses, his eyes shifting across Thara and over to the *Desierto* crew. "Tell you what," Silva says. "If you'd like, you and your sister can both walk into the Sonoran Sea, same as the rest of these hands who won't crew up. This time of year, past the thick of winter, you can grab a stray plank and have at least three or four hours before you freeze to death."

Not much, but it's something. If we end up in the Sonoran, we'll have to pray the sun shines down and we find an island hilltop or another trawler pulling through. Probably better than whatever he has planned for us on his ship. I bend down in front of the first suit, my arm extending toward the forearm pad with the thumbprint lock, when behind me, I hear: "Jin, don't!"

Taim and Saanvi emerge topside from a starboard ladder, and relief floods my chest.

Stars and moon, they're alive.

I squeal out a "Taim!" and it takes everything in me not to rush him, but he's shaking his head. Taim and Saanvi have their hands up, and they're immediately surrounded by Izzy, Jobs, and a half dozen other corsairs with pistols pointed.

Izzy orders them searched, and their pistols and knives are taken. Silva looks exasperated, tapping his bionic foot. "And who are you two, now—the brothers?"

"We're friends," Taim says, "and I have an offer for you!"

Damn if he doesn't sound all Coast Guard lieutenant right then.

Silva squints an eye. "And what's that, Navy boy."

"We're going after a treasure," Taim says. "We'll cut you in on it, but you agree to let us off—on land—after we find it."

"You'll cut me in on it?" Silva bellows. "It's my treasure to begin with!"

My blood boils. *Bhili.* She walked us right into this.

"Sure," Taim says. "But Bhili's gone, rode a skiff off the minute she saw your ship. Now those girls are the only people who know the location of the vault."

We know the location of the vault? I certainly don't. Bhili refused to tell me. Though maybe she confided in Thara. They got close. Either way, it's a good bluff.

Silva rips back the slide on his pistol, pointing it over Thara's shoulder at Taim. "Let's say that's true. Why, then, do I still need the pair of you blue suits?"

"Because we're not in the Navy," Taim says, arms still in the air. "We're in the Coast Guard. And with us, you'll sail straight past the cordon at Vegas-Drowned."

12

Two hours later, Silva's crew has near splintered the *Desierto* in two, searching for Bhili. Of course, she isn't here. She's probably set a course for the Angeles Outer Banks, where she'll long-con some other sucker and her sister into diving for non-existent gold.

Swamping parasitic lamprey.

Silva's pissed. He didn't shoot Taim and Saanvi. He hasn't shot me or Thara. We're all huddled together on the trawl deck, guarded by two corsairs, and my only conclusion is that Silva must think Taim's right. If he's planning a wrecking job into Treasure Island and Bhili's not here . . . well, then the four of us really are his best hope.

It was a smart play by Taim. This way, we're valuable to Silva; he needs us. Still, I can't shake the fear twisting through me, the memory of Silva lifting Thara's hood, and that piercing voice in my head that says: *Don't take your sister on that man's ship.* Of course, the more rational part of me says something else. The odds on surviving a swim in the Sonoran are twenty to one, maybe a hundred to one.

Live through today. Deal with Silva tomorrow.

I asked Thara if Silva spoke to her while she was on the midship platform (we need something we can use against him). She shrugged, saying, "He just asked for my name."

Right now, the man himself is pacing the trawl deck. His crew is in front of him; fallen hands and corsairs have been tossed into the sea. The rain cuts straight down, and I can feel the rage pouring off his skin. "All right, then!" Silva says. "If she's not here, she's not here." The remaining hands of the *Desierto* are lined up along the portside gunwale on their knees. The clouds have faded to an ominous gray. "We'll catch up with Bhili in the end," Silva says. "All Earth's little fish drown someday, and I plan to be the one to hold Bhili under."

Not exactly the sentiment of someone working *with* Bhili. Suppose I was wrong about that.

Silva looks up at the sky and huffs. "In the meantime, Izzy, you figure out which of the hands are joining and which are walking. Jobs, you pick a crew of three to sail this trawler beast down to Nogales, see what we can get for her. Rest of us—and the treasure seekers—I want back aboard the *Bandeira* in ten."

Izzy offers every hand on the *Desierto* a chance to join Silva's crew. Two accept, and they're told they'll be swabbing belowdecks until they prove themselves worthy. The other five, including Renato, walk a plank out into the Sonoran Sea. Many grab hold of the bodies of their fallen bloated compatriots; they flail in the black waters, chasing down chunks of polywood and debris from the melee earlier, faces grave, probably hoping they'll survive the night . . . knowing there's every chance they won't.

I watch them with shallow breath and a heavy heart. There's honor in what they do; they could have crewed up with Silva, saved their skins, if not their souls. But they didn't. The water made its plans—it brought Silva to the *Desierto*—and they accepted their fate. The water would choose whether to wash them ashore or drown them in an evening storm.

In my head, I keep blaming this entire fiasco on Bhili. But watching the hands choose between plank and crew, it reminds me—we all have a choice. The water may have brought Bhili to Coconino on that warm August morning near eight months ago. But I accepted her coin. I welcomed her into our home. I chose.

With the last of the hands in the Sonoran, Izzy leads Taim, Thara, Saanvi, and me across the black ladders that Silva used to board the *Desierto* and onto the deck of the *Bandeira*, the massive black cutter that Silva commands.

As we cross, Taim informs us that the *Bandeira* is one of the Coast Guard's storm-class cutters, two hundred and fifty feet in length and another fifty abeam. All steel and aluminum, the ship can travel thirty knots on battery-powered engines, and it supports a crew of up to seventy-five. Silva's crew appears to be fifty at the most, and we board aft-ship onto the drone flight deck. To the rear there's a ramp for the launch and recovery of two small inflatable craft, and midship there's a large bridge with two levels and what appears to be a pilothouse on the topmost with black-tinted windows surrounding it.

Izzy speaks with several corsairs, and we stand on the drone deck for a few moments.

"See that?" Saanvi whispers to me, pointing to a rear section of the bridge that looks like someone reached down through the clouds and punched a hole through it. "We did that," he says, smiling. "Had to wait until they were practically boarding. Shoulder assault weapons have limited range. Missed the turret, but at least we put a dent somewhere."

Taim shakes his head. "Lot of good it did."

"Don't lose heart." Saanvi bumps Taim in the shoulder. "You know my mom has this saying: *an eighth for a quarter for a half for a whole.* Know what it means?"

"No," Taim says without glancing at Saanvi.

"It's a gambler's ditty. Means there's always hope. Even the smallest win can be turned into another and another, and before you know it, you've stolen the pot."

"Isn't your mom banned from Agua Fria for counting cards?" Thara says.

That's the local rumor—never knew if it was true.

"Damn right she is," Saanvi says, grinning ear to ear. "Took three hundred ounces off them in a single day. She's my hero."

Right then, I decide to let go of all my ill will toward Saanvi. Any boy who stays positive through this, who declares his mom his personal hero—well, he's okay with me.

We cross the flight deck, and I keep my head down to avoid the leers and scowls from the several dozen rain-drenched corsairs that man the ship. From there, Izzy leads us into a compartment marked Captain's Quarters just beneath the bridge.

"Sit down!" Izzy says, the high pitch of her voice like a scrape in my skull. "The captain will be in shortly, and if I find you touched anything, I'll have an ear from each of you." With that pleasant order delivered, Izzy exits the room, and we're left with a moment to breathe before Silva's arrival.

The cabin is a compact, garish thing. A large ashen polywood desk lines the far wall with several maps, pens, and a squat lamp that offers a hazy green light. A few benches are in front of the desk with all of us smushed together on one. Three round portholes fit the forward bulkhead and look out onto the weapons deck near the ship's bow. In the middle of the weapons deck is the mounted turret gun that could have torn the entire trawler in half if it wanted to. The rest of the cabin's bulkheads are covered in paintings in gilded frames, maybe twenty of them in total, some the size of my torso, some no bigger than my hand.

The paintings are stunning, mostly seascapes, and they're nothing like the paintings that hang in tea-bars around Coconino. These, well—the abstraction of shapes, the purposeful lines, the raw emotion pouring out from each makes it clear: these are masterpieces, more akin to the old, famous paintings in Thara's Reader than anything else I've seen.

My first thought goes to Silva. These are his quarters. *Could he have painted these?* Though my next thought is more absurd. *Are these wrecking prizes?* It seems incredible that paintings could survive so long beneath the sea, but I also can't imagine where else he got them. Their beauty seems from another world . . . or another time.

Taim reaches out, snaring us into his arms, squeezing the rain out of our twitching, sogging frames. It's what I should be doing for Thara. She's shivering, her teeth clattering, and maybe it's because we were blasted by the rain topside for over two hours while the corsairs searched for Bhili, but more likely, it's because we just sailed six inches from death itself.

Seconds pass within the security of Taim's arms, but we may only have seconds, so I pull away, turning to Thara, asking the question that needs to be asked. "Did Bhili tell you where the vault is?"

She nods. "I'm sorry, Jin. I didn't think she'd—that *this* would happen."

"Thara," I say in my sternest voice possible. "I love you, and this is not your fault. Now, it's good that you know the location of the vault. Do not tell that to *anyone*, especially Silva. Not yet. Understood?"

"Agreed," Taim says. "We need to play along like we're going to give Silva the vault location, but only at the last minute, before the dive. Same as Bhili planned. Hopefully things never get that far. Saanvi and I should be able to tip off the officers stationed at Castle Mountain when we go for the patrol boat. After that, we leave it to the Guard to rescue us."

I knew Taim would say this. It's a decent plan, the quickest path to rescue, but the wrong one. "No."

"No, what?" Taim says. "You want to take on Silva's crew ourselves? With weapons we don't have? The four of us against however many dozens of corsairs?"

"We're not taking on Silva's crew," I say, "but we're also not tipping off the Coast Guard. Silva's smart. Luz shook her head, telling me not to unlock the suits—Silva killed her. I hesitated again, Silva brought Thara to his side. You told Silva he needs us for the dive, instead he searched the ship for Bhili. No. If Silva so much as sees the Coast Guard approaching, we'll be one shot to the temple, like Luz."

"Then what's your plan?" Taim asks.

I grab hold of Thara's shoulders. "We go after the treasure." My eyes pass over Saanvi's, Taim's. "We dive down. I dive down, with Silva, and we get it."

Taim rubs his eyes with his thumb and forefinger. "Why are you like this? Why can't you just—"

Saanvi clears his throat, interrupting. "Jin's right, Taim. The Guard doesn't have any subtlety, and they don't negotiate with corsairs. Our odds are better diving into Treasure Island, seeing if we can find the gold."

Taim sighs. "What if the gold's not there?"

"Doesn't matter," I say, full bluster.

"Doesn't matter?" Taim laughs. "You see us coming up empty-handed and Silva letting us sail free?"

"You're not understanding how this plays." I run my hand across my buzzed scalp. "Number one, we'll find *something* of value . . . even if it's not the gold."

"Okay . . ."

"Number two, we don't negotiate with Silva; we negotiate with his crew."

"And how's that?" Taim says.

"Because once I'm down there with Silva, I kill him."

Taim stares at me, his mouth hanging open. He inhales, about to respond—

Slam. The door to the captain's quarters is thrown open, and a very much alive Silva strides through. My breath catches as he hurls his mariner's cap onto an armchair in the corner. *Did he hear me?* His face doesn't betray anything if he did, and Izzy follows shortly behind him, dropping our bags next to the bench we're perched on, slamming the door on her way back out.

"All right, out with it, then," Silva says, running a hand over his head. His scalp's buzzed a quarter inch like mine, but the hair's white as lightning. Without the hat on, I also see a pearl-stud earring in the top of his right ear. "Start talking," he says. "What's your angle, where's the vault, and how do you get past the cordon?"

Thara's been keeping the maps in our dry bags, and she pulls them out and talks Silva through most of it. How Taim's a lieutenant and together with Saanvi they pick up a patrol boat from Castle Mountain in Mojave Main. From there we cruise through the Coast Guard checkpoint at Blue Diamond on the eastern shores of La Madre. Then a day-trip in. It's a three-person dive job into Treasure Island, but we only have two suits. We were hoping to recover another from Once-Havasu, and so on, and so on.

Silva nods mostly, and at one point clicks on a little battery-powered kettle on the corner of his desk. Looking directly at Thara, he says, "Cup-a-tea?"

She shakes her head quickly, and no one else answers except Saanvi, who replies, "Yeah, that'd be great."

I'm half-worried he's going to drop dead, poisoned on his first sip, but he doesn't, and Thara wraps up, saying she won't reveal the vault's exact location, but Bhili told her, and the gold will be there.

Silva sighs. "Bhili's mind's a murky one, full of lies and

deceit and one con or the other, but she has a nose for gold, and that's why we waited her out."

"How long have you been tracking us?" I say.

Silva licks his lips. "We first had eyes on Bhili up in Carson City more than a year back when she was researching this job. She must have caught our scent, though. We lost her. Until word got round the tea-bars about a gripper lady haunting a coastal in Arizona." Silva throws his feet up on the desk, the bionic crossed on top of the other as he kicks back in his chair. "Got a drone from Pew several weeks back saying he found old Bhili in a small bay by the name of Coconino. Waited for word, but when Pew didn't come back, I knew Bhili would make her run." Silva pumps his eyebrows. "We started trailing you when the trawler shoved out of Tonto, but waited until you anchored near Once-Havasu to close in."

"So Bhili served with you?" Thara says.

Stay focused, Thara! We don't need their whole story; we just need him to trust ours.

Silva stretches his arms out. "It'll be told one day up and down the Pacific Rim. Mates to lovers, lovers to enemies. That was before her teeth went black." Silva flashes a grin, his mustache lifting. "Doesn't matter to this haul. Now, who's taking me to the vault?"

Taim stands up. "I am."

Overeager jerk-off. I stand myself, shove Taim back onto the bench, and lock eyes with Silva. "They're my suits, and you want *me* down there."

Silva laces his fingers together. "And why's that? Coasties spend dozens of hours dive training." He taps Taim's shoulder with his bionic foot. "Plus, this one seems carved from stone. Better suited for hauling up my coin."

"No one's better suited than me," I say.

"Jin, let it go." Taim leans forward. "I'll dive."

"No," I say. "These two may be in the Guard"—I gesture at Taim and Saanvi—"but I've spent thousands of hours diving."

"Thousands, huh? And who taught you?"

"My dad."

"Where's *he* now?"

"Still down there," I say. "Like all the best divers."

"Ain't that the truth," Silva says, swigging back his maté. "All right, then, well, that's decided."

Taim stands. "But—"

"Sit down, boy!" Silva roars. "It's decided." I swallow, Taim sits, and Silva calmly continues. "Now, it's a decent plan. Few changes, though. First, we're not checking in at Blue Diamond. Too many Coasties on the southern half of La Madre." He draws his feet off the table, sits upright, pulls a knife from his thigh, and starts dragging it across the map. "We'll circle round the western and northern sides of La Madre, and then drop in an anchorage west of Yucca Cape. You, Lieutenant, bring the patrol boat round there." Silva jabs the knife at Taim. "Do it quietly, or you won't be seeing the sisters again. From there, we'll take a crew of me, six of my hands, the Coasty, and little miss thousand hours—"

"Name's Jin," I say. (Not entirely sure why I'm telling him my actual name; maybe because he already knows Thara's.)

"All right, then, Jinny. Once we're over Vegas, me, you, and four of my crew dive down."

"And how does that happen? We only have two suits."

"*You* have two suits," Silva says, wagging the knife at me. "We have another four." He winks. "So that's two of my crew that'll be watching the Coasty, and we'll keep young Thara safe in the brig as . . . insurance."

The way he says her name, like he's known her for years—it makes my skin crawl.

"Now there's just one thing that's not quite adding up." Silva scrapes the blade of the knife across his cheek, like he's attempting a dry shave. "Everybody has a part, a good part, except you there, friend." Silva cocks his head toward Saanvi, who looks completely stricken.

My breath halts, and I can feel the heat peeling off Taim.

"Now what do you think your part is?"

But before Saanvi has half a second to answer, Silva reaches down, pulls his pistol, and fires one shot straight into Saanvi's forehead.

Taim leaps off his bench, but Silva's around the desk too quickly, and he grabs Thara, pinning his knife under her chin.

"Hold yourself there, Coasty," Silva screams. "The little girl has a part, but she can play that part just as well without an ear." Silva's knife slides up to the edge of Thara's cheek, right at the wisps of her sideburns.

My heart's about to rocket out of my chest, my leg muscles are coiled, desperate to hurl me on top of Silva. I want to stomp his bloody face in, but I can't, I can't, because—I glance at Saanvi, and my eyes shut immediately. The sight is too terrible to behold.

My eyes open; my hands reach out to Taim on reflex, wrapping around his wrist, yanking him back. Then the words emerge from my lips, harsh and cold. "Let my sister go, Silva."

Silva doesn't move, the knife still at Thara's neck, and with his other hand, he pinches a lock of her hair, rubbing it between his thumb and forefinger.

"Don't touch her!" I scream.

Silva drops the hank of hair as if pulled from a thought, and the door to his cabin creaks open. In my periphery, I see the barrel of a gun pressed up against Taim's skull.

"Let's all just settle down," Izzy says from behind me. "Ertzo! Nyguenée! Bring some zip ties for our guests here."

Taim is steaming, his body taut and tense, as we're led into the *Bandeira*'s orlop, the lowest deck on the ship, below the waterline. Thara's behind me, silent; Silva released her once Taim's wrists were zipped behind his back and ours pinioned in front of us.

And then there's me, chest tight, breath shallow, swallowing, trying to force the truth of what happened down, like if I just keep trying it'll finally settle in.

Silva just killed Saanvi. Shot him point-blank, for no reason. Or rather, because Silva didn't see a reason for keeping him around.

"Step down, you," Nyguenée says, pushing Taim into the orlop. Taim steps down the ladder, but his hands are pinned at his back, so Nyguenée has a rope looped around Taim's chest to keep him from falling. Nyguenée's a young, wiry corsair with copper skin, a bald head, and a neck tattoo of a giant gull with wings spread and beak agape. "Don't get so jumpy round the captain next time, and we won't have to cinch your hands so tight."

Thara and I, with our hands tied in front, manage our way down the ladder on our own, descending into the deck, which is a sodden mess. Thin puddles dapple the floor, giant spools of cable and rigging are piled starboard, barrels are stacked aft in rows, and in the center, there's a square cage, six feet by six feet, with rusted iron bars running deck to overhead. We step inside. Behind us, Nyguenée throws the cage door shut, fitting a lock through the hasp. "Montserrat will be down in a few hours with food and drink."

"How's he supposed to eat?" I say, motioning to Taim, whose hands are still manacled behind him.

"Ain't my problem," Nyguenée says. Then she strides off, climbing back up the ladder and throwing the overhead hatch.

Taim flops down on the floor, leaning sideways against a corner of the tightly packed bars. Thara slides down as well. The entire deck is dim as dawn, only two crusty bulbs sconced on either side of the foremost ladder that we just climbed. The place smells of rot and salt and something sour, and you can hear the sea slapping against the hull outside.

"We should have taken the plank," Taim whispers.

"Don't say that." I sit down next to Taim, folding my legs together. "We'd all be dead. You did a smart thing, offering up the treasure, keeping us alive."

"Not all of us," Taim says.

Thara's crying now, a muffled, quiet thing. I picture Silva rubbing her hair again, and I motion her over. She sits beside me, and then it's the three of us thigh to thigh: Taim in the corner, then me, then Thara.

"I'm sorry, Taim," Thara finally says. "I got us into this, and—"

"No one needs to be sorry," I say, trying to be strong. "Except Silva, who I'm going to bury beneath fifty thousand tons of waterlogged concrete."

I can feel the blood pulsing in my neck, my toes curled, my calves tight, my teeth ground down on each other, like the way I'm going to leave Silva ground beneath that swamping tower.

The anger feels good. Better than the hurt.

"Saanvi wanted to be here," Taim says, his breath heavy as he shifts, leaning into me. His head drifts down on my shoulder, his lashes fluttering against my skin, and my body slackens with that delicate touch. "He told me on the *Desierto*. Enough money gets in the pot, doesn't matter what kind of luck you have; you stay in, you roll the dice." Taim shifts farther, and his head's on my lap now, his knees curled into his chest. "I just keep thinking." He stops, and I can see the faint lines of water, his tears, streaming off my thighs. "He was an only child, you know."

We know. Saanvi's mother used to buy some of our wreck-found goods, try to resell them. It's how I first met Taim, actually; went over when I was nine, with Dad, and even back then Taim and Saanvi were sail-to-mast, boots to knees covered in mud on account of some oysters they'd dug up in Cottonwood Bay.

"Tell me something about him," Thara says. She's nestled up against my rib cage now on the other side. "If you want to. I didn't know him the way you did."

My heart warms as she says that.

"He was learning Spanish." Taim's voice steadies as he

speaks. "For me. We were gonna travel to Durango on our next leave. I've never been, and Saanvi thought maybe I could find some relatives, learn more about Mamá."

I didn't know about that trip.

"We were friends for so long, he remembered her rolling out barley flour tortillas, us dunking them in her shrimp caldillo. He remembered her telling us this bedtime story about Santiago, an old fisherman doing battle with a marlin." Taim pauses, and I can feel his throat shift on my leg. "I'll never have another friend who knew her." It's such an awful thought, and Taim gasps for breath like he's been holding it this whole time. "All I can think now is—how do I tell *his* mother? How do I tell her that I—I couldn't stop it."

We don't say anything, and Taim's still for several moments, his eyes open but blank, empty. "Maybe I won't have a chance to tell her."

I trace a finger along Taim's forehead, to his temple, around his ear, down his neck. It's something I used to do when we just lay together. I'd retrace that line, over and over. And, at last, I whisper, "You will. I'll make sure of it."

13

The next morning, we're still in a pile. Thara leaning on my side, Taim's head in my lap, my back sore from sleeping seated and in restless thirty-minute intervals.

My dreams were a terrifying mess. Visions of Dad and Taim and Thara, all sunk in the deep, unsuited, standing on the ocean bottom with heads blown apart like Saanvi's and black eels swimming through them, in and out, in and out, until at last one eel swims straight toward me, snake-mouth opening, and then—I'm awake, and the only remnant of the dream is the sick, desperate desire to touch my face.

To make sure it's still there.

Clouds above. *Saanvi.*

He didn't deserve that. He was the first Coconino kid to make it into the Guard in five years. He mentored Taim—took him away from me, maybe, but also helped him toward a better life. Saanvi was a good person. An affinity for gambling, sure, but who doesn't need a little chance and hope in this bleary world?

The iron bars of our cage press into my back. Taim and Thara are curled up at my sides, breath ragged, sleeping.

Across from me, near the orlop's foremost ladder, is a young, gangly corsair, Montserrat, slumped in a wishbone chair. He has pale skin, a long neck, and a prosthetic glove bearing mechanical fourth and fifth fingers on his right hand. He dropped off dinner and some brackish tea late in the night. Thara and I fed Taim, then we resumed our pile and let the white noise of the waves wash away all thought.

The overhead hatch flies open, and Montserrat jerks awake.

"Monty?" Silva's square-toe metal foot is the first thing I see as he steps down the ladder. "You sleeping on my watch?"

Monty jerks up. "Never, Captain. Watched them the whole night."

Silva leaps down the last four rungs, landing like a bear on ice, all power and certainty. He's likely going on sixty, but that bionic must give him tremendous lower body strength. People say intelligence officers in the Navy get them sometimes, even if they haven't lost the leg. An elective job's as expensive as land is rare, though; I've never met someone who did it voluntarily.

Silva sticks a finger under Montserrat's chin. He's a good three inches taller than our cell-guard, and he pokes Monty right at the corner of his lips. "You're drooling, Monty."

Monty wipes his sleeve across his cheek. "Yes, Captain. Sorry, Captain."

Silva nods toward the ladder, and Monty climbs up quick.

Izzy takes his place, grabbing the rails and sliding straight down. She squints at the three of us, shakes her head, which jingles from the clash of her face rings, and yells at us in her dolphin-pitch, "Get up!" We do, and Izzy cuts all our zip ties.

Then Silva steps forward. "We tossed your friend over last night. Pair of kitefin sharks were glowing their neon blue near the rudder. They tore him up quick enough."

Taim's jaw is clenched beside me, but he's still, and I try not to picture Saanvi's body in the water.

"Good," Silva says. "Calmer today. Well then, let's lay about our business. Visibility is crack all, so we've crept up just five miles off Mojave Main. There's an inflatable already in the water for you . . . Lieutenant. You'll row out. I'm not wasting a battery on you, but you'll get there. Once you have the patrol boat, you meet us up in the Fingers of Southern Nevada at three, six, dot, eight, seven, three, zero, zero, four North by one, one, five, dot, five, nine, three, four, zero, five West. You can remember that, right? You're a diver."

Taim nods, asking Silva to repeat the numbers back twice. After a bit of mumbling to himself, he says, "Okay, I have it. But are you sure you want to meet up there? Southern Nevada is all privately owned according to the Guard. Dangerous and off-limits."

"That's exactly why," Silva says. "Place is desolate as a drowned city. Nice spot to tuck away while we wait for your vessel."

"Fine," Taim says. "Just stay put. Will be late tonight by the time I pull in."

"We'll be there," Silva drawls. "Don't get smart on me, though. I sniff a storm, and I won't hesitate to feed the sisters to the kitefins too."

Taim draws a long, deep breath. Then he leans across me and pecks a kiss on my lips.

I don't kiss him back. At least, I don't think I do. I'm not sure. All I can focus on right now is the tingly residue of his lips on mine. The faint acceleration of my heart.

"I *will* return," Taim says. "You and Thara stay safe."

I see Silva grinning behind Taim (asshole), then he steps toward the cage, speaking directly to Thara. "I'm going to ask Monty to bring something down for you. It's special to me. Please take good care of it."

My right fist squeezes as I speak for my sister. "We don't need it. Whatever it is."

Silva tilts his head. "Monty will bring it down. You two can decide then." He pulls a key from his pocket (*Remember that,* I think, *he keeps a brig key on him*), and his gaze shifts to Taim. "Ready, Lieutenant?"

Thara and I spend the rest of the morning in the brig. She's withdrawn and despondent, and I can see she's filled with guilt over what's happened, what she thinks she caused.

Meanwhile, I spend at least an hour with my lips frozen

still, letting the sensations of Taim's kiss fade to numb. My mind keeps drifting. What did it mean? Should I have kissed him back?

Which is pure idiocy. Because Thara and I are locked in this brig and Saanvi is dead, and Taim—well, he might not make it back.

Maybe that's why I can't stop thinking about it. I may never see him again—may never get to ask what it meant. Was it a calculated thing, meant to give me strength? A spontaneous thing, meant to satisfy his urge? Or maybe he's the one who needed strength . . . after his body and spirit crumpled last night.

It doesn't matter. I can't let myself get lost in feelings for Taim right now. If I lose focus, people die. Dad died when I didn't keep focus, when I stopped digging.

I can't let it happen to Thara. I won't.

I cozy up next to my sister, placing an arm around her. We sit in silence for a long time, until I hear Monty return, and he's holding something between the bars. I glance up, and my breath catches because the thing—it's stunning. A long white comb, translucent, with twisting veins of some semiprecious stone—maybe agate, because of the prism of colors: muted reds and oranges and yellows. The entire piece feels like an ancient heirloom, and Thara takes it from Monty, staring at it with awe.

"For your hair," Monty says to Thara. "Captain wants you to look nice for later."

My entire body goes rigid on that last line—my lungs hollow out.

There's a part of me that wants to grab that comb from Thara, shatter it into a hundred pieces, and tell Monty there won't be a later. We're not going anywhere, and his captain will not be coming within six inches of my sister. My *fourteen-year-old* sister.

But I know it's not the right play, and I release a ragged breath. Thara and I have been in these situations before. We've been running the inn alone for over three years. Every man who's looked at Thara like that has been bigger, stronger. They could easily have overpowered us. They could have . . . except that I always maintained our advantage.

Surprise.

"Thank you, Monty," I say as kindly as possible. "Please tell Captain Silva that we appreciate the comb."

Thara looks at me like *who are you and what have you done with my sister?*

"And one other thing, Monty?" I say.

"Yeah."

"Is there anything for lunch? We want to keep our energy up for . . . later."

* * *

Another hour, and Montserrat drops off a steel plate piled with grilled prawns—probably the same ones we were swimming in, but I could give two bits. We devour them ravenously, like shark on seal, and after we're done, I start working the comb through Thara's hair.

It really is a beautiful piece. Twenty teeth, wide set, each two digits long, sharp, and I'm thinking the whole thing was carved from bone and glazed. I've seen jewelry like this at markets where Dad and I would hawk our wreck-found goods. Lots of whalebone pieces out there, though more crude, and never with the stone inlay. This item must be worth dozens of ounces.

I dig out several prawn bits from Thara's hair, and what must be eggs (though I don't tell her that much). About twenty minutes into the combing, and I'm steeling myself for the conversation we need to have, when abruptly, Thara says, "So what do I do later? Stab him with his fancy comb?"

I start laughing for some half-drowned reason, and Thara starts laughing too. "What? You don't think I could stab him?" she says. "I could totally stab him. Death by comb. Try to touch my hair again, see what happens."

I'm still laughing. "I don't doubt you for a second."

"But," she says.

"But I think we should play this like that judge from Flagstaff. We flatter him, listen to his stories, get him gripping from the matés or drunk if he has alcohol." I sniff and point left. "I'm thinking that's the sour smell coming out of those barrels."

"Right."

"Anyway, we coax him along until his guard's down."

"Then?"

"Well—just like the Flagstaff judge. We'll be drinking, laughing, I'll climb into his lap at some point, pretend I'm having fun."

The thought of his hands on my body makes me shudder, but I pull the comb through Thara's hair, thankful that she can't see me. "Then you slip behind him," I say. "You pull the pistol right off his thigh." I pause the combing, imagining the scene. "You'll want to rip the slide back hard and fast. You know how to do that, yes?"

She nods. "Taim showed me on Auntie Ximena's gun once."

The things she's had to learn . . .

"Good. It'll let him know you're serious. From there, we have him walk us aft-ship toward one of those rigid-hull inflatables. We take that, send a drone out to the Guard, and let Taim know not to come back."

"What if you're not there?" Thara says. "I mean—what if he only invites me up?"

My heart slams in my chest, but I respond as confidently as I can. "That's not going to happen, Thara."

"Just, what if it does? What do I do?"

I walk around in front of her then, pressing a sharp tooth from the comb into the pad of my finger until it draws blood. "Then you stab him like you said. The first chance you get, you put this fucking comb in his eye."

Sometime several hours after lunch, Izzy comes down, her rings jangling on the ladder. She says, "The captain requests your presence for supper."

"Both of us?" Thara says so quickly.

"Yes, the both of you. Now, get up." Izzy's shriek pierces my temples, but the truth is I couldn't be happier. Thara doesn't have to face this alone.

Izzy unlocks the cage and motions for Thara and me to climb the ladder ahead of her. The *Bandeira*'s a true battle craft, functional and lethal, with cramped, narrow passageways, bright lighting built into the overheads, sophisticated instruments lining the bulkheads, and clear signage for personnel, directing them to the engine room, the weapons hold, cabins, sanitary compartments, and more. I take it in as we climb from passage to passage, trying to build my own mental map of the ship.

At last, Izzy opens a door as we move below the foredeck, motions for us to enter, and then pulls three strings hanging from the overhead. Lights buzz on, casting a pale white glow, and the compartment can only be a laundry. A deep basin lines the far-side bulkhead, with a washing machine and dryer beside it, and the machines are so massive it looks like they could handle the whole crew's laundry in a single load. The rest of the bulkheads are covered in clothing. Jackets of every size and shape hang from rods, most in dark shades like sea green and thunder gray and black, and all shimmering in a way that speaks to the anti-salt stain and water repellent that's applied to mariner outerwear. Above and below the jackets are shelves piled with undergarments, socks, pants, and boots rowed in tidy pairs.

Izzy strides in, grabs several items from the shelves, and throws them at Thara and me. "You both smell like prawns." She nods at Thara. "And you—do you still have his comb?" Thara nods; she tucked it into her waistband earlier. "Good, then clean well." Izzy gestures to a bar of soap and the basin. "The captain did the mess up nice. Consider yourselves lucky he wants to host you in private."

After a good twenty minutes of scrubbing, we're ready to emerge. Izzy tossed each of us pantsuits, like we're heading to some naval gala. Thara's is teal velvet, brass buttons on the sleeves, with a midnight blouse beneath, and mine is black vinyl, but I ditched the blouse, so it's just a V cut at my neckline and a matte blush sash across the waist. (If I can redirect his attention to me, then that's what I'm going to do.) All the fabrics are synthetic. Cotton and leather and that stuff is only for the wealthiest inlanders. Still, these are fancy synthetics, soft on our skin, and it's both wonderful and terrifying putting on clothes like this. I remember the rank breath of that Flagstaff judge in my ear. "I like your shirt," he told me. "But the thing about nice clothing is . . . it's meant to be removed."

I close my eyes and try to shut out that thought. *Don't go there. It's not going to get that far.* Thankfully, it never got that far with the judge, either. While I was sitting in his lap, Thara came up behind him and knocked him out with her cast-iron fillet pan. We left him on the street outside the inn with a concussion, no pants, an oyster knife buried in his inner thigh, and a note that read: *Come back and the next knife won't miss.*

I rub Thara's shoulder as we slip on naval-grade sea boots. "Ready?"

Thara pulls out the glass pyramid bead that she's been keeping in her pants pocket. "You think I should take it?" she says.

"For what?"

"For luck. It was Luz's lucky charm."

I hesitate a beat or two, hoping she'll hear how she sounds. Luz is dead. Nothing about what's happened to us is lucky. Unfortunately, Thara doesn't hear it, so I just say something to keep her confidence up. "Good idea. Bring it." I throw open the laundry's door to find Monty, who ogles us until I'm two beats away from cuffing him across the face. The upside: I know we look good. The down: we just got rain fresh so we can dine with the homicidal lecher of a sea captain who's holding us hostage.

Monty finally comes to and leads us to the end of the passage, dropping us with Izzy, who opens another door and follows us through. The mess is a spacious triangular compartment, consuming the entire main deck below the prow. About thirty feet at the widest, it runs port to starboard in the hull, and as you walk in, the left and right sides slope together, until they form an apex right at the chin of the ship. Large metal beams arc over the mess, and more of the paintings I saw in the captain's quarters coat the hull's interior. There are at least three dozen here, all depicting scenes of the sea.

Eight large portholes line the tip of the room's triangle, and the view through them is of a long stretch of coastline. I realize now that we are anchored deep in a bay that helps to form the Fingers of Southern Nevada. This makes my mind spin. I did not think that I would be here, out of the brig, hands uncuffed, and so near to land. It can't be more than a quarter mile swim, and suddenly the plan cements in my head. *Forget the inflatables. Jump ship, swim to shore, get onto land—escape.* The one thing between that plan and now: the captain who sits in the center of the mess, leering at my sister.

He's seated at a round table with a white polyester cloth and three cushioned chairs (his and presumably ones for Thara and me). There are ten other naked metal tables in the room, all bolted into the deck. Silva's table is set in a very refined way: three settings, with a light blue plate and bowl and better flatware than we keep at the inn. My eyes linger on that cutlery. A fork and a spoon. No knife. It's both disappointing and strangely pleasing. *Silva thinks us more capable than most men do.*

My eyes flick to Thara, and she's steady as a rock, her eyes locked onto Silva's, a coy smile on her face. There's a part of me that's so happy she's good at this, and another part that wishes she had no talent at all.

The table itself is piled with vessels containing crabs and whole fish, rice (haven't had rice in years), curries, a stew, and in the center of the table there's a beautiful ceramic teapot with an etched wavy pattern. The aromas are almost overwhelming—rich and salty and a distraction I don't need.

Silva motions to the chairs, saying, "Won't you join me?" His lips are in a thin, smug smile, and he's dressed as he was when we first met him: in the long black vinyl coat, his mariner's cap tilted down on his brow. I can't see if the gun's there on his thigh below the table, but it must be. Thara and I step forward, pulling out the chairs. Thara inches hers slightly closer to Silva. He studies her out of the corner of his eye but says nothing. Then Izzy closes the mess door, but stays inside, sitting on a stool in a corner behind us. *Shit.*

"You two clean up well," Silva says, and it comes out so swamping cocky that I can't help myself.

"And you're the fucking monster who shot my friend." My words roll forth, hot and vengeful, and I instantly regret them. I'm supposed to be attractive, demur, inviting. I'm supposed to play along. Thara kicks me under the table, and I yelp, and Silva sweeps his glance across the both of us, but for some reason, he shrugs it off.

"That I am," he says, lifting a small white ceramic teacup, filling it, and passing it to me.

"Do you have anything harder?" I say.

Silva squints at me. "I do." His lips purse. "Let's stick with the tea, though."

Damnit. I'm so freaking bad at this.

"Thank you for the comb," Thara says, batting her eye-lashes, coming to my rescue. "It's very beautiful." Thara draws the comb out from her hair at the nape of her neck, then tosses her hair from her right shoulder (the one next to Silva) and over to her left. I can smell the soap in her hair from here. Not her typical citrus, but something floral, like a water iris. I can only imagine the scent washes over Silva too.

Thara places the comb on the table, pushing it forward until it bumps into Silva's hand and her fingers graze off his. His eyes shoot up, meeting Thara's, and I'm half-terrified she's coming on too strong and he's going to lead her out of the mess and down to his quarters before we've had a chance to impair him.

He doesn't, though. Instead, he lifts the comb and examines it some. "It was my cousin's," he says. "Vitória." He waits several beats, as if he wants to say more, but eventually the moment passes and he fills a teacup for himself and one for Thara.

We wait for him to drink before doing the same. It would be rather pointless, poisoning us, but killing Saanvi also seemed pointless, and I'm not taking any chances.

"Where did you get the necklace?" Silva says, eyeing Thara.

She lifts the medallion off her collarbone, pinching it, holding it forward for Silva to see. "It was my mom's," she says. "Lakshmi, goddess of wealth and fortune."

Silva leans in. "Good we have her with us."

I really need his attention back on me. "My dad recovered it on his first wrecking job," I tell him, placing my hand on his. "Gave it to our mom. They're both gone now."

Yes, we're very vulnerable. No parents to protect us. Isn't that what you want to hear?

Silva swivels his head very slowly toward me, and maybe it's not what he wants to hear because he lifts my hand off his, draping it at my side.

My heart hammers away. *Maybe he's only interested in Thara. Disgusting cad.*

Silva points at the pearl stud in the cartilage of his right ear. "Got this just after my first job. Everyone remembers their first."

Several beats pass, and Thara reads him correctly. "What was yours?"

I realize only then—*he wants to tell us.*

Silva sits back in his chair and his eyes roll up. On the ceiling there's an etching similar to the one on the hull of this ship. Three shapes, all outlines—a white circle inside a white diamond inside a white rectangle. Silva stares at it for a moment, then speaks. "Was a long time ago. I was just a boy, seven years old, but my whole family were wreckers. We grew up on an island called Pico da Bandeira, not far from Rio-Lost. My family had hauled countless Brazilian artifacts up from the deep, but they'd never gotten the biggest: a giant, one-hundred-foot statue by the name *Cristo Redentor.*" Silva lets out a long sigh. "I wasn't supposed to go on the job—too young—but I caught my cousin Vitória sending a drone that morning. She was fifteen, shouldn't have been using drones, so I told her I'd keep it quiet if she smuggled me onto the ship." A calm smile spreads across his cheeks, and he turns to Thara. "Vitória had hair like yours. I admired her very much."

The man's sick.

Silva swallows, and Thara rubs his back. "Can you tell me more about her?"

Silva is silent. *Is he choked up?* I can't read it. After a while, he continues. "She was the family jewel. My parents said she'd be our best wrecker one day. I hoped so, because her father, my uncle, led the family. He was a hard man. . . ." A fat drop races down Silva's left cheek, and I think, *Is he . . . crying?*

This man shot my friend point-blank just yesterday.

"What happened on the job?" I say. It's abrupt, but this suddenly feels important. Like it might be the key to something.

"We get out to the site," Silva says. "Everyone dives. Just me, Vitória, and my aunt on deck. That's when two frigates showed up, started firing. It was another wrecking crew, rivals." Silva shakes his head. "I lost every family member I had that day—all of them except for Vitória."

I stifle a gasp. It's a sad story, no doubt, and Thara and I sit in silence after. *So many have been lost to the deep.* Still, I can't allow myself to feel sympathy for this man. What I need to be doing is focusing on our plan. The one where Silva relaxes his guard, and—

The man just cried in front of us. His guard's already down.

With the dawning of that realization, I stand up, and my eyes flash over to Thara's. She sees me and nods once. *It's now. We're doing this, right now.*

Silva scrunches up his face, looking rather confused, but he'll settle into it.

Men are men are men.

I take a step toward Silva, eyeing the small gap between

his chair and the table. It's just wide enough, and I squeeze in, lowering myself onto his lap. His hands connect to my hips, and then he shoves me to the right. "What are you doing?" he barks.

"I thought you might like some entertainment with your dinner," I say.

Thara's already up, moving into place, just behind him.

"Sit down," Silva says. "Now. You too, Thara. In your seat."

"But—isn't that why you called us up here?" I say. "Isn't that why you sent the comb? Why you offered us these clothes?"

Silva kicks his head back and cackles. From the corner behind me, I hear Izzy's high-pitched shriek as well. "Izzy, can you believe these two?" Silva says.

"It's too much, Captain!" Izzy's hollering now, hysterical laughs rolling out.

What the . . . ?

Silva straightens his back, getting serious. "I gave you the comb because I could see the prawns in your sister's hair from thirty feet out. I gave you the clothes because you both smelled like fish guts. I called you up here because we're going diving tomorrow, and I'd like to know about your experience." *My god. Did I really just misread this entire situation?*

"Now, sit back down, eat, and answer a few of my questions."

"Hold on," I say. "Why were you touching my sister's hair yesterday?"

"What's that?" Silva spoons rice onto my plate and Thara's,

along with a thin green curry containing kelp and squid rounds.

"In your quarters. You were touching her hair."

Silva shrugs. "You don't see long hair often. My cousin Vitória had long hair. Just got caught in a memory is all. Didn't mean anything by it."

Rust take me. I'm a complete fool.

I see the relief pouring out of Thara as she hangs her head and sits back down, starting to eat. I do the same, and Silva gives us a few minutes to wallow in our shame. Then, about halfway through my food (maybe only a tenth of the way through my embarrassment), Silva starts firing from the bow.

"*How deep have you been?*"

"Four thousand feet," I say, bluffing.

"And your biggest haul?" he says.

"Ten solar panels off a roof in Phoenix-Below."

"Sell them to a drone dealer, did you?"

"Yeah."

"You ever gone hypoxic?"

Eight months ago. "Am I here?" I say instead.

"People survive the thing. But if I'm going down with you, best know you can handle it."

"I can."

"Best you do," Silva says. "I put my life in your hands."

That's what I'm counting on.

"You planning to kill me?" Silva asks.

And with that, he finally catches me short. I take two gulps of tea, and it's too much. Still, I respond. "You planning to let us free once we haul it up?"

"Good as my word, I am," Silva says.

"Don't think our friend Saanvi would put much coin in your word." I slug back the rest of the tea.

"Well, thing is, it doesn't matter what you believe. Matters what I do, and I don't suffer freeloaders. Never said, you all come aboard, you live. Said I'd hear you out. And I did, and I didn't see a part for the boy, and that's that. Now I'm telling you, we haul it up, you and your sister and your dreamboat Coasty can swim to shore. Swear it on the sun-shining heavens. I'll even toss in a few coin for your troubles after. But you get funny down there, and I'll evac to the surface, pop a drone in the sky, and then Izzy, what's your orders?"

I glance over my shoulder, and Izzy's sitting in the corner, calm, legs crossed, silver smile hooked into her frowning face.

"Well," Izzy says, "then I'm afraid little Thara's gonna be fodder for the kitefins too."

14

As we leave the mess, Silva's cracking crabs, and I'm feeling like an idiot. That was our chance, and I misread the entire situation. We didn't get the key from his pocket. We didn't get the gun. But Nevada's close, a ten-minute swim or less. And that's the one saving grace because I think, maybe, I have a better plan.

Izzy leads us straight down the hall to the laundry. "Back into your prawn clothes," she says, shoving us in and closing the door.

I turn to Thara, whispering, "New plan."

She gives me a look like, *Please, let it be better than your last.*

I shake my head and continue, "You saw it, right, we're a quarter mile from Nevada. Can you make the swim?"

"Yeah, but how?" She waves her arms across the compartment. "This place is practically a second brig: no portholes, no other exits but the front door—with Izzy outside."

"Don't need one," I say. "We're going out the front door." I shuffle over to one of the two giant machines, lower my shoulder, drive my feet into the ground, and it budges. "These things are massive. We're going to use it as a wedge, and—"

"Finish up!" Izzy calls from outside. "Big day tomorrow, and I don't want Jinny nodding off down under."

At this point, there's no time left to explain. I yank a clothing rod off the wall, dump the hangers, and snap the thing in two across my knee. The short piece I shove through the front door's handle, so that it's horizontal across the doorjamb, barring Izzy from pulling the door open.

I hustle back over to the washing machine, yanking plugs, wrenching pipes, Thara staring on. Water rushes forth from the broken piping, and Izzy's screaming outside, jostling the door. "You two open this right now, or I'll have you swimming with the kitefins *tonight*."

Little does she know, that's our plan too.

I motion Thara to one side of the machine. "Drive it straight through the door and into the passage."

"Is it going to fit?" she says.

"They got it in here, didn't they?"

"But Izzy's directly outside."

"Exactly." I walk back to the door, yank the clothing rod out of the handle, and then I call to Izzy. "Okay, we're opening up. It's flooded in here, though. Stand back!" I hurl the door open, and in seconds I'm back behind the washing machine with Thara. Izzy strides through the doorway, and that's when we burst forward, driving the machine across the deck, directly at her.

She leaps backward, but that's the wrong move—she should have leaped to the side—because we plow the machine straight into Izzy, then out of the laundry, pinning her against the passageway wall. Thara and I squeeze out, hook left, and I glance back at Izzy, seeing a gun in her right hand. The hand is just in front of the washing machine, mobile. Izzy's shifting her wrist, trying to take aim, and that's when I punch her straight in that exposed wrist. She screams, drops the gun, I grab it, and then Thara and I are racing down the passageway. Two corsairs stand far ahead of us, so I yank open another door. It's some type of storage compartment, but there's a large, round porthole, and that's all we need. I raise the gun and fire—one, two, three, four, five, six shots. The pistol's out, the porthole must have been reinforced, but it's cracked and splintered now. Thara raises a leg, kicks, and—boom! The whole thing tumbles three levels into the water outside.

"Ready?" I say. Thara doesn't even respond. She just leaps, arms forward in a dive, and now I'm thinking I really should have checked for kitefins first.

I follow, dropping the empty gun and hurtling myself through the hole. It's a twenty-five-foot plunge at least, but the kind we've made hundreds of times as kids off the Admiral's bluff stairs.

In an instant, the frigid water claims my body. I'm beside Thara, scanning for ferocious, radiant blue creatures, but they're not here, and anyway, what good is scanning going to do? If they find us, we're dead. If not, well, we might still be dead.

Screams and yells bellow down to us from the *Bandeira's* main deck.

"Aye, there's a splash!"

"Crew overboard!"

"Who fired shots?"

"Throw them a rope!"

And then the unmistakable screech of Izzy. "It's not our crew! They're our prisoners. Now in with you all. After them! And take 'em alive!"

With that last sentence, a surge of hope floods through my veins. Izzy and Silva can't kill us. Not yet. We know the location of the vault. Which just means we have to outswim them. "Go, Thara! Go!"

My arms pound the water, my feet flipping like a seal's; adrenaline courses through my limbs, and my sister's keeping pace at my side. We can do this. We *can* do this.

I risk a glance back and already the *Bandeira's* shape is fading in the distance. I can't see the corsairs chasing us, but judging by the commotion they're making, it's at least a half dozen.

My hands keep pounding, cupping the water, shoving it past me, again, again, again. Thara's slowing down, she's a half-length behind me, our heads swiveling, face in the water, gulp a breath to the side, face down again, repeat. We're trying to keep form—the way to maintain swimming speed is to keep form—but it's also swamp-all impossible with a pack of corsairs in your wake.

I risk a glance up again—my face is stinging cold, the tips of my fingers growing numb—and then a wave hits me from behind, and another, and normally this would be horrible, waves flooding our mouths, stealing our breath, but waves near shore are good. Waves near shore mean—we're close to land.

I stand up because—I can stand. The shore's thirty feet ahead. I jerk Thara up by that sodden, midnight-black blouse she's wearing, and we're running, our lower bodies underwater, and then we're out of the water, feet on sand, and off across a black craggy terrain awash in mist that freezes the sea to our bodies. My feet aren't frozen, though; I'm running too hard for that. Thara's heaving at my side, but I keep my fingers laced in hers, running, pulling, running. I can't hear the corsairs anymore, but that may just be the blood pounding in my head. There's no one here. No stray buildings, shacks, no faint lights from an outpost, there's just—*clunk*.

I hit something. Like, I actually run straight into it. My shoulder's pulsing. Thara pulls up at my side, and I'm placing hands on it—a wall, a massive black metal wall that's smooth, almost polished. The mist is heavy here, but the wall seems to run in every direction, left and right, and then I'm craning my head back, back, back, looking up, because the wall—I can't see where it stops.

Thara's eyes are wide next to me, her mouth agape. "What is . . . and how high do you think . . ." Her voice trails off in the mixture of the two questions, both of which I have no answer to. I've heard of rich landowners who build walls around their coastal property to hold back the seas. But *this*, well—it's enormous. It must rise several hundred feet into the air. It's hard to say because it's a black wall leading into a black, starless sky. I can't see if there's a way around it.

Or maybe through it?

I'm trying to puzzle the thing out, when I swivel around and see a scattering of light approaching from the shore.

"You think those are people who can help us?" Thara says.

She's so hopeful, always. "No," I say, and then I'm grabbing her hand and sprinting along the wall, my left hand tight in Thara's, my right hand brushing the wall as we run its length. I peer back after a few minutes, and the lights are closer now, approaching the wall, not fifty feet behind us.

My feet slow, and Thara opens her mouth. "Why don't we—"

"Shhh." I put a finger to her lips, my eyes darting across the terrain. Is there a crater somewhere we can curl into? Someplace, any place, to hide. Between the mist and the pitch-black night, we just need a tiny hovel to shield us from view.

But there's nothing, and I turn around as the lights grow stronger again—they're almost on top of us when a blinding beam hits my eyes. I close them on instinct, and then Silva's melodic voice echoes off the wall. "Why, hello there." The beam shifts off me, and I open my eyes to see Silva and five other corsairs with headlamps across their brows. "Now, as you can see, there is nobody here to let you in. Even if you knock." Silva raps his knuckles against the wall. "Satisfied?" He pulls his pistol and then turns toward us. "Let's all head back to the ship now. The Coasty sent a drone. He'll be back soon with my boat. And you have the way to my gold."

15

Thara and I ride back to the *Bandeira* in a rigid-hull inflatable along with Silva and six corsairs: one of them conning the craft, and the other five soaking wet, half-frozen, and beneath blankets, like us.

I'm shivering, but more than the cold, it's the fear. We just blew out a porthole and forced a half dozen corsairs into the water at night. Silva seemed carefree enough when he caught us, but that man's emotions change quicker than a summer storm. And I'm shaking, wondering—*What are the consequences for an attempted escape?*

I don't linger on that thought. I can't. I'm so swamping tired from the swim. My eyelids keep drifting down, and wow, is that a contrast to Silva. The man looks so alert, so full of energy, so . . . powerful. We arrive at the *Bandeira* and pull directly onto the rear ramp. In moments, we're up onto the drone deck and greeted by Izzy, who sucker punches me in the gut. I fall to the deck, and she stands over me. "Time to be through with these girls, Captain."

My body clenches, my eyes drift to Thara, but thankfully, the wry old Silva waves Izzy off. "Just because she got the best of you?" Silva laughs. "No, they're worth the trouble. For fifty thousand coin, I'd have the whole crew in the water."

"Respectfully, Captain, I disagree, and—"

Silva steps up close to Izzy, looking like he might bite her nose off. "That's enough. Now lead young Thara down to the brig, while I have a talk with the big sister. Tomorrow we dive, and *then* we're done with them."

True to his word, indeed.

Izzy snorts, the rings on her face crashing into each other, then she pulls her pistol (I should have thrown that thing in the water) and shoves Thara forward.

Go, I mouth. *I'll be okay.*

Thara grimaces, but she doesn't protest, and Silva motions for me to get up and follow. The wind lashes rain down the deck as we walk, and it feels like tiny specks of shattered glass flung at my body. Maybe I should be more concerned about being led somewhere alone with Silva, but with the shame of capture still fresh, and with the orders to take us alive during our escape attempt, I'm starting to realize—this dive is going to happen. Silva's intent on it. And he needs me to make it happen.

I have to stop trying to survive the next few hours . . . and start planning to survive Treasure Island.

Tomorrow we dive, and then we're done with them.

Silva leads me up to the pilothouse on the second level of the bridge. It's a large space, with a giant pillar in the center, a dizzying array of nautical instruments, and black-tinted windows on all four sides. We're anchored, so there's a single corsair there, sleeping on a stool. Silva tells her to clear out, and then we have the ship's command center to ourselves.

On the pillar that pierces the center of the pilothouse, there are twelve of Silva's paintings in varying sizes, three on each side of the pillar, and Silva nods at them. "I wanted to show you these," he says. "I keep my favorites here. A reminder to my crew who steer the ship. Never forget what she's capable of."

"What who's capable of?" I say.

"The sea."

I walk around the pillar, taking them in.

"Pick one, and I'll tell you its provenance," he says.

Silva's head swivels with mine, and I see his eyes studying a pretty painting, large with warm tones, a menacing sea, sailors clinging to the debris from a wreckage, but it's the dawn of a new morning and the sun is gleaming so bright, blasting through clouds that submit to its glory. *"The Ninth Wave,"* he says, and I'm guessing that's the name. Doesn't matter, though. It's beautiful, but far too hopeful.

My eyes roam farther, and then I see it: a tiny thing, rectangular, perhaps one foot by slightly more, depicting a monstrous cresting rogue wave with white foam talons hooked, hungry, and reaching for three longboats in the swell beneath. There's a snow-capped mountain in the distance, thunderous clouds on the horizon, and the clouds are reaching out, spreading forth, no sun, ready to consume the sky.

This is the one. Despite its small proportions, the blue-striped wave captures the way I feel about our world. *Terror.*

Silva sees me staring, and he lifts the painting from its hook, bringing it to me. My entire body tenses, my hands clenched, and the weight of my chest shifts, stilling my heart, as I remember that one day, the claws of the world's oceans will pull us all below.

"An excellent choice," Silva says. "*The Great Wave off Kanagawa.*" He mulls over the words. "I recovered it from an ancient place in the mid-Atlantic: York-Lost. Pair of wreckers working the Colorado shores put me on to it. Said they knew of a horde of artwork, pressure-sealed, lying in a castle of a building called the Metropolitan Museum of Art."

Silva closes his eyes, as if recalling the moment. "Izzy and I made the trip. Was about forty-two hundred feet down, but well worth the risk on account of recovering such beauty."

Clouds above. *Forty-two hundred feet!* That's about as deep as wreckers go. My real max is thirty-six hundred, and that means—well, it means whatever illusions I have of Silva panicking under the pressure of the Vegas dive . . . they're just—illusions.

"You know what the most amazing part of it is?" He steps toward the pillar, hanging *The Great Wave* back on its hook. "The person who did it, Hokusai, he was born on an island nation, east of the Tibetan Plateau, in the eighteenth century . . . nearly three hundred years *before* the Stitching."

Stars and moon.

At this point, I can't resist. "How do you even know this?"

"There was a note," he says, "in the container the work came in. The people who packaged it, they wanted to preserve not just the work . . . but what it meant to those of the time." Silva pauses, stepping back, admiring *The Great Wave*. "Tremendous painter, Hokusai. To capture the sea for what it is . . . even before it was."

After a long pause, I turn back to the pillar. "Which is your favorite?"

He walks around it, stopping in front of a larger painting, just over three foot by five. "*The Monk by the Sea*, this is called. Pulled it from Berlin-Lost." Silva beckons me closer, and it's a bleak seascape. At the bottom, there's a lone, tiny monk on a rocky bluff with a thin, dark strip of sea stretching horizontally. Specs of white caps in the sea and an ominous sky above it, occupying almost the entire canvas. The sky's a hostile green at the horizon, and then gray clouds lashing up, as if to dome the Earth. "Take a good look," Silva says. "Nothing worse than being alone in this world." The monk in the painting is hunched, sad, with robes the same deep green as the sea. It makes the monk feel lost, insignificant, hopeless even. The image is remarkable, severe in its beauty, but still—I'm standing here, soaking wet from our escape attempt, huddled under a blanket, near shivering, and losing my patience. "Why did you want to show me these?"

Silva stares out the windows toward the sea. "I asked you earlier, in the mess, if you'll try to kill me tomorrow. I see how you are—protective of your sister, unafraid of death, willing to leap into the Gulf of Nevada in the pitch-black of night if it gives you a shadow of a chance at escape." He smiles. "I like that. And if I was you, I'd try to kill me too. But I want you to know two things. The first is that I know how to dive. The recovery of these works speaks to that."

Understatement of the century. If he really recovered all these pieces, then Silva is one of the best divers in the Archipelago, maybe the world.

He sighs and turns back to me. "The second is what I'm sure you already know. The way to kill an experienced wrecker is to collapse the building they're in. Be easy enough to crumble Treasure Island to bits, but you do that, then you're going to trap yourself in there too. You'll be just as dead as me. And when you're thinking about that, I want you to picture the monk right here." He points back at his favorite painting. "Imagine it's your sister. There's no pain worse than being the last in your family. She'll doubt herself for the rest of her years, always wondering what she should have done differently."

I scoff. "What do you care?"

But Silva's calm, looking through me. "I live with that pain every day. Don't wish it on anyone."

My first instinct is to shout at him, to demand our release, to tell him I don't give a damn about his pain. He killed my friend. Shot him in the face! But as I take another breath to digest his words, I realize something.

They're genuine. Self-interested, yes, he doesn't want the tower to collapse; he wants his gold. But the sentiment, marked by whatever tortured past he has, is real. And that makes me recall the comb and that story of his first wrecking job.

"What happened to you and Vitória, your cousin?" I say. "After the frigates arrived, you said you lost your family, but what happened?"

Silva walks back up to the monk painting, studying it, and finally he speaks. "Vitória found me hiding in the engine room. I was just seven, as I said. Not as courageous as today." A smile peeks out beneath his mustache. "She led me to a skiff that she'd already loaded with supplies, including two atmo suits. I told her we should dive, warn our parents and siblings, but I didn't know how, and Vitória shook her head. It's too late, she told me. 'É tarde demais. Vamos, João.'" Silva turns and his lips are pursed into a hard grimace. "She saved me, but we abandoned everyone else. Rode out to a small island, Ilha Tinguá, which Vitória said was the rendezvous point if a job went bad." Silva stops, as if considering something. "None of our family ever came, and I knew in my heart they were dead. After a few days, Vitória said not to worry, her boyfriend would come, bring coin, and we'd join his crew." He pauses there, and I wait him out, but he doesn't say anything else.

"Did the boyfriend come?"

"Yes," Silva says.

"And you joined his crew?"

"Not his, but another one. Swore I'd build myself into a wrecker who was worthy of my family's respect." Then he looks back at his paintings. "Guess I did all right."

"What happened to Vitória?" I say, sensing that it's important. I can't say exactly why, but he's taken the time to tell the story and he delivers it with such emotion.

Silva looks up at the ceiling. "Been a long time since I've seen her. We had a falling out." The words are laden with regret. "What you need to remember, though"—Silva prods me in the collarbone with one finger—"is if you die down there tomorrow, your sister becomes the last in your family.

Don't do that to her. You don't want her growing up the way little João did."

A short while later, Silva drops me off with Monty, who deposits me back in the orlop. Thara's there, inside the cage. My prawn clothes are piled next to her, and she's already changed out of her drenched naval-gala attire. *Guess I should do the same.* Monty opens the cage, locks it, then disappears up the hatch. In moments, Thara and I are huddled together beneath our rain-wet blankets, with bars in our backs—again.

"You okay?" Thara says, pulling out the glass bead, which it seems survived our swim. *Swamp all.* Was really hoping she'd lose that thing. She squeezes it in her fist, as if it can generate heat and fire and make us warm. "He didn't—do anything— did he?"

"No, sorry I misread that earlier. I feel like a fool."

"It's okay," Thara says. "The look on his face, though, when you tried to sit on his lap . . ." She howls, and a yelp escapes from my lips too. I can feel the heat in my cheeks. Thara's never going to let me live this down. (Which I realize is actually the best outcome . . . because it means we live through *this.*)

At last, Thara wipes the massive grin from her face. "So . . . what did he want, then?"

"To show me his paintings. Let me know that he's this

incredible wrecker. Which he is"—I roll my eyes—"but I think the real purpose was something different. He wanted to tell me more about his cousin Vitória, the one whose comb we used."

"What about her?"

"He said they got away to some island, met her boyfriend, but they had a falling out. He regrets it, that much is clear, but it's important somehow, and I don't think he gave me the full story."

"What do you mean, important?"

"I don't know. But Silva likes us. And we remind him of Vitória. There's something about it. There were two of them. Two of us. Last in our families."

"You think you can use it against him?"

"Yes. Maybe. But I need to understand what happened to Vitória. I think it's affecting his judgment, like—when he's thinking about us, he's thinking about her."

Thara yawns. "Makes sense, but I'm exhausted from that swim. Maybe some sleep will help us figure it out."

"Maybe . . ." I let the silence linger for several seconds while Thara nestles into my side.

"I hope Taim's back soon," she whispers. "Think he'll know what that wall was?"

I shrug. "It was—immense."

Thara grumbles something I can't make out. A minute later, she's snoring.

* * *

I wake with a jolt as the sconces flicker on and Taim slides down the ladder in the middle of the night.

Izzy's quick behind him, with a pistol trained on his head. "Your boyfriend did good. Nice little patrol boat moored along our starboard. And not a peep of Coasties following as we can see."

"You two okay?" Taim says, still dripping wet, topknot tendrils plastered to his face.

We are not okay.

Still, I'm much too exhausted to explain. So I nod.

Izzy opens the cage and Taim walks in. Then Izzy's double smile is in full effect. "Come here, all three of you." Thara and I stand, and Izzy tosses each of us a zip tie. "Best you're all zipped up tight. Not taking any more chances before our big day." We cinch the ties on our wrists, hands in front of us, at least. Then Izzy climbs the ladder, snapping the hatch shut.

"What are those?" Taim says, nodding at the crumpled pantsuits.

I sigh, but Thara fills Taim in on our escape attempt and the conversations with Silva.

"Do you know what's beyond that wall?" Thara says after.

Taim shrugs. "Didn't even know there was a wall. Place is foggy as the sky. Can't see anything from shore."

"The Guard doesn't talk about it?" Thara says.

"Not much. Just that the property in Southern Nevada is private owned. We're to steer clear, and if you're found up there, you're discharged for misconduct."

What is in there?

Taim steps toward me, inches from my face, his toes touching mine. "Jin, are you sure you're okay?" He wants me to lean in, to seek comfort in him, but I've had the entire day and half the night to realize what a horrible decision that would be.

"Don't do that," I say, shoving him back.

"Don't what? Don't show you how I feel?"

Are we really doing this? Now? When all our lives are at stake?

"We're over, Taim. We've been over. You left me for the Guard."

"Don't you see—I can be in the Guard *and* with you?"

"No." I have to be firm now. I need my mind clear—focused—for the dive. "You're going to get us all killed with your—your—recklessness."

Hurt shines in his eyes. But I don't care. I can't.

"If I actually mattered to you, then you'd let me focus on trying to live, instead of whatever twisted *moment* you're trying to have hoping that—that it'll smother your feelings about Saanvi."

Taim sinks down against the bars. "*My* recklessness." He shakes his head. "You know, I came down for you on that freedive. I pulled you up when your dad died. Your air was empty in Phoenix, and I hauled you out. Me."

"I know I could have searched longer. I still had air left."

He stares me down. "Blame me if you want, but I gave you more time than any sane person should."

I swallow the lump in my throat, turning my back to him. "Don't worry. I do blame you."

It felt good to finally admit that to myself. For so long we were together, and I kept telling myself: *You can't blame him; it wasn't his fault.*

But I blame him, as I blame myself.

The rest of the night is like the opposite of last night. Instead of the three of us piled on top of each other, we've each claimed a separate wall of the cage, and the empty fourth wall makes Saanvi's absence even more pronounced.

There's no one guarding us tonight. Maybe the crew is busy repairing the porthole we blew out? Regardless, the hours tick on until sometime in the early morning I wake to find Thara and Taim both staring at me. At last, Thara breaks the tension in the damp, dark compartment. "Dad's dead," she says. "Saanvi too. But the three of us are still here. Jin, you're going down there today, and that means the two of you need to get over your rust, and we need to talk about how we survive this." I shrug, and Thara continues, "How'd it go at Castle Mountain, Taim?"

"Fine. I got the patrol boat, obviously, but I'd never met the two folks posted there. The Guard has a strict policy against negotiation with corsairs, so I couldn't tell them about our situation. They would have run the whole thing up the mast, and I wouldn't have made it back. I thought, yesterday, when Saanvi was still—I thought I'd leave him at Castle Mountain to tell the officers after I'd stolen the boat. Then I could make it back, and we could still get rescued by the Guard." Taim closes his eyes. "That wasn't an option anymore."

Several moments pass, and a lone tear stripes Taim's cheek. Then he opens his eyes again. "There's one other thing. I stole a suit."

"A diving suit?" Thara says.

"Yeah, nicked it after dark; it's why I was so late."

Thara twists strands of hair in her fingers. "Did Silva find it?"

"I don't know. He sent two corsairs onboard after I pulled up. Told them to search the craft. I stashed several pistols too, so I'm hoping they find those and think they did their job. The suit's in a hull hatch, only accessible from under the ship." He wipes his eyes. "It's not much, but something. Maybe if I can dispatch the corsairs who stay behind, I can grab the suit and come down after you, Jin."

"No," I say, my voice hard. "You promise me right now. If you manage to take control of the boat, you come back for Thara. You dive under the *Bandeira*, come up at the hull. Thara, you be listening for Taim's knocks. Once you find her, cut in, and use the suit's thrusters to cruise a few miles down the coast and get ashore. Somewhere beyond that blasted wall."

Taim heaves a long sigh, his eyes roll up, and several seconds tick by before he speaks again. "Jin, do you remember the first time I went diving with you and your dad? Auntie had made that arrangement where I cleaned the inn each afternoon, and in exchange, your dad let me stay there after school until she got off work."

The thought of ten-year-old Taim mopping the parlor makes me crack a smile. "Yeah."

"I knew you all went wrecking. I was so intimidated . . . especially by you."

He was?

"Then, a few months in, your dad invited me out to Once-Scottsdale. Auntie almost bit his head off for proposing something so dangerous."

Auntie's fierce as a winter storm.

"I still don't know how he got her to agree," I say.

Taim swallows. "I asked Auntie once, shortly after your emancipation. I asked her what changed her mind, and she said your dad showed up at our doorstep one evening. It was pouring buckets. He was soaking wet, and he said one thing, 'Ximena—he wants to go. And if he's down there with me, I'll protect him like my own son.'"

My heart beats so heavy inside me.

"That's how it has to be, Jin. We look after each other. We protect each other. If I can escape, I'll come down after you."

I bite my lip, considering it. But then I see Thara at the edge of my vision. "Silva told me what he fears. He's worried I'll collapse the tower. And that's exactly what I'm going to do. Now, what floor's the vault on, Thara?"

"Twenty-two."

"Perfect. I'll lead them in deep, then collapse several walls, and I'll trap the entire dive party down there. Good chance I'll get trapped myself, which means you, Taim, need to come back for my sister."

Thara's sweet face is bulging, outraged. "No! You don't get to decide that! You told me you'd figure out how to manipulate him. You don't get to just die down there."

"If I can figure it out, I will. I'll ask him about Vitória. Try to catch him off-balance. It's a sun-shining prayer, though, Thara. A long shot, and you know it."

That finally does it. Thara leaps across the brig, hitting me while I throw my hands over my head. "You swore to Dad that you'd keep me safe!"

I mutter while her tied hands rain down. "That's what I'm doing."

Eventually all that hitting tires her out, and she collapses on top of me, sobbing, her hair a veil around us. I try to hug her, loop my arms around her shoulders, let her feel my beating heart, let her know it will be okay. She just ducks out and takes a seat back against her wall of the brig.

The rest of the early morning is a restless one: coastal waves slamming the hull, the scream of the wind whipping past the ship, the whole thing creaking, crying, rocking in the water like a baby that won't hush. Izzy and Monty come eventually, and they cut our ties. Then Taim and I are led out of the brig, and I give a last kiss to Thara on the forehead, the way Dad used to do. I tell her, "Build that greenhouse one day. Promise me you will."

"Promise *me* you'll be back." She whips the words at me, but I can't promise her that I'll return. I can't have the last thing I say be a lie. She's right: I promised Dad I'd keep her safe. That's the only promise I'm keeping, so with my heart feeling like an anvil, I just pat my hands awkwardly on her shoulders. "I'm sorry, Thara."

She doesn't respond, and I ascend the ladder with Monty ahead of me and Taim and Izzy behind. About halfway up the ladder, I turn for a final glance at Thara, and maybe she realizes that this is it—we may never see each other again. Maybe she just knows how to reach me, the unspoken bond between sisters. Whatever it is, she stares back, holds a fist in the air, bumps it against the bars of the brig, and then holds it over her heart. The gesture almost makes me crumble. Because there are people like me—who have to grow up before they're ready, who become responsible for someone, who have it thrust on them. And there are people like her.

She had twenty years on me the day she was born.

I wish she had been the older sister. She would have done a better job.

I bump my own fist on the ladder, holding it to my heart. *I love you too, Thara.*

My hip slams against the portside gunwale as Izzy shoves me forward. We're topside now, on the drone deck, the air wet and leaden, the sky above dark, threatening, and the eastern horizon striped in a faint pearled gray. It's dawn. A dozen hands are on the deck with us. A rope ladder hangs over the gunwale, and Silva's down in the patrol craft along with six corsairs. Monty nods at the sea, and quick as that, Taim is over the rails, and then I am as well.

It's forty feet down to the surface, and the wind's cutting hard north, smearing the hood of my poncho across my right cheek. There's a part of me that just wants to hop down on the patrol boat and make our stand right here, but that's incredibly foolish. We have no weapons, it'd be Taim and me against eighteen corsairs; we'd end up dead before the whole thing even began.

After a few slips, I'm boots down on the craft. It feels like a small thing alongside the *Bandeira*: a thirty-foot aluminum hull, seafoam-green collar, an inboard/outboard engine, battery powered, and a single enclosed cabin rising in a square box about seven feet off the forward portion of the deck.

This is the type of craft that's sometimes anchored at the mouth of Coconino Bay. A fully loaded patrol boat, capable of chasing down littoral smugglers in small bays, but not the type of thing you want to take across the open Pacific.

Silva steps up, his long coat slick with rain. "Welcome aboard! Or perhaps it's you who should be welcoming us, Lieutenant?" Silva nods at Taim, who just stares back. "Well then, allow me to introduce you to our treasure hunting crew. Near the cabin, we have the Dongo brothers, Piasu and Triasu. They'll be looking after the boat and the lieutenant while the rest of us take a swim."

The Dongo brothers look like giants; one of them is maybe six foot eight, the other near seven foot; both with thick black beards, tight skull caps, and they're lifting the heavy atmo suits one-handed, stowing them in cargo holds built into the deck.

"Now, Lieutenant," Silva continues. "We found several pistols and a few knives stowed around the ship. Very naughty. I promised the Dongos here they could give you a taste of what's to come if you get cute on us again."

One of the brothers, maybe Piasu, I'm not sure, walks up

and hits Taim hard across the face. Taim's entire head snaps left, hanging limp over his shoulder, while the other brother bends low and launches a terrible uppercut into his stomach.

Taim falls forward, grunting, slams into the deck, and receives one more kick to the ribs, though a part of me wonders if he's laying his reaction on thick. Silva doesn't bring up the diving suit that Taim said is stashed in a hull compartment. Still, the chances of a manacled Taim escaping from these two half-walrus, half-human brothers seems slim, and my stomach's squirming as I realize just how fragile my plan is.

If I fail to kill Silva—Thara's dead. If Taim fails to escape the walrus brothers—Thara's dead. Everything goes to plan— I'm dead, and Taim and Thara are wandering cold and alone in Southern Nevada.

But they'll have each other. They'll survive.

They have to.

"As for the diving crew, we have Cao, Hitesh, Mayra, and Khaddhi." Silva motions round the boat, port to starboard, at the four normal size people with us. "Cao and Hitesh have the tools. Once we reach the vault, which Jinny will lead us straight to, they do the cutting."

Cao and Hitesh are both shaved bald but with long facial hair twisted into thin locs and draped off their chins. Mayra's petite but muscular, with a cloud of black hair that sprays up in defiance of the rain. Khaddhi has a setting sun tattoo across her left cheek and a long cutlass scar running from her right ear down to the point of her chin.

Cao's testing the communications equipment inside each helmet that we'll use for the dive. Our suits probably need to be put on the same stream as Silva's so that we can all speak together below. Hitesh is packing two duffels with immersible torches and plasma saws—everything we'll need to breach the vault (not that I intend on letting things run that far). Then I see Hitesh slip another device into a side pocket.

"What's the eliminator for?" I ask.

"Old vaults sometimes have security systems," Hitesh responds. "They were designed to withstand the elements. If the system's still active, an eliminator can drain the system's battery and take it down."

That's smart, actually. Bhili hadn't thought of that.

Mayra and Khaddhi fit three suits with harpoons. Because while the people I'm diving with are dangerous, the creatures that live down there are far more deadly.

"Mayra and Khaddhi, they're security," Silva says. "We encounter anything predatory, they stay behind and handle it." Silva tosses several rolled neoprene bags to Cao, and he stuffs them into the duffels.

"Now these Treasure Island coins are two ounces apiece. That right, Jinny?"

I nod.

"Okay, then, so fifty thousand coin will run us a good three tons," Silva says. "But we spread it out across ten bags, should be able to haul it out with the extra push from the atmo suit thrusters. What do you think, Lieutenant? Can this patrol boat handle the weight?"

"She'll hold," Taim says, his voice stiff.

Silva slaps the boat's green collar. "Well, let's get on, then." He cocks his head back till he's looking straight up the eel-black hull of the *Bandeira*. Izzy's silver smile flashes down from the deck. Thara's arm is held tight in her grip.

"Remember, Izzy! You don't hear from me by dark, then it's time to feed the fish."

16

The next thirty minutes are spent winding along the coast of Southern Nevada. I hug a seat near the portside collar, staring down the crenulated shoreline. The place looks desolate. Such a strange sight, with land being so precious. No seaside shanties, coastal inns, outposts for battery recharge, or floating docks. I can't see the wall, either (though the mist seems to hang thick here, day and night). It's just stretch after stretch of craggy, unpopulated scrubland, which begs several questions, like: *Who owns these lands? What do they keep here behind sky-high walls? And why does the American Archipelago allow hundreds of square miles to be privately owned and free from human habitation?*

After a time, I shift into the cabin with Taim, who's at the helm. Mayra sits behind him, a pistol trained at the back of his neck.

Silva's there as well, and he says to Taim, "How far?"

Before we can chart a course over Vegas-Drowned, we have

to check in with the Guard, who've cordoned off the area. The check-in we're using is at a promontory at the southern tip of Yucca Cape. Hitesh handed out blue-white Coast Guard ponchos for each of us to don. The Dongo brothers look ridiculous in theirs, like giants wearing doll clothes; their ponchos will rip apart if they flex too hard.

"Ten at the most," Taim says. "I suggest most of you sit quietly on one of the aft benches. They'll only need my identification and the boat's. But they hear you talking and . . . well, best not to talk."

"The crew will sit tight," Silva says. "Me and you can do the talking."

"I meant you too, Silva," Taim says, curling the wheel so we scoot round a channel marker.

"You don't think I can play the part? I have an excellent Coastal accent." Silva's wry smile emerges, and he pulls his pistol. "Besides, someone has to be close enough to fit a blade between your ribs, should you get smart." Then he motions at Mayra. "Fill the crew in. Tell them to be tight and quiet."

We round another headland and Taim trims the boat, slowing us down as the Yucca Post emerges—a floating dock with two structures and ten slips, most sized for lifeboats or small cutters. But there's also a large ship, maybe a sky-class; it's about one hundred and fifty feet long and moored on the far side of the dock.

"Did you know that would be there?" Silva says, tapping a

knife against Taim's back. "Remember, don't get smart, Lieutenant. Few cuts and I'll spill the blood from your body faster than a cloud spills rain."

"I didn't know," Taim grunts. "Never been here. You chose this check point, remember? I wanted to use Blue Diamond off La Madre."

Silva pulls the knife, twirls it, and drives it back into the sheath on his boot. "I suppose that's right. Okay, then, talk it out smooth. I don't mind a sky ship, so long as it stays put."

The patrol boat slows further as we pull up alongside a long cement quay with two Coast Guard types in fatigues emerging from a lean-to at the end.

"Jinny, you keep in the cabin," Silva says.

Taim steps out with Silva on his heels, the cabin door remains open, and I hear a big, hearty "Ahoy there, Guardsmen!" from Taim.

The guard in the lead has an old, wizened face, her hair in a close gray shave and a sidearm strapped to her thigh. "Identification, please."

"Just mine or the ship's too?"

"We'll take the ship's off the bow," the other guard says. She's a young, slender thing, and she shuffles up to our craft with a scanning device.

"What's your orders?" the older one says.

Taim passes a plastic card over the collar. "Few locals say they spotted a pod of orca heading west, near the Canyon

River Delta." This is the backstory he and Silva agreed to. "Higher-ups worried they might topple a tower if they get over Vegas-Drowned and dive too deep. Don't make much sense to me. Never known an orca to dive below five hundred feet." Taim shrugs. "We do as ordered. Supposed to sight, dive, recon, and get a drone out to confirm."

"Uh-huh."

The guard who scanned the patrol boat speaks up. "And you took this craft out of Castle Mountain in Mojave Main yesterday? That right?"

"That's correct."

"Why didn't you check in at Blue Diamond, then?" the older guard asks. "La Madre is a whole lot closer."

Taim knew we should have done Blue Diamond. We're a good thirty miles off course, and it doesn't make sense if the mission's over Vegas-Drowned. Did he know this would happen? Hope it would?

The thoughts are swirling, and I'm wondering what to do when Silva says, "Excuse me ma'am, hope I'm not speaking out of turn, but you ever been through Blue Diamond? I been a good two dozen times and, no offense to a fellow guardsman, but the place just ain't run right. Two or three hour waits, lots of confusion 'bout who makes decisions." His drawl's thick, but friendly, like he's attempting seashore bumpkin. "You all do things right, so I say to the lieutenant here, we gotta get a few supplies up north. How about we just check in with the fine people at Yucca Cape after?"

"I have heard that a time or two," the young guard says, winking at us.

The other one pipes in. "We also heard about a corsair sighting up in the Fingers. See anything strange there?"

"Corsairs?" Taim says, like they're some kind of imaginary villains. "Can't say that we have."

And at that moment I see three other guards down the dock. That's five total, plus Taim and me, seven . . . against seven corsairs. The odds seem like the best we'll have, and I'm emerging from the cabin, right next to Taim and Silva, trying to catch Taim's eye, to signal him, as I open my mouth and—

Silva slams into me awkwardly, and my head clips the wet cabin door. My ears are ringing, but faintly over the din, I hear Silva. "Fool klutzy sea legs."

"You okay there?" the lead guard says.

And I'm trying to speak, to say something, anything, but Silva's hand is practically over my mouth as he says, "She's fine, she's fine. Duck your head now," and he shoves me into the cabin, calling back, "We got a med pack under the conn. I'll get her fixed up good."

"All right, then," the older guard says. "You're clear, Lieutenant. Steady on."

Silva pushes the ignition switch, and the engine growls to life.

17

My knees dig into the cabin floor as the tip of Silva's knife edges between two of my ribs. We're kneeling, and he's thrown the door shut. I doubt the guards can see us from here; the thing's a steel box from the waist down. If I could stand, they'd see the panic on me right through the cabin's portholes, but the chances of standing without this knife plunging into my gut are about as good as having the rain stop today.

Moments later, Taim slides into the cabin, waving back at the two guards, flashing every tooth he has, and it's a good fifteen or twenty seconds before we're clear of the quay. Then Taim shoves the throttle down hard, Silva and I slide back into the cabin's aft wall, and Taim finally looks back, saying, "What kinda rust was that?"

"That was our chance!" I say. I'm so furious, I don't even care if Silva hears. "You just blew it!"

Silva scrapes the knife ever so lightly across one of my ribs; the pain is a sharp, blinding bolt that rips through my chest.

"Careful with your words, Jinny."

"Our chance is with Silva," Taim says, his eyes shifting to the captain. "He's already told us: we find the gold, we all walk."

"The lieutenant sees the right of it. If you tipped the Coasties off to our excursion, I'd off you both—one, two, quick." He lifts the knife just a hair off my body. "As for young Thara, I'm sure under the right pressure she'd give up the location of the vault." Silva stands, yanking me up with him. "Should we turn around and ask her? Maybe *she'd* like to dive."

I shake my head and gulp, while Silva throws the cabin door open. "Piasu, Triasu—bring your ugly selves in here. Zip up these two youths."

The rest of the ride, Taim and I are separated. I'm in a seat on the aft deck with Mayra three feet away, her pistol trained on me. Taim's in the cabin with Silva and Piasu.

The rain feels like it's coming in horizontal, but really that's just our speed. At least forty knots, the force of the wind pelting tiny droplets into my cheeks, so hard I can't keep my hood on. The waters over Vegas-Drowned are vast and empty. Not a craft in sight. Visibility can't be high, maybe a mile or two, but Taim says the Guard uses drones to run checks here, which means they don't need a physical cordon of ships to keep folks out.

So a drone will likely spot us at some point today, though

that should be fine, since the Guard up at Yucca Cape will radio our approval through.

The whole thing feels almost too easy, particularly with Taim and the patrol boat. Which brings me back to the question that after thirty minutes of ripping through dark-green rollers, I still have no answer to: *Why didn't Taim alert those guards?*

He could have done it. He was alone with them.

And the more the water whips my face, the salt builds on the starboard side of my cheek, the more I'm wondering: *Why didn't he plan for an escape there?* He must have known there'd be a half dozen guards stationed at Yucca Cape. More than enough for us to make a play. And early enough that, if we survived, we could go back, cut the *Bandeira's* hull, and pull Thara free well before Izzy's even expecting a drone from Silva.

The replay of that Yucca Cape sequence disgusts me, and as the patrol boat rages across the water, freezing my face, I feel my heart trembling beneath the most awful thought. *Could Taim be in league with Silva?* Just the idea sends bile surging up my throat. It can't be true. It's not. I clench my stomach, try to swallow, settle my nerves and my spinning mind, but it won't stop. Taim's too smart to miss that opportunity. And I can't breathe as his words return to me.

Our chance is with Silva.

He sounded like he meant it.

Did he?

The patrol boat starts to slow, the wake flattening at our sides, and Silva throws open the cabin door. "We're here. Ready the suits. In a few hours, we'll all be richer than a pair of Rocky Mountain goat herders!"

Grunts and cheers erupt as Silva walks aft, stopping at the anchor winch, a tightly bound drum of steel wire near the stern. The patrol craft's engine cuts out; Silva pulls a folded piece of paper from his long black coat and calls back to the cabin, "Read out the lats and longs, Taim."

Taim? He's dispensed with the nicknames. . . .

Piasu, stooping in the cabin, slides back the aft glass, and Taim calls out the numbers one by one, "Three, six, dot, one, two, four, seven, two, zero North by one, one, five, dot, one, seven, one, eight, six, zero West."

Silva's holding a wide blue sheet of paper, which I realize is Bhili's Treasure Island blueprint. He must have taken it from our things.

"That's it," Silva says. "Read it again now, Taim, and the rest of you put those numbers in your head. Get lost down under, you'll find no other way back."

Taim reads the numbers a few more times, my stomach surging with the sound of his steady voice. Mayra, Cao, Hitesh, and Khaddhi mutter to themselves, making sure they have the location, and I force myself to do the same.

Silva fingers the anchor winch. "How much cable, Taim?"

He feels like part of their crew, and I want to scream: *Stop using his fucking name!*

"Twenty-five hundred feet."

"Good. Triasu, clip that horn and drop her in."

Triasu grabs a squat trapezoidal anchor the size of my head. It's caution yellow and has an embossed *100lbs* on its face. He clips the winch cable into the horn that tops the anchor, and then throws it overboard, like a fish too small to keep. The winch rips round and round, emitting a low buzz, and my stomach flips right along with it.

We had numbers. We had opportunity. And he did nothing.

My eyes track Taim. Cold, confident Taim. Unafraid Taim. Who could possibly hide their fear in a situation like this?

Only someone who doesn't have to be afraid.

Only someone who has made a deal.

"All right," Silva says. "If Bhili's papers are accurate, then we'll slide straight down the anchor cable to the Treasure Island roof. No tethers, since we're entering the building. Now, suit up. Poor Jinny only has eight hours before her sister's shark meat. Best be quick about it."

Ten minutes later and we're suits on, staring over the patrol boat's seafoam-green collar into the black waters of Vegas-Drowned.

Waters I've puked into twice.

The whole crew's been laughing at me, and I told them I always puke before a dive, but that's a blatant lie. The puking is because of him.

Because, in my head, I keep telling myself—there's no way Taim's with them. Not possible. But my stomach, my gut, is sending a whole different message. It's got a terrible feeling about this. A frothy, acidic feeling that's gonna burn my insides until I confront it.

Until I confront Taim.

I don't want to. Because if it's true, I know what those words will do. Crack my ribs open, yank my heart out, rip it in half, and feed it to the deep. I'm not sure how I continue with that knowledge.

But I have to know. Because if Taim's not on my side . . . who goes back for Thara?

I'm standing next to Mayra, who's next to Khaddhi, then Cao, Hitesh, and then Silva. Piasu's behind us loading air tanks (two per suit) and doing final checks. I'm in my suit, the one I wore for the Once-Havasu dive. Cao is wearing Dad's old suit. Hitesh, Mayra, Khaddhi, and Silva all have on similar frames, probably aluminum alloy, though theirs are palest gray, like abalone, with bright blue bindings and steel helmets. Mayra, Khaddhi, and Silva each have recoil harpoons strapped to their sides, and Hitesh and Cao have the tool bags. Silva's suit is some kind of custom job with the right leg cut off below the knee and fixed directly into the calf so the bionic's exposed. Taim's behind us, bound at the hands and feet, sitting on a bench with Triasu.

My mind tries to justify that: *Why tie him up if he's part of their crew?*

"All right, turn around," Piasu says. "Shut your blow holes."

Down the row of us, viewports are clamping on, and I realize this is it—now or never. I peer around Piasu, which is like peering around a bluff, and finally catch Taim's eyes. "Why didn't you alert the Guard at Yucca Cape? Tell me the real reason."

Taim bites his lip, then shoots a glance over to Silva. I look down our row to see that Silva's viewport is closed, meaning he can't hear us, so Taim can be honest.

"I'm sorry, Jin," Taim finally says, his hands on his face, barely looking at me. "Silva offered me the ten thousand coin that Bhili promised if I secured the patrol boat and took us clear through Yucca Cape." He lifts his face and makes it hard, impassive.

My stomach twists like a sea snake, my vision blurs, my heart sputters, and I'm trying to process those words, let them sink in. But I can't believe them, I can't. "But you—you tried to comfort me. You said you wanted to be together."

"I said what I needed to . . . to get you here."

"So I could dive for your money?"

"Just bring it back, Jin."

"And if I don't? If I just bring the building down on all of us?"

"Then you know what happens to Thara."

Fuck!

How can he sit there like that and deadpan it back to me, all tied up, and—that's right. "Why's Silva still have you tied up, then?"

"Doesn't trust me, I suppose. I wouldn't, either. It's like you said, Jin. He sees everything. You can't outmaneuver someone like that . . . you have to be on their side."

My body's taut, my hands clawed in my exo-gloves, my eyes staring him down, looking for that crack in the veneer, the one that will tell me—he's lying, he's lying, you know he's lying. At last, I say it. "I don't believe you."

He scoffs. "You're the one who said I always put myself first. And you know what Mamá told me. There are two kinds of power: money and authority." Taim leans forward, his dark eyes blazing. "After this, I'll have both."

My heart dissolves in my chest right then. Just melts away into my other organs, roiling my insides, and I'd keel right over if I wasn't held up by the suit. *How could he?!* Those three words peal through me, like they didn't come from my mind; they came from my ruined soul.

All I can think of is Thara's statement: *If you don't find the courage to trust someone . . . you're gonna have a life that's not even worth living.*

She was wrong. She was so wrong. God help me, I will never trust *anyone* again.

Triasu leans forward and plows an elbow into Taim's gut. "Enough talk. Girl's gotta get on." Taim spits, then sits up straight, resuming his icy mask. I'm seething, broken, my mind clinging to one word to keep it from wasting away just like my heart.

Thara.

I have to regain control. Shut off all emotion, all feeling. Don't need a heart—just my mind and body. One way or the other, I'm going into the deep with five other suited corsairs. I'm doing that, and I need to focus and do it well.

Because no one is going back for Thara now. No one except me.

So I stow my rage, close my viewport; the world goes silent, and I travel to that soulless place that knows how to survive. It's the place I inhabited after Dad died. It doesn't need to feel. It just needs to live.

I *will* stay alive. I'm going to dive down and kill Silva and dispatch these four other corsairs. I'll steal a harpoon, hold it to Taim's rusted, treacherous heart.

I can make it back. I must.

And good luck to the swamping Dongos taking me down when I surface in an atmo suit. Bullets rebound off these things like rain on shingles.

At last, I center myself again on the suit and the dive. I don't dare look at Taim, but I use the instrument panel inlaid into my right glove to flick through comms channels. Each suit can tune in to a local wireless channel. My suit and Thara's are always on the same one, but Cao and Hitesh were testing the comms earlier to tune us in to theirs. That means we should be able to hear each other within the standard fifty-foot, unobstructed radius. Keyword: unobstructed (which will be swamping near impossible since we'll be *inside* a building).

Finally, a few clicks farther, I hear Silva. "Pressure on now."

I flick another switch in the glove, feeling the air tighten around my skin, the suit securing at one atmosphere. Then I hear Cao's nasal voice. "This suit stinks worse than a bloated jelly."

"What?" I know the suit doesn't smell, but I can't help responding to his bait.

"The suit," Cao says. "This is your sister's?"

"It's not my sister's."

"Dad's, then. Sure was a foul bastard," Cao continues. "Whole thing smells of rot and decay."

"That's because he died in it," I say, breathing steady, letting the torrent of anger for Taim and Silva and every corsair at my side filter slowly down my arms, out to the tips of my fingers. I'll be down there with them all soon. In the dark. And then one by one by one . . .

My breath settles into calm, even puffs. "Maybe you will too."

Cao, Khaddhi, Hitesh, and Mayra are already in the water, sliding down the anchor cable. I'm next up, then Silva after. I turn my head to the right and take a small pull of water from the hose that pokes up in the helmet's interior. Enough to wet my lips, but no more. (We'll be down there for hours; too much water, and I'll be relieving myself in the suit too.)

Piasu steps up, and it occurs to me that he and his brother, with their behemoth frames, look like they're just permanently wearing exoskeletons. Piasu grabs a short little three-foot cable that extends from a ring embedded in my chest. Then he clips it around the anchor cable, gives me two pats on the helmet, and forms a circle with his thumb and forefinger to indicate I'm good.

"Hop in, Jinny," Silva says through the comm link. The rest of the corsairs are out of comms range.

I tip my head forward, staring into the swirling green-black waters. I swore to myself so many times that I would never put this suit back on, not unless I absolutely had to.

I almost laugh. *Twice in about forty-eight hours. Doing real well on that promise.*

I leap into the water, and my body hits with a large displacement. I barely feel it through the suit, though. My head tilts back, my eyes roll up, and I stare at the faint specs of light, bubbles sparkling at the surface. The light fades quickly, and then my vision shifts forward, and the only visible thing is the chain running from the embed in my chest to the anchor cable.

I check the comms channel, but no one's in range. Then I flick on the dashboard that prints my status across the viewport: latitude, longitude, depth, speed, air, pressure, battery, date, time, and compass. Everything looks good, so I move the display to the side in resting mode, and I burst my foot thrusters for a slow descent. I already got jerked out of the water much too quickly in Once-Havasu. Need to be careful with pressure acclimation on the way down.

My descent slows and everything's going to plan, until—*thump*—my feet knock into something. For a moment, I think I've hit the ground, but the suit only reads fifteen hundred feet deep, so that can't be. Then—*thump, thump*—two hits across my back, my suit starts beeping, and I catch something out of my lower periphery. I'm in a gentle end-over-end spin, still attached to the anchor cable. I'm trying to locate the source of the beeping and slow the spin; I tap the thrusters on my feet when a giant gray thing slams into my chest. I'm yanked forward, ripped free of the anchor cable. My head clouds and I'm flung into a violent, twisting spin. My breathing goes shallow, my chest tightens, my vision blurs.

I tap several thrusters, but I can hardly think straight and I can't get a bearing on the spin. *Which way am I rotating?*

The alarm is blaring in my ears. I close my eyes to try and center myself, but all I can feel is the crushing pressure of my brain colliding into my skull with every lurch. Like a blow to the head, again and again, and there's one word swarming in that head now. *Blackout, blackout, blackout.* I know it's coming. My mind's about to shut down, and if I don't arrest this spin, then I'm going to plow into a building. It'll collapse, and when I come to, I'll slowly breathe out the rest of my air and die.

I try to open my eyes, but the pressure from the spin is too much. My lids are glued shut, I can't open my mouth, my stomach is the only thing that's mobile, and it ricochets across my chest until I'm so nauseous, I realize it's not long before I vomit again. *Not enough that I die. I'm going to do it while suffocating beneath my own stink too.*

This is it. I'm alone, in the deep, where—

My head snaps back as my body plows into a hard surface. Haptics rumble through the suit. I skid across something (a building, the ground?), and then, at last, my body comes to rest, and I'm seated, upright, my back against a giant metallic object.

My head's still pounding, but with the spinning stopped, the pressure's gone and my eyelids finally find the strength to open. To my immediate left and right there are five cars, two trucks, and a jeep, all rusted and barnacled to oblivion. I gaze down, and the ground's smooth—paved, I realize—with faint white lines dashed across. I turn around, and there's a car behind me as well (that's what stopped my slide). I try to stare out beyond the road, but my suit lights only carry so far. Still, I can feel something out there. Something immense. *What are those? Creatures? Structures?*

The steel cord that ran to the anchor cable hangs limp off my chest. The beeping continues, knifing through my temples, and I finally scan the digital readout on my viewport. It says I'm twenty-five hundred feet deep (this must be the ocean floor), my pressure's dropped to ninety-nine percent (lucky it's not worse), and I have less than four hours of air remaining. That's definitely the source of the beeping, and I know instantly that I've lost an air tank. My whole body tenses with that thought, but I still have power, I still have pressure, I didn't black out. Not yet. *Stay focused, Jin.* Blackouts often come five or ten minutes later, after a spin stops. I hover up to get my bearings, and I bump my helmet on a large metal pole with a long green sign. It's hanging crooked over the road below me, and I lean back, shifting my chest lights onto the sign. It reads: S Las Vegas BLVD, 3200.

I've arrived.

18

Through a haze, I flick a switch in my glove and turn off the alarm. My mind's still an utter fog, but I realize that I'm *here*— smack in the middle of Vegas-Drowned. I lower myself back to the road, trying to think through my options, when a blur of white light skids to a stop in front of me, and a lilting voice carries through my comm.

"You all right, Jinny?" Silva says. "I saw you spin off into the dark."

The terror of being alone in the deep is still fresh, and a flood of sputtering relief hits my voice. "Something hit me. My tether clip broke, and—"

"And you lost an air tank, by the look of things." Silva thrusts up beside me, and I can see his wry face bent in a smirk, his long white mustache shining from the helmet's interior lights. "It happens. Whales, sharks, maybe one of those giant Pacific octopi. This is their home, after all. They don't like us down here . . . intruding."

"Yeah." My nerves are still splintered, my head a dizzy wreck. "How far off are we?"

"Not far, I think. You get a bearing yet?"

I point up at the street sign, and Silva glides toward it and back down. "Very good," he says. "They used to call this the Strip. Now if it was just me and you, I'd say we surface, find the lats and longs, get a new tank, and sink again. Rest of the crew won't know what's happening, though. They'll start a search, get lost themselves, and we risk scuttling the mission. No, best thing now is to make our way through Vegas. Treasure Island won't be far, and I studied Bhili's maps well enough. We'll find it."

It's awful to say, but I'm so immensely relieved that Silva's here, taking control. That spin shook all the courage right out of me, and it's a sharp reminder of what being this deep is really like.

The dive two days ago in Once-Havasu was so beautiful.

Most dives are the opposite of that.

Most dives are this: The sheer terror that accompanies a reduction in all your senses. No sound but the tinny gurgle of words whispered through a comm. No sight but the shadows illuminated in a fifty-foot hemisphere in front of you. No touch but the faint haptics of the suit. No smell but the stale sweat that clings to your body. And no taste but the blood in your mouth from biting the insides of your cheeks raw, hoping to shunt the anxiety back down your throat, into your stomach, where you'll keep it in a hard, dull pit until, may the light shine down upon you, you emerge back above the surface.

Dad loved this feeling; said it made him sharper, more aware, more appreciative of the full glory of the world above.

I wanted to be like him. I spent so many years with him, diving, hoping I'd see the glory of it, the contrast that gave him so much optimism; how little we have below . . . and how much we have above.

That never happened.

What I feel most often down here is just—less. Less of my senses, less like myself, less alive . . . and closer to death.

The pounding in my head continues, and blackout belatedly sinks its claws into my skin as I drift, drift . . .

"Engage!" A faint screaming sound coming from Silva. "Engage! You didn't spin that hard. Focus on my voice. Engage your thrusters, Jinny. Engage!"

And strange as it sounds, Silva's voice leads me back. I wrap my hand tight around his left forearm, and then with a few taps in my glove, I engage all four thrusters for a soft burn and we're gliding forward, twisting around cars, as we maneuver Las Vegas Boulevard.

After another thirty seconds, the pounding in my head finally dissolves, and I whisper into the comm, "Thank you."

Perhaps it's the worst thing to say. Thanking my captor, the person I plan to kill, the person I'm so certain will kill me when I've served my purpose. But it's just what comes out. What feels right. Silva went into the void to follow me here. And had he not, there's a strong chance I'd be lying senseless on Las Vegas Boulevard right now. Sipping the last of my air till the end.

"It was a freak thing," Silva says. "Sure you'd do the same for me."

He's mocking me with those words. Silva and I are not on the same team. Silva saved me because he needs me to lead him to the vault. And if he gets hurled down this sunken street by a giant oarfish, flipping him end over end in a blackout spin, well then, there's only one thing I need to do: leave him to his fate.

"Can you really guide us to Treasure Island from here?" I ask Silva.

"Not in the dark," he says. "Be like searching for the sun in the sky. I have a flashbang, though." He taps a long, thin tube on his thigh. "Cao has three more, smaller ones. We'll use mine, see if we can spot a landmark, and we'll move forward from there."

Flashbangs are single-use transient blasts of projected light. Dad and I occasionally acquired them so we could assess a big mansion for point of entry. Most drowned cities aren't like

Once-Havasu, with bioluminescent fungi lighting the whole place up. So instead, you buy a flashbang and use it wisely. They're expensive, and the ones we used to get were tiny, half a foot squares.

"How big is it?" I say.

Silva uncaps the tube on his thigh, pulling out a long, thin metal sheet that he unrolls. It's huge, and I've never seen them unroll like that, either.

"Two feet by four. Should give us a thousand feet of wide-cast light. You've used them before?" He reverses on his thrusters.

"Yes, but how do you know which way to point it?"

"I don't," he says. "But I'll try one way, and if I don't recognize anything, then we go in the other direction. Don't turn around now, you'll be blind if you do."

I keep my eyes peeled forward, and seconds later a tremendous beam of light washes over the road in front of me. The road itself is cracked, buckled, and littered with dozens of rusted cars, trucks, and buses. On our immediate left, there are several low-lying buildings, windows busted, covered in prickly, yellow sea sponges. Ahead to the right, there's a massive striped tower, the word *Encore* written in the top left. The tower has a gaping hole in the middle, maybe a hundred feet across, like an eel gigantic swam straight through it. I shudder at that, thinking of the moray that almost devoured my arm. Farther in the distance, I see the shadows of some other massive structures, but can't make them out. And ahead on the left, there's an organic structure that's translucent and gelatinous. It's incredibly wide, perhaps five hundred feet; it rises like a pillar, higher than I can see, and it's formed from thin layers, stacked close and wriggling. A large black creature scuttles across it, I shudder, and then the light goes out.

Silva's voice comes through my comm. "Lucky you didn't land in that."

"What is it?"

"Web of sorts," Silva says. "Sea spider colossals make them to trap other giantics. It's a type of mimicry; they fashion them after drowned buildings. You get caught in one of those—you're never coming out."

My jaw quivers, and I turn to see Silva tossing the used flashbang to his side.

"Did you get a bearing?"

He nods. "That building with the hole. Encore. It's the second oldest in Vegas after Treasure Island. We move in the opposite direction of it. Treasure Island should be about a thousand feet down on our right." Silva zooms forward, grabbing my arm and dragging me with him. He thrusts up a few feet off the road so we can easily avoid the bumps and buckles. Mostly, we keep our chest lights pointed forward. Not trying to run into any sea spider colossals. Silva keeps flicking his lights to the right, though, reading the names off hotel signs as we pass. It's as good a time as any to push him. Just the two of us right now.

"Why'd you come down after me?" I say. We're gliding under a small, raised walkway that intersects with the boulevard. "You must have been thrusting very fast to keep up. Any number of creatures or buildings you could have slammed into. You should have just let me black out and die down here."

Silva chuckles through the comm. "You know what floor the vault's on. I need you."

It's more than that. I can feel it. "Do I remind you of her?" I say. "Of Vitória?"

Several moments pass, but he finally responds. "No. Your sister does. Not just the hair, but her height, shape of her face. Never thought I'd see that face again."

"What happened during your falling out?"

"Not important," he says quickly.

"I don't believe that."

"Don't piss me off, Jinny. I'll drag you back to the sea spider."

I gulp (he probably could), but I press on. "Answer one thing, then."

He grunts through the comm.

"Vitória's dead, isn't she?"

"Yes, she's dead."

I knew it. *Been a long time since I've seen her.* That was some obtuse gullshit.

"How'd she die?"

I wait him out several moments, but he doesn't respond, just thrusts us up and over a rusted traffic light.

I finally say, "How old was she when she died?"

He exhales, long and slow through the comm. "Fifteen. And don't ask about her again."

After several minutes, Silva's chest lights shine on a sign with two massive lowercase letters: *ti* (the *i* hangs horizontally), and beneath those letters, it reads: FREE PARKING. We've found it.

We hook right immediately and thrust up and very slightly forward until we can see the contours of the building. There are three sides to Treasure Island, as the building's shaped like a three-armed star. The side we're rising up is crusted over with so much sand, shells, and seafloor detritus that I can't even make out windows. I've seen that happen in Phoenix-Below. Depending on the pull of the current, one side of the structure becomes completely caked over.

"Mayra, Hitesh," Silva calls over the comm as we rise higher and higher.

No response.

"We'll land on the roof," Silva says. "Find the others, then determine the best point of entry."

I grunt a response, and moments later we edge over the roof. Dark here, which is very strange. We should be able to see the crew's lights. Or at least the faint specs of them.

Silva thrusts down, and I land beside him. Silt wafts up from our feet, but the ground's firm otherwise, and there's a boxy structure up ahead.

I pivot a full 360 degrees to get my bearings, but there aren't any other structures, and there's still no light from another suit. We should move toward the center of the building. That's where I'd go if I landed here first.

"Cao, Khaddhi," Silva calls, twisting on his bionic.

"Maybe they got thrown off course too?"

"Let's hope not . . . for your sister's sake." Silva plods forward, and I follow.

There's a saying in wrecking with visibility so nonexistent: *See something, move toward it—carefully.* Things often turn out to be very different than what you initially assumed.

This, however, does appear to be what we assume: a large rectangular structure, several wingspans across and perhaps twice our height; there's a ladder leading up to the top and slats built into the walls. *Perhaps a ventilation chamber of some kind?*

I step around a corner and whip back around as fast. There's a faint blue light glowing from the opposite end of the structure, about thirty feet forward.

"What's there?" Silva says.

"Bioluminescence," I say. "Creature. Big one."

Most bioluminescents are in the blue-violet range, but some do lighter hues as well, yellows and reds. A lot are plants, corals, or fungi like we saw in Once-Havasu, but there are also small luminescent creatures, like viperfish with their needle teeth, or the tiny Bougainvillia superciliaris. Commonly referred to as "brain jellies," they look like transparent blobs with a human brain glowing inside.

Some bioluminescents are large too, like kitefin sharks or the giant angler fish. The anglers are twenty feet across and lie flat on the ocean bottom, camouflaged, until you step on one, and it pulses a bright, screaming blue, right before it gobbles you whole.

"What kind you think?" Silva says, peering around the corner.

"Not sure. Maybe a vampire squid colossal. They put out a color like that."

"Yes, they do," Silva says. "Best we check it out, then." He bounds forward, leaping up above the structure in a move that's both reckless and terribly impressive. "Move, Jinny, before I flush out this vampire. You don't want those diamond charm tentacles to suck out your blood."

That's a joke. I think. I don't know. I'm pretty sure vampire squid don't suck blood. And anyway, I don't think it could break through an atmo suit. Though the colossals can grow up to forty feet in length. It could surely wrap a tentacle around me and smash me into this roof.

"Let's go, Jinny. Quit shaking in your suit and get over here."

So I do, one tentative step at a time. The right course of action would be to wait the thing out. Or try to go around. Still, Silva hasn't cried out in agony yet, so I step along the wall, slow, a side shuffle, my back to the structure, but my helmet turned and my eyes on the blue light that ebbs and flows in front of me. Finally, I'm inches away, about to round the corner, my fingers on the thruster triggers, ready to rocket off if need be. I lean forward, and then something leaps out, screaming. "ARGHHHHHH!"

My fingers smash the thrusters and I've shot twenty feet up before I hear the raucous sound of laughter through the comm. I glance back down only to see the rest of the corsairs: Mayra, Khaddhi, Hitesh, Cao, and Silva, all switching on their suit lights and waving me back down. All their suit lights are white . . . except for Khaddhi's, which are bright blue.

"Not funny," I finally say.

"It was very funny." Hitesh's voice is flat and humorless.

"You almost leaped the building!" Cao chimes in.

I make a few soft thruster taps to adjust my descent, and then I'm standing in front of them. "Who uses blue light on a suit?"

"I do," Khaddhi says. "I'm a shark, Jinny." The setting sun

tattoo on her cheek is visible through her viewport, but a thin-lipped, joyless smile distorts the image. "Don't forget that. Just like those kitefins that dined on your friend. I'll chomp your head off!" She bites the air in her helmet, and I hear the snap of her teeth through the comm.

Cao snickers, and then Hitesh says, "What took you two?"

"Something down here doesn't like Jinny," Silva says. "Knocked her clean off the cable into a spin. I tracked her down, and we made our way along the boulevard. Keep your wits about you now. There's some big life-forms down here. Saw a tower made entirely by a sea spider colossal." Silva runs his bionic across the floor, cutting an arc through the silt. "Now, did you krill scout anything while you wait? Jinny lost an air tank, so that leaves us with less than four hours."

"We took stock," Hitesh says. He seems the only one of the crew who's business down here. "Scouted the roof and two sides of the building. One has floor-caking. Thick layer too."

"We saw that," Silva says.

Hitesh nods. "There's a red algae forest on another side. Can't use that, either."

Most seaweeds grow near the surface where they can get some light, but a few survive in the deep. They're prime hunting grounds for predators, and my entire body tenses thinking about that moray snaking up my legs. *Thank god we're not going through there.*

"And the third side?" Silva says.

Khaddhi thrusts ahead with her blue lights. "Haven't checked it yet. Follow me."

We all follow, and Khaddhi leads us off the roof, far enough that I can't see the edge of it anymore. Then she sinks down about twenty feet and twists until she's staring back at us. She keeps tapping her thrusters, keeping herself level, and heading back toward the building. The rest of us pull up behind her, and slowly, our lights illuminate three letters *URE*. Beyond the letters, you can see the shadow of the building below. "Cao, hand me the flashbang," Khaddhi says. "I'm going to reverse thirty feet or so. You all keep your eyes forward and down."

"You've used the other two?" Silva says.

Hitesh responds. "Yes, when we checked the other sides."

Silva huffs. "This is our last, then. Jinny and I used one to navigate Vegas."

"Not to worry," Khaddhi calls. "We'll light her up and make it count."

Cao fishes into his pack, then hands Khaddhi a thin vertical sheet about two by three. Khaddhi zooms backward.

I turn back around, staring forward at the large black thing that's a shadow in front of me.

"Eyes forward," Khaddhi says.

Suddenly, an enormous pillar of light streams from behind me, falling upon the sunken building that is a crumbling replica of the structure in Bhili's blueprints. The letters *T URE ND* remain across the top. The structure is encrusted with all manner of sea sponges, coral, and anemone, and, from this view, the side of the building has a slight curve to it, like a U but tipped forward and with the ends bowed out. The windows are visible. Or at least, the holes where the windows once were. Bhili's prints put the tower at thirty-six floors, and the holes cascade in rows across the entire façade. The bottom right of the U has crumbled from the roof about ten floors down, and a jagged mess of rebar and concrete protrudes there, as if in warning for all those who dare enter. On the far left there's a jagged crack running roof to ground, like a bolt of lightning ripped down through the sea and split a seam through the building. And far below, there's something on the ground in front of the building, directly beneath us.

At first, I'm thinking it's a smaller, domed structure, at least a hundred feet in diameter, and I'm staring down, trying to get a sense for what it is (this was not in Bhili's blueprints), when a lid flicks open, a giant bulbous eye locks on to my own, and then the flashbang goes out and all's black.

"Roof," my voice trembles. "We need to get back on the roof."

"What you mean?" Cao says. "You said the vault's in the building. Simplest way in is through one of those busted windows."

"Can't go through there." My thrusters are already on, and I've lifted ten feet over the rest.

"Now hold on. I'm not squirming my way down floor by floor if I don't have to," Cao says. "You just tell us the floor, and—"

"What did you see, Jinny?" Silva's words are sharp, direct.

"There's something down there," I say. "Something big. And *it saw me*."

"What?" Cao says. "Khaddhi's behind you, and ain't no kitefins down there."

"This wasn't a kitefin," I say. "It was much larger and it . . . wasn't luminescent." I'm twenty feet above them now. "We go in through the roof. And we do it quietly."

"Silva, you listening to this?" Mayra says. "We shouldn't of come down with the girl. She's a spook, danger to herself and us. Now, the quickest way in is straight through those window frames. We all saw it."

"That's true," Silva says, "but the girl's wrecked enough to know something suspicious." Silva's lips smack across the comm. "I want you to drift down a shade, Mayra. Fifty feet or so, stay within comm's range, and you tell me what you see."

"Wastin' our time, Silva," Mayra says. "Already a half hour down on my air tanks." But she goes, drifting ten feet, twenty, thirty. "Ain't nothing," Mayra says. "Maybe one of them old parking decks we seen before. I'll go a bit farther and check it."

"Don't go out of comms," Silva orders.

Mayra's white light fades a bit further beneath us. "Probably just a stretch of sea grass or—something. It's swaying like. Hold there—swamping mother of a—engage! All of you, engage, engage!"

Suddenly, a massive creature below us shifts into a bright, screaming color, like an ochre sea star. With each passing second, the hues keep shifting, from deepest blue to orange to lavender. A swirl of tentacles writhes, flailing.

Mayra shrieks, and with the comm in my helmet, it's like the blood-chilling cry came from my own soul. Then we're hit with a current of water surging upward toward all of us. The comm's patchy, crackling, with the sounds of metal crunching and Mayra's screaming.

I arrest my spin, my reaction time heightened since the descent, and Silva's at my side, Cao, Hitesh, and Khaddhi ten feet or so up from us.

The comm is still clicking with Mayra's screams as she goes in and out of comms range. The creature's pulsing, but more slowly, in dark shades.

"Mayra! Mayra, pull out of there," Khaddhi says. "Mayra, pull—"

There's a sound like a burst of liquid across the comm, a gurgling, and I'm thinking some part of Mayra just, just— exploded.

"Engage your thrusters!" Cao says. "We're—"

Silva slashes a hand across his neck in a diver hand signal that tells Cao to stop talking—immediately. "She can't hear you no more. Now, everyone, cut your lights."

We all do, and suddenly, the creature goes black, the luminescence abruptly ending like the flick of a light switch. Then we stare down in silence, in horror, waiting, waiting . . .

After a minute or so, I finally put my hands on Silva's shoulders, whispering, "We *need* to get back to the roof."

He nods. "Cao, Hitesh, Khaddhi . . . and Jinny. Switch to helmet lights only and make your way to the roof—slowly."

"We're just leaving her?" Cao says. "What if—what if whatever it is doesn't kill her for a while?"

"You don't understand," Silva says. "That sound. The creature burst her suit. She's already dead."

19

"I'm goin' down after it," Khaddhi says.

We're back on the roof. Our chest lights are on. Visibility is still swamp all, and the silt's ankle deep. Silva, Hitesh, Cao, and Khaddhi are all in front of me.

I can see their faces at close range, but even when I can't, their voices are clear enough: Silva's lilt, Hitesh's stiffness, Cao's concern, Khaddhi's bravado.

"And how's that going to go?" Silva asks. "You saw the thing. Was a hundred feet across and blinking colors like a siren. You plan to spear it with a harpoon?"

Khaddhi's blue chest lights swivel toward the group. "I like my chances, Silva. Stick it right in the heart, I would."

"I don't think so," I say.

Khaddhi gets right in my face, the blue blinding. "Who asked you? Perhaps I stick you in the heart."

I close my eyes but keep my voice flat and firm. "My

guess—it was some kind of cephalopod. Likely a gigantic form of Humboldt squid. Those things blink colors to communicate with each other. And if that's so, if it is a Humboldt, you can't kill it with a harpoon to the heart."

"Why's that?" Khaddhi says.

"Because Humboldts have three hearts."

Khaddhi tips her helmet into mine. "You one of them smart ones, ain't you."

"Funny too," I say, shoving her off.

"Swamping cephalopods," Cao mutters. "I hate them slimy, long limbed—"

Silva cuts back in. "That's enough. Now, we haven't gone to all this trouble to get distracted trying to take on gigantics. There's a thing there. It snatched Mayra. But we have a job. Hitesh, you scouted the roof. Where's the entrance?"

I check the readout on my viewport as Hitesh leads us single file across the roof.

Three hours and twenty minutes remaining on my air supply. Not good losing one of my tanks. Thankfully, my pressure's still at 99 percent. Standard pressure is one atmosphere, but if the suit takes a hard hit (say from the tail of a massive sea creature that rips you free of an anchor cable), even the tiniest fracture can cause pressurization to slide. If pressure keeps slipping, that means there's a leak. And leaks are serious. Once pressurization slips below 95 percent, you're on death watch: headaches, nausea, nose bleeds, spots in your vision. The only option is to break for the surface, and for most divers, if you don't make it within the hour, you're dead.

The last indicator I check is my battery level, which is also fine at 92 percent. A suit will maintain pressure without any battery; you can even keep sucking down your air. But if you're out of power, then your thrusters don't work. No thrusters and, if you're in an untethered dive like we are, then you have no means of ascension.

Hitesh curves us around several small structures until we stop at one with a door embedded that reads: Treasure Island, Casino & Hotel, Center Stairwell A.

Silva kicks the door in with his bionic. "All right, then, Jinny. What floor?"

"If I tell you now, what good am I? I'll lead you down."

"You think we'll just feed you to the cephy once you tell us?" Khaddhi says, grinning through her viewport.

"Maybe."

"Come, now," Khaddhi says. "Daddy didn't teach you to trust nobody?"

"Not the likes of you."

Silva swivels around. "I told you, Jinny. I keep my word. We find the treasure, you and sister Thara will be *just* fine."

"Good to know," I say, not believing him for a minute. Then I step through the open door and into the stairwell. There's a rusted railing on my right side with two red cap jellies sucking on it. Red caps are little translucent jellyfish, like mushrooms with wispy trailing tendrils and glowing red tops. Each is tiny; can't be longer than my thumb. Years ago, I saw a giant smack of them near a drowned hardware store in Once-Maricopa. Dad moved us on quickly because the things are alloy parasites, devouring all kinds of metal. They're lethal to wreckers in large numbers, but innocent enough when there's just two.

I squish these two between my thumb and forefinger as I peer down the center of the stairwell. There's a staircase landing below me, then the stairs hook right, another flight, and that appears to keep up, down and down in a tight spiral. I'm trying to remember the blueprints Bhili had as I step down, Silva and crew following, but not four steps in, my foot clips off something and I stumble forward. My body splays out in the water, no footing, and my left hand pierces the drywall next to me on instinct. I'm clawing through it, like teeth through urchin, the entire thing melting into the water as my hand pulls down, and finally, I pump my thrusters and stop on the staircase landing.

What did I even trip on?

I glance back up, and Khaddhi kicks a hulking metal thing off the flight above. It floats toward me, and as I lift my lights, I see a yellow-black atmo suit with a half-decomposed human skull inside the helmet. The suit descends in slow motion, arms spread wide, fingers outstretched like the ghost of this diver is reaching out.

But it's just in my head. This person died years ago. The suit's intact, but flooded, probably lost pressure over time. My chest compresses, thinking, *This is what Dad's face would look like now*. Devoured by water and pressure.

I step aside and let the suit fall at my feet; the arms drag on my legs, setting off soft haptics that rip shivers up my spine. I hear Dad's voice screaming: *Jina!*

It's not real. And I blow out a long exhale.

Steady, Jin. You're in enough trouble. Don't start hallucinating.

"Lookie here," Cao says, reaching down to a step where the suit first lay and pinching a shiny object in his finger. He holds it up to his helmet, and as he steps down the stairs, I can see that it's a coin, an exact replica of the coins Bhili paid us with: gold with a grizzled parrot stamped on one side and the words *Treasure Island* on the other.

"Our first lucky charm," Cao says with a guffaw. "Perhaps that rooftop entry was right after all."

Silva arrives and stomps his bionic on the viewport of the dead diver's suit. The shield shatters, and then Silva's silver foot has stabbed a gaping hole into the skull, connecting the two black eye sockets.

"What you do that for?" Cao says.

"To make my point," Silva says. "We don't stop for every

glint of gold. That's the mistake our friend Bhili made. Probably same one caused this diver to run out of battery. You don't snatch at krill when there's a fat vat of prawns below. No, we make our way to the vault. We do it fast and quiet. Then we haul out fifty thousand coin with only the sun to be jealous of our golden glory."

"Aye, like the sound of that," Cao says, pocketing the gold coin anyway.

Silva waves a hand forward. "Lead, Jinny."

After a few more flights, my mind starts racing as it occurs to me that this stairwell may descend straight down to floor twenty-two. And then what? I still need to off four corsairs that are in near impenetrable exoskeletons.

My objective was a whole lot easier back when I could try to collapse a part of the building with all of us inside. Use my suit (thrusters at full) to crash through several floors and a few dozen walls. I'm dead, they're dead. Taim goes back for Thara. Job's done.

Now, with what Taim's done, well—I can't count on him to go back for Thara. *I really do need to make it out of here.* Which means I need to pick them off one by one, and this casual descent down a much too well-functioning underwater stairwell is not helping.

We pass the next landing, and this one has a door marked

with a 30. Perhaps if I can get us into a more open space where we're less on top of each other . . .

"So, Khaddhi, were you and Mayra close?" I say. Khaddhi's clearly the hothead of the crew, and if I have a chance, it's with her.

"Some," Khaddhi says. "We had our moments."

"And did she always do things so utterly stupid?"

"Watch the way you talk about the dead," Khaddhi says from behind me. "Lest you fancy becoming such."

"It's like the old wrecker saying: You don't die from the deep, you die from the dumb shit you do there. And Mayra seemed clownfish-level stupid."

Khaddhi shoves me in the shoulder, and I stumble down a step. "I said, watch the way you're talking."

"I mean, I told her I saw something big; something that saw me. What'd she think? That we could float on past it and tuck into a window? Did she get her helmet bashed in on a previous tour? Because I can't imagine any diver with such thickheaded, doltish thinking. You know what that word *doltish* means, Khaddhi?"

"Means I'm gonna put this harpoon through your thick head if you don't shut your swamping hole." Khaddhi shoves me down another three steps to the next landing.

"Settle down now, Khaddhi," Silva says. "Jinny's just trying to rile you."

I howl a laugh. "Now *you* must be as ignorant a cretin as Mayra if you think that harpoon's gonna do anything but clink off my helmet."

"What you call me," Khaddhi says, using her thrusters to shoot down to the landing I'm on.

"I said you're an ignorant, witless, jelly-brained cretin whose head I'd bash in if I thought there was anything there to bash." I knock twice on Khaddhi's steel helmet, and I can see the long cutlass scar running across her right cheek, glowing white-hot from the lights off my suit. "You there, Khaddhi? Harpoons don't work on atmo suits." *Knock, knock, knock.* "You get that?"

She growls low, then picks me up (just as I'd hoped), grabbing the crotch and armpit of my suit; she engages her thrusters, shoots forward, stops short, and then hurls me through the stairwell wall.

20

There's a story featured prominently in the Rigveda, one that never made sense to me. In it, Indra (Dad's favorite god) slays the evil demon Vritra, who had imprisoned the world's water. Indra accomplishes the task using a mighty weapon (the elixir, Soma) and a fierce determination (he destroys ninety-nine fortresses). At last, when Vritra is killed, torrents of rain fall from the sky and the world rejoices.

But why? I thought. *Why praise the god who released the rains? Isn't he the villain?* I remember getting indignant with Dad once, telling him as much. We were in the parlor, electric fireplace glowing, suits waxed, last guest had just gone upstairs. I was eleven, and Dad was reading in his reupholstered recliner. He had a certain smile when I really dug in on something. He'd cup his right hand to his jaw, cover half his mouth, so the smile came from his eyes and the lift of his left cheek. This is the only memory I have where I can still see that smile.

When I finished my speech, Dad closed his book, saying, "Do not take things so literally, Jina. See the heart of the story. Vritra is the obstacle; Indra, the will to overcome." He got up then and walked over to one of the oldest maps. "When these words were first spoken, the world was a drier place. It needed rain, and Indra provided. For us, we need the clouds dispelled. And though it feels impossible, one day this too will be accomplished." Then Dad walked back to me, taking my hand. Because of the arthritis, he'd hold your hand in the most gentle way. "For you, Jina, I want you to remember this story. Use it to think about your own life. What obstacles will you face? How will you overcome them?"

How will I overcome them?

Dad's deep voice echoes in my head as my body plows through three sections of wall, my head swimming, haptics rumbling. Finally, I stop about two dozen feet from the crew.

How will I overcome them?

Behind me are two rusty nightstands and a half-disintegrated bed frame covered in some grotesque purple algae. In front of me, there's a tunnel of wreckage leading back to the stairwell: rotted wooden slats, piping, wires, steel beams, a blasted sheet of plaster, and drywall dissolving through it all. The water's growing hazy, but the ceiling hasn't come down, and I can see Khaddhi's blue lights like a target in the distance.

How will I overcome them?

"Stay put, Jinny," Silva calls out over the comm. "Don't do something stupid, now."

How will I overcome them?

I grind my palms into the floor, eyeing my suit—my mighty weapon.

Do not take things so literally, Jina.

Well, sorry to say, Dad, but you raised a literal person. One who has her weapon. One who's gathering the only other thing she needs: determination.

Get up, Jin. Get up.

I shake my head in the helmet, responding to Silva. "I'm okay. Coming back now." Then I stand, engage my thrusters, full speed, and I dare any obstacle to step in my way right now. Slats and beams splinter as I roar back through the tunnel.

"Slow down, Jinny!"

"Something's wrong with my suit," I lie. "I'm out of control!"

Then I explode this mighty weapon into Khaddhi, crashing the both of us through the concrete stairs behind her. Khaddhi comes to, engaging the thrusters on her feet, and then we're up through the staircase above us. She throws me off, but I respond quickly, smashing into her, fixing my hands to the neck of her suit and engaging my right-wing thruster only, so I start spinning a circle on a pivot. Then I cut the right thruster, pump the left, and fling Khaddhi up through another staircase, at which point the entire well begins to crumble.

I know a collapse when I see one, so I rocket back down to Silva, Hitesh, and Cao, who are staring up at the slow-motion plummet of rubble and rebar and concrete blocks drifting toward us. "Get through the wall!" I scream, grabbing Hitesh's hand and pulling him toward the tunnel into the hotel room. *Need to at least pretend like I'm still on their side.* Hitesh pumps his thrusters, halting my advance, and like the cool, collected jackass he is, he turns back to Silva and says, "Orders, Captain?"

Silva takes a final look up, then blasts off into the tunnel, saying, "Follow me. And once we're through, Hitesh, you tether a cord to Jinny. From here on, she doesn't move more than six feet without my say-so."

Two corsairs down, three to go.

I'm leashed to Hitesh now. A cable runs from the tether ring in my back to the ring in his chest.

We're in a hallway of some sort, about eight feet wide and running straight ahead farther than our lights shine.

Cao's behind us, still poking at stairwell rubble and speaking into the comm. "Khaddhi, you there? Khaddhi! Tell me how to reach you. We'll dig you out." He's been talking that way for the last five minutes, and finally, Silva says, "How much air do you have, Jinny?"

"Two hours," I lie. It reads three, but I need us moving . . . taking risks.

Silva grumbles. "We need to go."

"But Khaddhi?" Cao asks, turning from digging in the rubble.

"She made her grave."

The rest stand in silence. Unbelieving, I suppose, that Silva could turn on a crewmate so quickly.

Silva pivots on his bionic, facing me. "Now as for you, I don't suffer fools gladly. We keep you leashed to Hitesh now. One wrong step and I'll ask Cao to pull the eliminator out of his pack and shock the power right out of your suit."

Good god. That's why they brought the eliminator.

Silva steps up to me, touching his viewport to mine, and his eyes are as hard as I've ever seen them. "I'll leave you here, Jinny. I'll leave you, and then Thara's fate will be sealed."

My mouth is like chalk, but I don't blink. I don't even tip my viewport back. I find something—a strength I wasn't sure was there, and I stare back at Silva, helmet to helmet. "I don't suffer fools, either. And Khaddhi was a swamping fool if ever there was one. Now, I said I'd take you down to the vault. I keep my word just like you . . . Captain Silva."

Silva looks like he could rip my helmet clean off the suit, but after a time, he just taps my viewport with two fingers. "Lead on."

We resume the journey, walking down the hall, passing room after room.

"You think this is where people stayed?" Cao asks. He's

up ahead, kicking in doors, and as I pass them, I can see the moldering remnants of couches, beds, dressers, and several foggy mirrors that Dad would have liked.

"Yes," Silva says, one word, and I can feel the tension through the comm as an alarm sounds in my suit.

High-pitched beeping, same as when I'd gotten ripped from the anchor cable, but this time it's not my air. I glance at my viewport, and the fruits of my idiocy are finally coming to bear. I gasp, and Hitesh, perceptive as a dolphin, calls out, "Speak, Jinny."

Guess his life's tied to mine now, quite literally. I turn around. "My pressure's down to ninety-seven percent. Could have been a one-time burst, what with the, uhh—disturbance—back in the stairs."

"More likely you have a leak," Hitesh says.

He knows it, I know it. The only question is how bad.

Silva lifts off the ground. "*Move* faster."

I thrust forward and my lights reach the end of the hall. The skeletal frames of two armchairs and a rusted metal console table lie ahead. Dad would try to salvage those.

Cao hooks around the hall's end and says, "There's a door with one of them staircase drawings on it over here. Probably another well."

But I look back and see Silva standing in front of two large steel sheets embedded in the hallway wall. He says, "No.

We're taking a straight shot down. Then Jinny can finally tell us which floor." Silva tilts his bionic and jams it into the vertical crack between the two steel sheets. He digs both sets of his fingers into the crack and pulls in opposing directions, until slowly, the sheets separate and recess into the surrounding walls. Silva's standing in front of a gaping rectangular hole that's lined with concrete and several black and silver cables running up and down.

Not so different from the cables that operate our lift back at the inn.

"How'd you know it was there?" Cao says, panting as he arrives.

Silva chuckles to himself. "The architects mark them on the blueprints. These days, you see lifts mostly on the coast, built into cliffsides. But the old sunken towers all have them too."

Silva steps forward, engaging his thrusters to keep from sinking. "Everyone in. Hitesh, you and Jinny first, since she's leading, then myself; Cao, you trail from the top."

I drop in, tapping lightly on the thrusters until Hitesh steps into the shaft as well. The shaft has a thick black center cable, and the far-side wall opposite the entry is lined with wires and cables, at least ten different ones, and three silver, rail-like beams. It's a hollow rectangular pillar, about ten by ten, and I sink slowly, descending past the backside of more silver doors, each with wide red letters that can only be noting the floors: 29, 28, 27.

My jaw clamps down. *This route is way too direct.*

"The elevator will be somewhere below us," Silva says. "Hitesh, you make sure Jinny doesn't plow into it. Don't want it ripping free and falling to the ground. That cephalopod's already given us too much attention."

"Understood," Hitesh says, tapping his thrusters.

"Feels good not to be walking anymore," Cao says from above. "These suits were made for swimming."

I spin around, staring down the insides of the shaft. The cabling is pretty beat up, probably broken down by the pressure. Maybe I could use those cables somehow? Tie Silva, Hitesh, and Cao into the shaft together, or—swamp all. I'm reaching. They're in atmo suits, have strength five times what they have aboveground. No rotted cable's going to hold them down even if I manage to do it.

We pass floors twenty-six and twenty-five. My heart's pounding, my skin tight beneath the suit. We're minutes from twenty-two and it's still the three of them against me . . . and I'm swamping lashed to Hitesh, removing all chance of escape. We float past twenty-four, and then—buzz. The haptics in my feet vibrate as I land on the elevator.

"Hold there, Jinny," Silva says, as he, Hitesh, and Cao land as well.

The thick black center cable connects directly to the roof of the elevator, and the thing occupies the entire space of the shaft, no chance of descending around it. Though maybe I could break that center cable somehow? If Cao or Silva gets inside, I could collapse the shaft on top of them?

Silva cocks his head and tugs lightly on the center cable. "Seems stable. Take out the torch, Cao. We cut through the box. Delicate like. I don't want us stomping through only to have the whole thing come crashing down."

Cao reaches for his tool bag and Silva says, "Steady, Jinny. If you decide to stomp, then Cao pulls the eliminator and your last two hours will be at the bottom of this shaft."

Heat flames across my face. Damn that man. He's in my swamping head!

Cao removes the eliminator, flashing it for me to see. It's handheld, black, and shaped like the base of an electric kettle. He tucks it away and hands a torch to Silva, who works a wide square on one side of the elevator, easily big enough for us to fit with the suits. Silva's careful not to go near the center cable, and after a few minutes, the entire square's glowing red from the heat. The elevator roof seems like it's made from plastic as the burned edges are all curling and melting. All it requires is a tap of Silva's bionic and it'll fall through into the elevator.

"Ready, then?" Silva says. Hitesh nods, Cao too, and Silva's not looking for my opinion. He raises his bionic, and as I glance down at the top of the elevator, I see a corner of the cut square has already fallen in. Around that corner are three little red cap jellies, the alloy parasites. Second time I've seen them in Treasure Island.

And then I realize . . . there's metal all up and down this shaft. This cabling seemed rotted, but maybe it's half-devoured. The elevator itself is probably metal, but the interior . . . the roof. The roof *melted*; it's plastic. *It was holding them back.*

The three red caps float toward Silva's bionic. He sees them too now, and he pauses. The mushroom-like bodies latch on to his limb, wispy tendrils tucking in, and I see several more squirm out from the caved-in corner that Silva torched. I look up at Silva, and I can see worry contorting his face; he must know.

But I recognized them first. I take two steps forward, saying, "What you waiting for, Silva?" Then I smash the torched square down with my foot.

As soon as I do, I slam my thrusters, shooting up, pulling Hitesh behind me, as a wave of red cap jellies erupt from within the elevator.

There must be thousands—tens of thousands. Despite my head start, I'm swallowed by the swarm—my entire field of vision consumed by their gelatinous bodies. Their red caps are pulsing. My suit shrieks out an alarm in a way that is entirely unnecessary because I can see the jellies already sucking on it. Hitesh and Cao are screaming below me, and I can hardly think, so I switch off my comm, trying to focus.

I swat through throngs of them, and they blob easily out of the way. But there are so many, it feels like they've become the water itself. I glance down my chest and see dozens leeched on. Then I feel a rush of something through the haptics in my feet, then up my legs; there's something moving quickly below me, and with a whoosh that almost pins me against the back rails, Silva rushes past, his thrusters on full as he shoots up the shaft.

He has the right idea, moving so quickly. I race up behind him, still jerking Hitesh along. Silva stops alongside one of the walls. The jellies are less dense here, though there are still thousands of them in our immediate vicinity. He jams his bionic into a crack in the wall . . . a wall that is covered in jellies.

He's trying to exit onto another floor, but he also has something in his hand, and he's not willing to put down whatever he's holding to get the leverage he needs. I thrust up next to Silva, while Hitesh (or a red-transparent-pulsing thing that resembles the shape of Hitesh) is still dangling limp below me. My hands sink into the crack in the doors that Silva's trying to pry open; I yank hard, two-handed, to my right side, while Silva pulls to the left, and the door slides open.

Silva squeezes through immediately; I follow, turning

sideways to fit through, and after a few steps I'm pulled back by Hitesh, whose body swings horizontal and catches in the crack that Silva and I squeezed through. I reach back for him—jellies are floating through, attaching to my hands and arms—but Silva shakes his head. He pushes me back into the hallway, Hitesh swivels, and I see his viewport, the only thing not covered in jellies. His face is stricken in horror. Silva lifts his bionic and kicks Hitesh hard in the chest, propelling him back into the elevator shaft and slamming me against the doors. The force of the bionic kick causes the tether that bound Hitesh and me to rip free, and then Silva shoves me out of the way as he presses the doors back together.

Silva's mouthing something to me, and I see him swishing his hands up and down across his suit, removing jellies by the dozens, and then slowly, painstakingly, crushing them with his hands. I stand up, beginning to do the same, and, in silence, we eliminate the few hundred jellies that snuck through the crack in the elevator shaft doors.

At the end of it, Silva picks up the bag that he was holding in the shaft. It's the same one that Cao lugged down here; the one with the tools we need to cut into the vault. Silva points to the side of his helmet, his lips moving, and I finally switch back to our comms channel.

Hitesh and Cao are still screaming back in the shaft, and I almost flick the comm off again, until Silva says, "The sea jellies are almost through their suits. Cao and Hitesh will depressurize shortly. The least we can do is bear witness."

The cries of Hitesh and Cao don't fade slowly, like someone drifting off to sleep in the night. They build to a terrifying crescendo, the pitch and fever of their screams accelerating, until there are suddenly several deep pops and echoes of splattering . . . and, just like Mayra, silence.

I close my eyes. The jellies may have killed them, but I set the jellies free.

Silva knocks on my viewport, jarring me out of that moment. "What's your pressure read?"

"Ninety-six percent," I say, scanning down my suit. The thing looks less like an exoskeleton and more like a half-eaten metal carcass. "You?"

"High enough." Silva studies me, then asks, "You've seen red caps before, haven't you?"

He knows. He saw me make the choice that killed two of his crew. Denying it's only going to piss him off more.

"I've seen them," I say.

"So you knew what you were doing when you smashed that square on the elevator?" His lips are pressed together, his mustache a flat white line above.

I stare him down. "I did."

He nods slowly. "Horrible thing, to kill, but sometimes you

think . . . it needs to be done. There's no other way." He takes a long breath, clearly thinking about something. "Just be careful where it leads you."

At first, I'm not quite sure what he's trying to tell me.

It needs to be done.

There's no other way.

My question to him echoes back to me. The question about Vitória.

How old was she when she died?

Fifteen.

"*You* killed her, didn't you?"

He raises his head, his green eyes locked on to mine, but he doesn't say anything.

"Vitória. She'd be alive today except . . . tell me what happened," I say.

The soft hum of his consideration rolls through the comm, and I wait, but still he doesn't speak; instead his eyes roll up, as if watching the memory.

"You were only seven, and you caught Vitória sending that drone in the morning—" I pause then, all the pieces coming together. "The drone had the coordinates for the dive."

His eyes fix back on to mine.

"Who'd she send it to?"

"Wasn't all her fault," Silva says. "Her father, my uncle, was a rough man. Beat everyone who got close enough for him to land the blows. The boyfriend, Luiz, probably put the idea in her head—told her she had to leave, one way or another." Silva shakes his head. "On the island, stranded, I kept believing our family would come. A few days in, though, Vitória told me to accept their death. 'Nossa família está morta, João.'" Silva pauses, and all I hear is his breath on the comm. "She said her boyfriend would come, and he'd bring coin. That last part was when I knew. Why would he bring coin? Only one reason— because she sold out our family. That night, I stashed a gun. I waited until Vitória ran to his boat by the shoreline. They embraced." Silva's voice becomes a whisper. "I walked up and fired twice. That was the end of them."

My god. He was seven years old. . . .

"From there, I took the two atmo suits, plus our remaining supplies, and made for Mantiqueira, the largest island chain near Rio-Lost. I bartered one dive suit with a wrecking crew who agreed to berth and train me. Built myself into the man I am today." He closes his eyes and draws several breaths. "Was a terrible thing I did." That low hum emerges again. "Some acts you can't take back. Some you regret your whole life."

I let his words wash over me, and my thoughts drift to Thara. What did Silva say to me? *Never thought I'd see that face again.* He's haunted by her, by Vitória. And seeing Thara—it's affected his judgment. I was right, and—the realization finally dawns.

"I don't think you could kill Thara."

His eyes open, and the hurt's there, those eyes wet, red, and tortured. "Probably not," he says.

"What are Izzy's real orders, then? What happens to her?"

Silva picks up his tool bag, sighing. "If we don't get back, I told Izzy to set her free at sundown. Release her on the Nevada shores."

The moment ebbs. The only sound is Silva's soft breathing and the echo of my own lips opening, closing.

"Had to talk it right. Get you to cooperate."

So what does that mean? I force myself to think. Thara's in the brig, and she'll be released into Nevada in several hours. She's safe. And, as for me, I'm in an atmo suit. I could thrust out of here, make it back to the *Bandeira*. I could break Thara out or track the skiff Izzy uses to release her. I don't need to be here in Vegas.

I can leave.

"One other thing you should know about Vitória." Silva steps toward me. "This pearl stud of hers"—he stops a foot away, swiveling his head so I can see the earring—"she recovered it after eight hours below." He pauses. "Vitória would never leave a job unfished. And neither will you." Silva extends his arm, and he's holding something black, a disc, pressing it to my suit. The haptics across my chest burst; vibrations thrumming through my ribs. Half a second later, my lights go out, my viewport blinks off, my heart accelerates, my legs and arms stiffen, and my breath catches in my throat as I realize what happened.

Silva used the eliminator.

He drained the battery on my suit.

No battery means no thrusters, no way to surface.

And, at last, the truth of the situation hits me: Silva said he couldn't kill Thara.

He never said anything about me.

21

Well, I'm dead.

So stupid. How did I think for a moment that he was going to let me carry on after taking down three of his crew? That's why he stood here so long, talking. He was wrestling the eliminator from the bag.

I fall to my knees, but Silva yanks me up. He's mouthing something, but I can't hear it (no power for comms). Then Silva switches to diver hand signals, many of which Dad taught me for emergencies (like loss of power), but it's been so long that I can scarcely follow what Silva's saying. Finally, he drags me up by my armpits. Points at a 26 on the wall (the twenty-sixth floor, I presume), and then shoves me forward. It's the silent equivalent of *Lead on.*

I can still walk in the suit, and it still maintains air (whatever little I have left; maybe two hours?) and pressure (which, given the condition of my suit, can't be much more than my last reading at 96 percent). But the reality is, I'm dead. There's no surfacing without Silva hauling me up. And he's the one who just eliminated me, so a whale's chance of that happening.

There is one consolation, however. *Thara will live.*

That knowledge makes my cheeks rise and my heart beat firm inside this suit. Maybe Silva thinks that's an awful outcome, Thara being the last in our family, but that's not the way I see it. Silva's not haunted by being the last in his family. He's haunted by what he did to Vitória. The decision to take the life of the only other family member he had. That is truly an unthinkable burden to carry. And it's one that Thara won't carry. She'll make it into Nevada, she'll find her way back to Coconino, and I'll meet her again one day, beneath a blue sky, sun shining in my next life.

With that hopeful thought, I walk forward through this underwater hallway. Rusted sconces line the walls, the floor is covered in an algae film, and Silva keeps prodding me in the back. I could still try to kill him. It's just me and him left, and I'm dead here anyway. But without thrusters, without the strength from my fully powered suit, collapsing the tower would be impossible, not to mention pointless.

Still, in some brazen act of defiance it occurs to me: *Why lead him to the vault? Why let him win?* So I pause, turn, folding my arms across my chest, and you don't need a comm to interpret that. Silva rolls his eyes, clearly annoyed, and he points his bionic tip to the floor and starts swiping it in clean lines across the green algae. He works slowly, patiently, writing four letters: TAIM.

His name's like an electric jolt. I tried to put him out of my thoughts these last few hours, not willing to face what he's done. But those four letters send my emotions swirling, because I know the implication: move or Taim dies.

There's a cruel part of me that thinks Taim deserves to die. He betrayed me, took Silva's offer. He made his choice. But Silva's words from a moment ago echo in my head. *Some acts you can't take back. Some you regret your whole life.*

My chest collapses, thinking of those words.

No matter what Taim's done, I can't sentence him to death. So I uncross my arms, and I walk. I'll draw out my last breaths down here. I will lead Silva to his treasure.

Thara and Taim will live.

Robbed of power, the weight of the suit is immense but just manageable, as the water lightens the load. I trudge forward, and Silva puts an arm around my back, supporting me as I walk. It's strange—like a caring, fatherly thing, but I don't discourage it.

What would Dad be thinking if he were here? He'd be rooting for the treasure to be found. A soft smile comes to my lips, and I remember Dad recovering that silver jewelry box in Phoenix-Below. For weeks after, he glowed like the sun herself. Kept moving the box from the bar to the fireplace mantel to our tea shelf. Wanted the perfect place to show it off. Finally, he told Thara she could keep it in our room, place Mom's necklace in there at night. Thara did that for a week, tops . . . then she asked Dad if we could trade it for some grow bulbs. "I want to start a little garden," she said in the parlor one evening. I thought Dad would be devastated. Instead, he wrapped one hand across Thara's shoulders, cupped another to his bearded cheek, and I watched his eyes shift to the suits, twinkling, as he said, "Of course we can. And don't worry—I'll find you another."

That's how he thought about it. Treasure was out there— waiting to be found. It was supposed to be found.

The lights from Silva's suit guide our way, and we turn into a door marked Staircase C, winding down the stairwell in silence. I let the memory fade, and the reality of what's about to happen comes flooding back through.

I'm not coming back from this.

I guess I always knew that. I knew it deep in my bones, where the fear lives, where the hope dies. This is where Dad departed. This is where I'll go. This dark and vacuous place where people once played out their entire lives.

There's no sound now. Only the faint suction of air through my nostrils, the speedy beat of my heart. I open my mouth just to hear the separating of my dry, cracked lips, and slowly it's settling in that I will die alone, in the dark, without touch or smell or taste or sound.

Perhaps Silva will be there when I die. In some odd way, I imagine he's always been there. Not the man himself, but what he stands for: The desperate search for glory and riches. The pitiable need to believe we can influence our destiny. Whether Dad or Bhili or Silva, it was the same whisper in my ear: Descend into the deep. Seek and you shall find. Come, brave the underworld with me, and we will return with treasure.

I exit, finally, through a rusted door marked with another placard: 22. No sooner do I step onto the floor, than Silva whirls me around, his hands on my shoulders, his lights so close, blinding and warm. He's searching my face to confirm it's true—that this is *the* floor—and surely he must see it from the defeated drape of my cheeks, my inability to meet his eyes.

He spins me back and pushes on my shoulders, wanting me to sit down. I do, and then he thrusts off, carrying the bag with the torch and saw. The specs of light from his suit fade as he leaves. My world dims, and I wonder: *Will that be the last light I ever see?*

I'm lying down now, my eyes closed (not that it makes any difference). My breathing is soft, my head pounding, my jaw throbbing. I remember the passage from the Rigveda:

Desire . . . the primal seed and germ of Spirit.

The desire to continue. The desire to live.

I'll try to hold it off some, as Dad would want, but there's only so long you can fight the inevitable. *I probably have an hour, less.*

I read once what happens to a body if a suit ruptures in the deep and the diver doesn't ascend. It starts similar to free-diving, with an ache in your sinuses, your ears, your face, the fogging of your brain, the numbing of your hands and feet. But it escalates past that quickly, as freedivers are only ever exposed to single digit atmospheres. Down here, it's dozens of atmospheres, and that means your lungs compress, your chest grows heavy. Blood rushes to the lungs to compensate, so you develop the itches on your chest. Combine that with the delirium, and you might scratch your skin off, were it not for the metal suit.

Suddenly, a lung collapses, a sharp stabbing sensation, like a knife slipped between ribs. Your rib cage flattens, the remaining sacs in your lungs rupture, air bubbles enter your arteries, and then it's heart attack, stroke, oxygen toxicity to your nervous system, or all of the above. At that point, you're (thankfully) dead or unconscious, because the real event begins. Your tissues rupture (muscle, connective, nerve, and skin), your bones splinter, and ultimately your entire body explodes out across the canvas of the suit's interior, while slowly, the water seeps inside the suit, until the remnants of your corpse are floating inside.

Your suit—your coffin.

You won't feel it, I tell myself. After the lung, you won't feel a thing.

Except I do feel something—a kick to my side. It rolls me over. I open my eyes to see Silva's bionic hanging over me. His smile's spread wide into the white chops on his cheeks, and his right hand points one finger to his chest, and then with the pointer fingers on both hands, he gestures out in front of him with the sign of *follow me.*

I'm not sure how he thinks that's possible. I'm not sure if it *is* possible; my head screams with pain, like a drill's barreling into both temples, but Silva lugs me up with the immense strength of his powered suit. He throws one of my arms around him and then we shuffle down floor twenty-two, which is different from the above floors. It's not a narrow hallway with doors on either side; it's a wide expanse, with rotted tables and chairs and rows of barnacled slot machines. Most have levers and buttons and shattered screens. The red caps would feast in here.

I stagger for a moment, and I'm thinking about just keeling over. There's no need to go on. I can't do anything more for Silva besides weigh him down, waste his time. It doesn't even make sense why Silva would drag me forward. *Has he found it?*

Does he want me to see the treasure, to know it's his? One last gloat before my lungs collapse?

He turns into a smaller room with three hexagonal tables, like the card table Dad and I recovered, the one that Saanvi said finally served its purpose.

Saanvi, I'm sorry we couldn't make Silva see your purpose.

Around each table are six chairs with piles of silt in the seats, stacks of coins on the table in front of them. Card players who must have chosen to play until the bitter end, as the water levels rose and the hotel flooded. Their skeletons at last disintegrated.

Silva pulls me farther, almost carrying me now, until we enter an alcove room behind the card tables, and there, the entire back wall is steel, with a gaping black hole at the center. At first, Silva's suit lights shine only on the wall, and then upon a large circular door lying flat on the ground in front of the wall. The door is also metal, with a disc-shaped wheel protruding from the center. Beside the fallen door are Silva's torch, the immersible cut saw, and Cao's black tool bag. Then Silva takes three steps forward, stooping at first, toward the gaping hole in the back wall. Full of dramatics, he raises his chest, casting his suit's light through the hole and illuminating piles upon piles of glittering gold coins.

My heart swells with the sight of them, and I draw a long, deep breath, perhaps the only proper breath I've taken in the last ten minutes. Strange to think, but I'm thrilled and relieved at the sight of the gold. Silva found his treasure. Taim will have his money. Thara will be free.

Silva's lights swivel back to me and he motions for me to come forward. He bends down, reaches into Cao's bag, and my mind races forward. What's he going to do to me? I'm already dead.

Then Silva spins me around. I'm glancing over my shoulder, but I can't see him well. He's grabbing at something in my lower back. Then, abruptly, he shoves something else in. My viewport comes alive with the prints of my status, and Silva's lilting voice echoing in my ears, "Can't leave you for dead yet. Need you to haul my treasure up to the surface."

22

Silva had a spare battery in the tool bag. It feels like a swamping miracle. I would kiss him were he not a murderous, conniving liar still holding my sister hostage.

"What's your pressure read?" Silva says, pulling a rolled neoprene bag from the toolkit and unfurling it across the vault floor.

I glance at the corner of the viewport and realize just how dire the situation is. Ninety-five percent. I really am dead in an hour . . . probably less, as the suit's likely been at this level for some time. "Not good," I say.

Silva picks up his head as he mounds coins by the hundreds into his bag. "My suit's the same." He pulls three more neoprene bags from the toolkit, walks over, and hands two to me. "Get scraping, then. We pack everything we can and break for the surface."

"We won't be able to take it all," I say.

"Doesn't matter. Each bag will hold six hundred pounds. Across four bags, that's about twenty thousand coin. We take those, plus our lives, and we come back for the rest later."

"I'm never coming back here," I say.

"Nor me with you. Now pack the gold before I snatch that battery out your backside and leave you for the jellies to find."

The next ten minutes are some of the most bizarre of my life. Wading through pyramid piles of gold, scooping them into my duffels by the armful. The coins all have the same markings: the scruffy parrot, the words *Treasure Island*, and a glossy, unrusted sheen that makes it clear that these are 100 percent pure gold (pure gold doesn't rust . . . not even twenty-five hundred feet below).

But if I'm in shock wading through this shimmering golden dream, then Silva's gone gonzo, kicking up coins, flinging them about the room, tossing handfuls up through the water and letting them shower back down upon him. Perhaps he's short on air too, not just pressure, because he seems to be suffering some kind of delirium. He clearly knows that we need to jettison to the surface immediately; he's just unable to keep himself from lying down in the mess of gold and doing the backstroke.

Finally, I call out to him, "I'm almost packed. You ready?"

That seems to wrench him from his mania, as he goes

horizontal, engages his thrusters, and holds his bags open, zooming about the vault and scooping giant heaps of coins. A few minutes and several barreling handfuls later, and Silva's packed to the brim as well, and I'm not sure who's more the fool, myself for taking so long, or Silva in all his lunacy.

My head's pounding again (perhaps the adrenaline of the discovery is wearing off), and I lug the bags over my shoulders, engage my thrusters (there's no way to walk with this additional weight), and say to Silva, "We need to go—now."

"I'm ready," he says, tossing his bags out of the vault. He moves to the fallen door and says, "Put your gold down. We need to seal the vault."

"No one else is coming down here, Silva. It's fine."

"It's not fine," he says. "And it's not other wreckers I'm worried about. It's those jellies."

He's right. If the vault's open and the red caps find their way out of the elevator shaft, they'll sniff out the gold and devour it like they did our suits. And though I don't care, though I'm never coming back to this place again, it's easier to just heave the fallen door up than it is to argue.

So I squat down with Silva, thrust up, and we slam the giant circular steel vault door back into place.

"You realize the door's metal, Silva. They'll eat through it eventually."

"Yes, but not for a few months, maybe years. Time enough

for me to come back with Izzy for the rest."

Izzy. That makes me pause for a moment. Do I really trust Izzy to release Thara? Maybe those are her orders, but is she going to do it when we show up with four of her crew dead?

No time to linger on that thought as we hoist the duffels over our shoulders. Thrusters engaged, we zoom back through the card room, out onto floor twenty-two. Our pace is slowed by the additional weight of the gold, but we're moving, and we should be able to get up in ten minutes, maybe fifteen if we blow a thruster on the way.

We're passing rows of those metal slot machines, no sight of the jellies, and then Silva takes a hard left, away from the staircase, which is straight ahead, and he's full speed toward a wall lined with shattered windows.

Stars and moon. I know what he's doing and now I'm thinking that delirium in the vault wasn't just some temporary golden ecstasy. "Silva! Stop, we don't exit that way."

"We do now."

"Your brain's fogged, Silva. We need to climb the stairs, get back to the roof."

"No time. My pressure just dropped to ninety-four percent."

Swamp all.

"How are you still alive?"

"This body's built for wrecking. Even for me, though, there comes a time when you shoot straight to the surface."

"The cephalopod's gonna be waiting for us!" I say, realizing

I'll be at 94 shortly. As much as I've desired to escape Silva, in this moment, he's right—we surface now or we're dead.

"It sure is." Silva blasts through the broken window. "Punch your thrusters, Jinny!"

I do, and I'm out in front of Treasure Island, driving up hard with Silva above me.

"You remember the lats and longs?"

"Yes."

"Good, cause we're about to get separated." Silva jabs his finger down twice and I bend forward and look. Below me, shadows move against shadows, and then something white and round gleams, reflecting back the light from my suit.

The eye blinks twice, the creature swirls to a bright purple, and then a long, thick, white tentacle unfurls, roaring up toward us. My hand squeezes harder against the thrusters, but they're already at full. Silva's a few feet above me, and then, suddenly, I rocket past him.

I look down and a colossal prehensile tentacle is wrapped around Silva's suit leg, now pulsing a deep indigo, hues shifting by the second.

This is my chance. Leave Silva to the deep, blast up to the surface with the entire dive crew dead and ten thousand coin. I'll use the suit to seize the patrol boat, force the truth from Taim, use the gold to trade for Thara if Izzy doesn't follow orders.

My victory is waiting for me in the empty waters above,

Silva's screaming through the comm below, and I've won, I've won. . . .

But then I decide to get greedy.

The decision happens in a fraction of a second. I spent the last three years cowering inside the inn, telling myself to be careful, be smart, survive. *Don't be reckless like Dad.* Clouds above, I hate Taim, but he was right. I haven't been safe. I've been scared. I've been so fucking scared.

I'm still scared. But I'm also strong. I'm also *here.* I've defied all the odds, overcome every terror. I've risked everything and now I *want* everything. I want the gold *and* Thara, and I won't have to trade away an ounce . . .

. . . if I have Silva to trade instead.

So I jam my thrusters and cut my lights. Cephalopods don't have sonar or some magical underwater hunting abilities. They just have sight. Awesome sight that can detect pricks of light at five hundred feet out. But if my lights are off . . . then I'm black as the water around me.

The minute I cut my lights, the creature goes black as well. Then I float, silent, invisible, down toward Silva. He's still screaming, calling my name through the comm.

Don't worry, Silva. I'll be there soon.

The tentacle stops thrashing some. The eye below is a thin slit of white now. It's focused, intent. It has one of its prey ensnared; it's searching for the other. For me.

I can see Silva clearly, despite my lights being off. He's thrashing, and his lights wave out in wide arcs, like a lighthouse, calling me near. I tap my thrusters, ever so slightly, *tap, tap, tap.*

Another tentacle has come up, no color, though. The cephalopod knows I'm close. I think it's trying to feel me. Silva's lights swipe across the other tentacle, once, twice.

I'm lined up well now, sinking, just a few more feet. I'm coming up from behind Silva, his lights cast out in front, avoiding me. The tentacle wrapped around him has gone still . . . as if it's listening to the vibrations in the water.

"Cut your lights, Silva," I whisper into the comm. He does, and then I grab his bionic before I float past.

The tentacle shivers. It can feel my weight, I know it can. It's slithering along Silva's body, his arms pinned at his sides. I unhook Silva's harpoon. "Be ready," I say, lifting the tool bag off Silva's suit and attaching it to my own. "Thrust on my command." Gently, I load the band on the harpoon and then I let go of Silva's bionic, drifting down again.

"Where you going?" he says. His voice rattles, and I realize it's the first time I've ever heard him scared.

"I'm not planning to shoot the limb," I say. Just a few feet farther; I can't see anything now without Silva's lights, but I know it's down there. I just have to trust my instincts.

"What are you shooting, then?" Silva says.

And this is it, I must be right upon it. I bend forward, staring down, and flick my lights on while responding to Silva. "The eye."

The cephalopod's eye slams open with the blast of light, and I squeeze the trigger on the harpoon. The spear hails down, burying itself directly in the black pupil at the center of the eye, and though I can't hear anything through the suit, it's as if I do.

The monster's entire body jerks, pulsing with a bright, piercing blue. It writhes, tentacles pulling back, furiously lashing the water. I drop the harpoon, and I'm spinning when I cut my lights and punch my thrusters. "Now, Silva. Climb!"

I can only hope the thing's released Silva, but I'm not focused on him now. I'm focused on my own ascent, and the rolling waters I can feel below me through the haptics on my feet and shins. I risk a glance down, thinking the thing must be following me, but I don't see the giant squid hurtling up, and after two or three minutes, I risk restoring my lights.

As I near the surface, the pressure lessens, and my lats and longs come back in the viewport. I'm off course, but I correct, and then I'm headed back for the entry point. A few minutes later, the pounding in my head eases, then the water brightens, and a crackled voice comes over the comm. "So, you like me after all, Jinny? Or do you just have it out for the cephies?"

"I hate cephalopods," I say.

He chuckles. "Thought as much."

I thrust over to Silva. Only his legs, the bionic and the normal, are in the water, but I can see his body pressed against a lighted diver's buoy—a standard device, about twelve feet across, that's thrown in the water to make it easier for divers to return. It sits half-under, half-over the surface, and you can throw your arms over it and pop your helmet off (something I'm about desperate for) without having to wait for your craft to come around and haul you aboard.

I sidle up to Silva underwater, clipping my duffels to the buoy alongside his. But before breaking the surface, before that first rich breath of non-tanked air, there's a last thing I need to do. I unzip the tool bag I took off Silva, scrabble around for the eliminator, and then I shock him and wrench him free from the buoy.

His viewport's open (must have gasped a few proper breaths before I arrived), and he starts sinking immediately, his green eyes wide with hurt, like he believed I really did come back for him out of the goodness of my heart.

After he's dropped two dozen feet and has a moment to think I'm gonna let him drift down until his head caves in, I drop down myself, thrusters on, grabbing him under the arms, and then haul him back up above the surface to the buoy. Maybe I should let him sink into the deep. Maybe the world would be a safer place without him. That's what a young Silva would do: take his revenge, eliminate his enemies.

Didn't bring him peace, though. *And it won't bring me any, either.*

Silva sputters as he comes to, water rushing out of his open viewport, hands clinging to the buoy. "I thought I felt a bit light," Silva says. "You took the tool bag—off me—before you blinded the cephalopod. That right?"

"Sure did," I say.

Silva's still coughing up water when I rest my gloved hand on top of his head. "Now, I want to be clear about something." I pause, and his coughing finally halts. I look him square in the face, his white mustache dripping salty tears into his mouth. "You're gonna serve *my* purpose. We're gonna race back to the *Bandeira*, Thara will board the patrol boat, you will tell Izzy and crew to stand down, and I walk with *all* the gold . . . otherwise, I will drop you down to that Vegas Strip." I poke him in the forehead several times. "Understood?"

"Your proposal is quite clear," he says. "Just one problem."

"And that is?"

"Look around, Jinny." Silva swivels his head. "There's no boat."

23

No patrol boat. Why? Did the Coast Guard figure out the truth of our plot and have everyone arrested? Or perhaps Taim and the Dongos are just watching us from the horizon with a spyglass, waiting for the rest of the crew to surface (not gonna happen).

In any case, I open my viewport and suck down a long drag of fresh, salty air to help myself think straight.

We're in the right place; the buoy is here; our lats and longs are correct.

"Where are they, Silva?"

"Don't know," he says in his most I'm-just-an-innocent-corsair tone.

"And I believe you because . . ."

"Well, I'd sure like to exit this water and not freeze to death."

Silva's soaked through after I eliminated him and let him sink with his viewport open. He'll die out here tonight if I leave him on the buoy. Not that I care.

Not really.

Anyway, the real issue is how to make it back to Thara. The nearest shore is fifteen miles away (La Madre to the west and Yucca Cape to the north). I could thrust myself there and get a boat. But there's no way I can thrust Silva, myself, and the four duffels of gold. I couldn't even carry the four bags on my own. Which means I could take two and leave Silva here with the others. But what if the patrol boat shows up? Then Silva's free and he has two bags of gold. I do think he'll release Thara tonight, but what then? She's left wandering the shores of Nevada in the dark, without coin, and I just hope she makes it back to Coconino?

Not an outcome I like.

But what's my other option? Just sit here above Vegas-Drowned with twenty thousand pieces of gold, the man who murdered my friend, no boat, and hope my back-stabbing ex-boyfriend shows up?

That seems to be what Silva wants.

"Mind hauling the gold up?" he says. "If we're here, best have our eyes on it. Don't want any little fish snapping holes in the bags."

I sigh, but I close my viewport, tuck under, and lug each bag up onto the buoy. The weight's heavy, pressing the buoy farther into the water, but this thing's designed for ten divers to haul up on, so it holds, and I remove my helmet.

"Sorry about the boat," Silva says. "Seems your sister's going to be wandering the Nevada shores cold and alone tonight."

"I can still drop you down to the ocean bottom, you know."

"You could," Silva says. "Maybe you'd kill me in cold blood. Though I'm not so sure. You stuck a cephalopod in the eye to save me."

"I didn't come back for you, Silva. I came back for the gold."

"Oh, is that it . . ."

Talking with this man is exasperating. "Do you have a suggestion or something? Otherwise, you may just freeze to death tonight."

"My suggestion is to sit tight. The Dongos are probably waiting this out on the horizon, make sure the whole crew surfaces. Probably spooked after seeing just me and you." Silva unzips one of the duffels and I can see his eyes sparkle. "Though we got what we came for . . ."

"And what about Taim?" I say. "Did you really offer him ten thousand coin to make sure we sailed through Yucca Cape?"

"Is that what he told you?"

"Is that a yes or no?"

Silva licks his upper lip. "It's a yes. I offered, but no, he didn't take it. Are you wondering why he didn't sound the alarm with those guards back at Yucca Cape?"

"You could say so, yeah."

"Well, if I recall, I had a knife in your ribs at the time. Seems to me he wanted you to stay with your insides on the inside."

Which is what I thought, but then I asked him, and . . . "He told me you cut him in on the treasure!"

"Coasties make for good liars," Silva says. "I was hoping for it, really. Your boyfriend knew, just as I did, how to prevent you from caving in the tower. Can't do it if you think you're *the only* one who can save your sister. Then you need to stay alive. Just as you've done."

My heart's racing, my jaw trembling. *Is that true?* But Taim held my stare and refused to back down, and—he found a way, a reason, to force me back up. My racing heart slows, the beats pounding steady and firm. *It's true.* I know it's true, because that's what Taim's always done. Pulled my tether. Made me surface. Willed me to live.

"Why don't you think on that while we wait." Silva sinks a gloved hand into the unzipped duffel, letting the coins clatter back into the pile as they spill through his fingers. "I'd like to enjoy my gold . . . before you snatch it back away."

Ten minutes later, something does appear on the water, a little black spot against the gray horizon, getting bigger and bigger. Silva zips the open duffel of gold, and I slide my helmet near, bracing myself for the Dongos or the Guard or whatever, whoever, I have to fight through to make my way back to Thara.

I call out to Silva, "No funny business, now."

He shakes his head, raindrops flying off the soggy white buzz. "Wouldn't think of it."

The black spot creeps closer, closer, and then, in an instant, it fades to a dark metallic gray, the patrol boat's cabin, surrounded by a seafoam-green collar, and a person at the prow. His shoulders are rolled back, his blue-and-white Guard issue poncho rippling in the wind—and a pistol trained on Silva.

"Taim!" I shriek it out, full of forgiveness and understanding.

He doesn't shift the gun off Silva for a moment, but turns to me as the patrol boat pulls up beside us. "I'm sorry, I—"

"I know," I say. And that's all we need between us.

Taim leans off the prow, reaching out to me, his round, wet cheeks sparkling. He grips the collar of my suit with one hand, right where the helmet twists in. Then he jerks me two feet toward him and, suspended between boat and buoy, he kisses me.

For all the strength it must have taken to heave me forward, the kiss is a soft, delicate thing—my eyes closed, our lips together, his nose grazing mine.

Taim's long lashes flutter on my skin, and then my eyes are open, watching his, so focused . . . on something behind me. He pulls back. "Hands in the air, Silva!"

I whirl around, and the captain slices a long thin smile across his face. "Afraid not, Lieutenant," Silva says. "Unless you want me on the ocean bottom."

"His suit's been eliminated," I say.

Taim's eyes shift back to Silva. "Where are the others?!"

"Still down there," Silva says, winking at me. "Like all the best divers."

Then the cabin door slides open, and a corsair steps out, but not one of the Dongos—this one's shorter, with a maroon slicker and thick salt-and-pepper locs. . . . "Bhili?"

"Ow, ow, ow!" Bhili steps out of the cabin, whistling, clapping, her massive smile spread so wide it almost overcomes the black rot of her teeth. "Did you kiss him back good, now, Jinny? Old Bhili can show you how it's done if you want?"

No, thank you.

Taim and Bhili haul me onto the boat, and Taim resumes his pistol pointing at Silva.

I get to my feet and spy the Dongo brothers tied up, face down on the aft deck.

"Like what I did with them?" Bhili says, nodding at the corsairs.

I shake my head. "You . . . came back?"

"Aye, well, you know I fancy the Cook. You all right too, I suppose."

I blink in disbelief, and Bhili plods on, wiping the rain off her shoulders. "Dongos ain't too hard to handle if you come up on 'em in a suit." She gestures to a gray-black atmo suit half disassembled in the aft deck. "Borrowed off a friend in Mojave Main. Or maybe stole at knifepoint is more accurate."

"But how did you find us?"

"Gave you the lats and longs myself, didn't I? Thrusted out with the suit this morning. Found the boat. Dongos tried to drive off, but I caught up and knocked them down not ten minutes ago. Your boyfriend was half-suited up, ready to dive when we spotted you and the captain." Bhili leans out over the collar and spins the buoy, so Silva's beside us. "How do you do, João?"

Silva shakes his head. "A pleasure, Bhili."

"We taking him?" Bhili says. "Think I heard you say his suit's been eliminated. Just as well with me, we sink him down, leave him in Vegas to rot."

"We're taking him," I say. "Izzy still has Thara. She's supposed to set her free at sundown, but four of her people are dead, and I'm not taking any chances. We'll trade Silva for Thara to make sure it goes smooth."

"Well, let's get on, then."

I start to remove my suit arms but pause almost immediately. "Why'd you come back, Bhili? You abandoned us."

"Yes, well, me and pretty João here, we ain't on the best of terms." Bhili puckers her lips and pops an air kiss at Silva.

"Didn't fancy getting strung up and made to walk a plank into the Sonoran. Tried to lead them off in the skiff, but they didn't follow. Shame, that." Bhili claps Silva twice on his wet cheek. "Keep that firearm trained on him, now."

Taim passes me the pistol, and I keep it on Silva while he and Bhili heave Silva onto the patrol boat. Then Taim tosses him two zip ties and takes the gun back. "Suit off and fit those around your wrists and ankles."

Bhili helps me out of my suit. "Where's the boy, Saanvi?"

I look down. "Gone."

I just leave it at that. Silva killed him, sure, but it wouldn't have happened if Bhili hadn't bolted. Or if I hadn't let Bhili stay at the inn.

"Aye. João's a heartless kinda sea beast. Don't lay that on yourself. You go whalin', somebody gonna get speared. Sometimes you, sometimes the whale, sometimes a nice boy like Saanvi."

There's a moment of silence, just the memory of Saanvi and the tapping of the rain on the patrol boat's metal cabin. Then Bhili glances back at Silva, who's tied up on the deck, unsuited. Bhili twirls, swings a leg, and sails a boot straight into Silva's ribs. "Don't bring him back, but it feels good. You go on, you get one too."

I take a deep breath, and at first, I want to. In a sense, Bhili's right; there are parts of Silva that are utterly heartless.

There are other parts too, though. Parts that are broken, that make me pity him. So, I pick my head up instead, and I catch Taim's fierce stare. He sees me. He knows. And then he looks past me, out into the sea.

"No," I say. "I just want to go get Thara."

"Suit yourself," Bhili says, launching another haymaker of a kick into Silva's gut. He curls up, coughing, and I take two steps toward the cabin before stopping myself. *There's something I'm forgetting.*

I reach back over the collar. "We'll want to get these aboard first."

"Your tools?" Bhili says. "Just leave 'em."

A broad smile slips across my face. "Not the tools. The treasure."

We're blasting across the Gulf of Nevada, the rain shattering against the cabin's windshield. The patrol boat's throttle is so far down that we keep skipping off the tops of the waves— *ba bump, ba bump, ba bump.* The day's light dims, and the black waters of the Gulf are frothy and rolling, like a squall's coming in.

Taim's in the cabin. I'm on the aft deck with Bhili, and Silva and the Dongos are prostrate beside us. It feels so good to hear again, to smell, to taste, to touch. I don't care if it's all salty seas, wet air, and the crush of a hull across water. After being that close to death, almost entirely without my senses for four hours, maybe I'm finally starting to understand Dad's sentiment that diving made him better appreciate the full glory of the world above.

I never thought of our world as glorious. This rotten, soggy, fetid place of sunken cities and sinking continents; it always felt—wrong, like it wasn't made for us. It was made for the cephalopods and sharks, the whales and jellies. The creatures of the deep, who can withstand the pressure, who can see hundreds of feet through black waters, who can hum and hear the shape of things.

But coming back aboard the boat, feeling Taim squeeze the breath out of me—well, there is still warmth. We are still here, alive, above the water, and light still pierces the clouds, and we are still making our way.

The first thing I did aboard the patrol boat was put a drone in the air, voiced by Silva himself, telling Izzy that we were returning with the gold. That the mission had been a success, and that Thara was to be given an inflatable and set free on our return.

Silva said his orders were to free Thara at sundown, but Silva wasn't the one holding Thara. Izzy had Thara, and I do not trust Izzy to follow orders. Best to have Thara waiting in an inflatable. Hopefully alone, but if not, we'll do an exchange. I told Silva he could walk with a thousand coin and the right to go after the rest. As for the remaining nineteen thousand, we'd split it five ways: one share each for Bhili, Taim, Thara, Saanvi, and me, and Taim will deliver Saanvi's share to his family.

Bhili's transferring that thousand coin from a duffel into the tool bag that I plan to send back with Silva. "You best hold to the bargain," Bhili says. "Make sure dear Izzy sees our shining generosity."

Silva nods from the deck floor. "She will. Thousand coin's a nice taste, and Izzy will release the girl. Especially once I tell her we're going back for thirty thousand more."

Bhili grumbles. She's not pleased with the arrangement, and there were several earlier comments in the vein of, "Perhaps I just put a sinker in the heads of Silva and the Dongos, keep the knowledge of the thirty thousand to myself, and we go break the Cook out with the suits as the lieutenant says we could."

Taim kept pushing that. Said we shouldn't trust Silva and Izzy to hand Thara over. We had two fully functioning suits (the one Taim stole from the Guard and the one Bhili "borrowed" from her friend in Mojave Main). Two of us could suit up, cut the *Bandeira*'s hull from below the ship, and break Thara from the brig as we originally planned.

I put my foot down, though. I'd just spent four hours diving in the deep with Silva. I knew the man now. He was cunning, yes. He was a survivor, certainly. He was a monster, most of all. But I also knew he wouldn't let harm come to Thara. It might just cleave him in two.

After we finish counting out the gold, I step into the cabin and sit down beside Taim, who has one hand on the steering wheel. I don't say anything, but I lace my fingers into his other hand while my mind runs with everything we've been through.

Ever since Dad died, I blamed Taim. I blamed him for Dad's death, for the collapse and pulling me out too soon. I blamed him for leaving me behind in Coconino, for getting into the Guard. I even blamed him for this trip, for indulging Thara and Bhili, for agreeing to it.

But as he squeezes my hand, the brutal truth emerges once again.

I was wrong. I've been wrong.

I wanted someone to blame. I wanted my life to be someone's fault. But that's no way to live, and the reality of me and Taim is the exact opposite.

Taim's always cared about me.

In Phoenix-Below, Taim saved me. I would never have stopped digging for Dad. He did it again on the Coconino freedive. *I've got you. Get it all out.* And, yeah, he left for the Guard, but it wasn't to abandon me. *Don't you see—I can be in the Guard and with you.* Even when Taim lied to me about being in league with Silva, he did it to keep me fighting. He refused to let me sink into despair. He held my gaze, accepted my hate, and he gave me a reason to live. Taim's always done that. Over and over, he keeps picking me up, no matter where or when or why, he—

Taim loves me.

"You love me," I say, turning to him.

He startles and looks over. "So that's what you were thinking about so deeply?"

"You do, don't you?"

For once, there's no taunt, just Taim's penetrating eyes locked on to mine. "I do."

"Even in my darkest moments, you've been there."

Taim's eyes well, and he takes my head in both hands. "You're the strongest person I've ever known. And, if you need me, I will *always* be there."

Before he can say a single additional thing, I kiss him on the lips and my face smears into his. Tears gush out, and I can feel them, the wet between our cheeks. My chest heaves, and I shift my mouth off his, wrapping my arms around him. Then, with shuddered breath, I whisper, "Thank you—for never giving up on me."

We pass by two Coast Guard craft on our way, as we cut up through a strait that's wedged between La Madre and Yucca

Cape. The Guard doesn't even pay us a second glance. They just flash headlights in a hello, and they cruise right past us as we rip into the Fingers of Southern Nevada at a terrible speed.

I'm at the patrol boat's prow when we arrive at the *Bandeira*. The death-black ship's half-shrouded in mist, still tucked into the same anchorage where we left her, but flipped around, so that the bow faces south, toward us. It juts through the vapor like a spear to the fog, and below, wrapping around the bow, are the tinted portholes of the mess-cum-gallery in which we dined with Silva.

The entire deck of the *Bandeira* is obscured in wisps of gray, but I can only imagine the full crew stationed there, sabers at the ready, prepared to swing down from lengths of rigging, board us should we get close enough, and run me through once they find out that I've dispatched with four of their mates and intend to give them only a sliver of the treasure they were promised.

All those thoughts and worries dissolve, though, when an inflatable emerges from the mist, and on it are Izzy, Montserrat, two corsairs I don't recognize, and Thara, bound and gagged.

"Let her go!" I scream out as the inflatable pulls along our starboard.

Izzy eyes the deck and, seeing Silva and the Dongos tied up, she says, "Well, now, that depends on someone explaining to me just what happened here."

"You okay?" I lean off the patrol boat, reaching for Thara.

Izzy yanks her back and slides a knife to her throat. "She's fine. Now start talking. This ain't exactly the little rendezvous I expected after the drone report of our great success."

"Thing about success is"—Bhili steps aft down the boat—"depends much on your perspective. Things worked out quite well . . . for *us*."

"Bhili? By what star's shame you doing here?"

"Here for my treasure," Bhili says. "One I found. One you tried to steal from what's mine."

"And where's the rest of our people?" Izzy says. "Mayra, Cao, Khaddhi, and Hitesh."

"Claimed. By the deep." I say.

"That right . . ." Izzy's silver rings lift, contorting her face into a rictus. "Well, I'd like to hear the captain's side of things."

I move to untie Silva's gag, but Bhili signals me off. "João's gone a bit . . . what's that word—apoplectic." Bhili shifts the bag of a thousand gold coins, and, unbidden, I'm transported back to the inn, to Bhili curled up on our lawn, shaking her purse just to hear the sweet sound of the coins clacking together. I roar back to the present as Bhili claps me on the shoulder. "Now, our Jinny here, she's dredged up a right fine bargain for you. You hand us Thara, we pass Silva and the

Dongos back your way, and we even toss in a thousand goldies for your troubles."

Izzy pulls on the ring in her nose. "I want five thousand."

"How 'bouts we give you nothing," Bhili spits back.

"How about I shove this here knife into little Thara," Izzy says. "Then we see what takes longer: her bleeding out or us striking a bargain?"

My heart skips two beats. *This is not going the way it's supposed to.* I pull the tie on Silva's gag, prodding him in the back of the head. "Talk."

"Izzy, no harm comes to the girl," he says. "I mean that."

"And no harm should have come to our people, but we're missing four of them. Now, I want five thousand, the captain, and the Dongos, and *then* you get your sister."

"Three thousand," I say.

Bhili swivels. "Shut it, Jinny. Leave the bargaining to me."

"Four thousand," Izzy says.

"Done."

"What the—you swamping fool, Jinny. She would have done it for one."

Silva cracks his neck, port and starboard. "Well done, Izzy. We'll take the four thousand, heal up, purchase ourselves a few new suits, and then we have first right to go back."

I realize then that Silva knew Izzy would negotiate. Maybe he meant for Thara to be safe, but he also planned to walk away with more than a thousand coin.

"Why we going back?" Izzy shouts over my thoughts.

Silva's cheeks lift. "To get the thirty thousand I left down there."

Three planks are laid between the inflatable and patrol boat, and when Thara's finally across, it's like a beam of sunlight, piercing the clouds and thawing the dread from my bones. Her gag and bonds are already cut, and she leans into my chest, sobbing endless tears that could fill oceans. I press her close, whispering into her hair. "I'm here," I say. "Haldar sisters to the end."

At that, Thara stills, her head shifting off my chest. She looks up, chokes off the tears, and stares me dead in the eyes. "To the end." She says the words full and fierce, and they vibrate through me. Part reminder that I should never have planned to sacrifice myself. Part affirmation that me and her— we can make it through anything.

On my left, Taim pushes Silva and the Dongo brothers forward. The Dongos carry a bag we've now filled with four thousand pieces. When Silva's across, Taim walks toward Thara and me, throwing his arms around us. My eyes close, my body relaxes, squeezed within Taim's embrace, and finally I hear Bhili say, "All right then, Izzy. That's that. Let's put the pistols down."

There's a churning of water, and Silva calling as his voice grows faint. "Goodbye, Jinny. You keep your sister close, now." I picture the painting I saw on Silva's bridge—the lonely monk staring out from the cliffside. "And Bhili!" Silva continues.

"What that?"

"I catch you skulking Vegas-Drowned, looking for my treasure, and you'll find a harpoon buried in your heart!"

That last jab pushes my eyes open, but my cheeks warm as I see the widest smile painted on Bhili. It's not bright exactly, it can't be with those black teeth. But it's stretched ear to ear, and her eyes are doing all the sparkling. "Don't need *your* treasure, Silva! I'm sailing away with the real treasure—the three of *them*, safe and sound."

Evening drifts down and the clouds shift into a solemn anchor gray. We're riding deep into a bay that's tucked between two promontories that stretch out like thumb and forefinger from the coast of Southern Nevada. The wind whips in sideways, and outside you can taste the cool, clean air of the squall's approach.

Right now, Thara and I are tucked under a blanket, all of us in the cabin, with Bhili guiding Taim toward her friend's place. *The friend who's seen the sun.*

My chest flutters with that thought. Just the idea of meeting someone who's seen it feels incredible. Bhili says we can shelter at her friend's place for the night and book the sun journey.

"Squint your weather eye, Lieutenant." Bhili points forward, to the starboard side of the prow. "You see the shore? We get off there, up a hill, then 'bout a half a mile inland there's a large wall where her compound begins."

A large wall? That jerks me out of my reverie.

"What wall?" I say.

"Big one. Lot of richy landowners have them. Will keep the place from floodin' when the seas rise up and creep into Nevada."

I shake my head. "The other night, Thara and I, we jumped ship, swam to Nevada, and we ran into a colossal wall. Who knows how high, and maybe several miles long. There's no way through."

"Oh, there's a way," Bhili says. "Just have to know how to knock is all." Bhili waves me up from the cabin floor. "Jinny, take the conn. Taim—need your help with the distress lamp. The lamp does the knockin'."

The squall descends and rain slams down upon the cabin. The resulting pings and tings are so loud, we scream to be heard. All four of us are tucked in here. Thirty minutes since we eased onto the sandy black Nevada shore, and all Bhili keeps saying is: *Hold tight, she comin'.*

On the aft deck, Bhili and Taim erected the boat's distress lamp. It's a wide, immensely powerful bulb that shoots a pillar of white light into the sky. Most expensive craft have them. The light pillar can be seen for several miles. They're used in emergencies when a ship loses power or if they're out of drones.

We still have drones. Taim sent one to Yucca Cape to give them the lats and longs on the *Bandeira* (though odds on Silva still being there are thinner than a skimming stone). As for using the drones to get in touch with Bhili's friend, it's not possible. Apparently, Bhili's friend shoots down all drones that fly over her compound. Which begs the question . . .

Who is this woman?

"How do you know her again?" Taim shouts at Bhili.

Bhili clicks on an electric kettle wedged into the corner near the cabin's controls. "Her name's Nyala, and I met her in me youth, doing wrecking tours in Delhi-Below. She was young then, still rich, though. She one of them born rich types. She'd just made the trip to see the sun via Nanda Devi. Found me holed up, suckin' down teas at an inn near Almora, town in the Himalayan foothills. She knew I was a wrecker somehow. Proposed a job. Wanted to get her hands on an ancient statue, prehistoric she calls it, made before time and writing itself. Was buried deep in the National Museum of Delhi-Below. Went by the name *Dancing Girl*."

"Did you get it?" Thara asks.

The kettle rumbles, and Bhili arranges a few cups. "Does gold glitter? Course I got it. Pretty little thing too: 'bout the size of my hand, long limbed girl, all bronze, twenty-five bangles molded up the one arm. Nyala paid me three hundred ounces for the job."

"Why didn't you get the Treasure Island gold with her?" Taim says, probing harder.

"Well, I done several jobs for Nyala, though not all of them well. And this ain't really her type of job—goes after unique items. And what's more, she ain't meet with no one unless they carrying enough—"

A bright light blasts through the cabin's aft-glass, and we all swivel round. Bhili knocks over two teacups as she throws the cabin's door open, and a harsh voice booms out from a megaphone. "Who are you, and what do you want?"

"Is that Nyala?" Thara asks, but Bhili doesn't bother to answer.

In seconds, Bhili's outside the cabin, rain pelting her face, clouds crackling above. She screams back at the man. "Name's Bhili Bones. I's an old friend of Nyala's. We interested in a trip up above the clouds, and we has coin to pay." Bhili walks toward the aft deck, and I'm fast behind her with the wind biting into my poncho. I peel my eyes off Bhili, scan the beach, and my pulse leaps forward as I realize that we're surrounded by a crew of twelve heavily armed security personnel. They have two jeeps, four all-terrain vehicles, and the headlights on every vehicle are pointed at the patrol boat. I swallow the knot in my throat as the wind howls, and the warning horns finally blare in my head. I've just been lounging, soaking in stories, while Bhili led us to a crew that could take every coin we have.

24

"Bhili!" I shout as my voice is gobbled by the rain. "What is going on, Bhili? These people are armed. Did you know they were coming?"

Bhili plants a foot on the aft deck, pivots, and cups her hands together, imploring me. "You have to trust me now, Jinny. You want to see the sun. I can help you. But we can't move all this gold on our own."

I bite down on my lip. "I don't like this, Bhili!"

"You got coin? Let's see it," the lead man says. "And turn around! I want to see your hands!" He has broad shoulders, a thick beard, and a silvery bionic right hand wrapped around the megaphone. With his left he draws a pistol from his thigh holster.

"Do you know these people?" I shout at Bhili.

"No."

No!

"What if they swipe it?"

"Rust take you, Jinny! Do you trust me *or not?*"

"Hands in the air!" the man screams, and Bhili's and my hands go up.

I glance behind me, seeing Taim holding Thara back inside the cabin.

All the while, I'm trying to think it through. *Do I trust Bhili?*

For so long, I thought Bhili was a con. Everything she did: asking about the dive suits, taking us out on Dad's anniversary, leading us to that grillman on Tonto, abandoning us on the *Desierto*. Every time, I thought she'd done us in.

And every time, she hadn't.

Thara's words come back to me now. *There are also good things, good people. There are people who care about us.*

And finally it sinks down deep. The truth of it seeps down, like the rain in my bones.

Thara was right.

"Show him!" I yell. "Show him the gold!"

Bhili's cheeks are mounded so high, like she's bursting with righteous joy. "Knew I'd crack that cold heart of yours, Jinny! You's a softy deep down. Knew it the first day I seen ya."

Worst person to own up to.

Bhili turns around, marching several steps forward until she's right in front of a duffel. Her hands are still up, palms out toward the man. "Now, I's gonna reach down and pull out fist

332

fulls a coins so shiny, you have to cover your eyes."

The man rolls his eyes.

"After that, you take us straight through the wall. We some richy clients of Nyala's, and we have important business of seeing the sun."

The next twenty minutes are completely surreal. Bhili shows the lead man a handful of coin. Then he hops up on the patrol boat, takes a gander in the duffels, and very kindly introduces himself as Yuri, Nyala's security chief.

Thara, Taim, and I pile into the back seat of one of the jeeps, with Yuri driving. Bhili's in another jeep along with all the gold (guess I'm really leaning into this trust thing), and several ATVs lead and trail us as we take off for the compound.

Thara rides in a car almost every day, carpooling into Prescott for school, but I get in one maybe two or three times a year. We're off the beach in no time, riding west along the wall, but with the pockmarked terrain and the squall's winds threatening to flip the jeep, my stomach sloshes around until I'm about to puke.

(Boat rocking I can handle, but land vehicles—it's the worst kinda movement.)

Thankfully, Yuri pulls over two minutes later. He lowers his window, punches a few buttons on a box staked in the ground, and then we drive down into a concrete tunnel. It's squat, narrow, pitch-dark, but we emerge shortly, riding an incline into a world that's so bright, like I'm indoors, with a view that steals my breath.

On our left and right are rows upon rows of trees—real trees—they have to be. None are more than ten feet tall, but there are thousands of them, with wide swathes of grasses and bushes and other plants in between. It's every shade of green: wakame and kelp, turtle and teal, all of it sparkling and spotted by pops of red and orange and yellow . . . flowers? *Are those flowers?*

It's more vegetation than I've seen in my entire life, and we're driving through it, on a double-wide paved road that's raised, perhaps ten feet off the ground, so we can see miles in every direction except behind us. Suddenly, it occurs to me that it's nighttime, and—*am I hallucinating? How am I even seeing?*

I glance out the jeep's back window, and I'm squinting, staring at hundreds of massive grow lights in rows fixed onto the inside of the perimeter wall. It's like an outdoor greenhouse, the kind the American Archipelago uses to farm non-oceanic produce, but it's private and outdoors. *How is it outdoors?* How has the topsoil not washed away with all the—the rain?

I pause, listening. I can't hear the rain. I look at Thara, who looks like her jaw might drop right off. She reaches a hand forward, claps Yuri's shoulder, and finally finds her voice. "Stop—stop the jeep. Stop the jeep!"

Yuri hits the brakes. He mumbles something, presses a finger into his earpiece, and says, "I'll give you ten minutes. Madame Nyala is waiting in the Musée."

I have no idea what a *Musée* is, nor do I care, because Thara, Taim, and I are tumbling out of the jeep and onto the road. Thara draws a breath so deep, it's like that one breath contained every moment of her life before.

And then there is now: life after.

I grab Thara's hand and Taim's, standing between them. Despite our proximity to the Gulf of Nevada, the air smells so clean, so rich, so—so full. Thara tips her head back and breathes again, long and through her nose. "There's so much," she says. "So much oxygen."

Faintly, I hear a door slam behind us, and then loudly, Bhili's voice. "Get on out there. Take yor boots off too!"

I look to Yuri for affirmation, he nods, and in seconds, Thara, Taim, and I are barefoot. I glance up, shielding my face, expecting raindrops to plunk into my eyes, but they don't. It's a black sky above, although it looks a little—blurry? I'm not sure. Maybe that's just the tears in my eyes and the flood of emotions as I find myself standing on a raised road, overlooking a place more beautiful than I have words to describe.

Thara manages another question. "Does—does it not rain inside the compound?" It sounds ludicrous as it leaves her mouth, of course it rains—it rains everywhere. Still, I'm standing here, silent, praying that this place defies all the world's rules. Let us be beyond science, beyond reason. Let the answer be: yes.

Of course it's not, and Bhili confirms it. "Bah! Course it rains. Just an overhang. It's clear to let light down, and a thousand feet up, which is why you can't hear the rain rattling."

Yuri nods. "It extends from the top of the wall across the Garden. It's something Madame Nyala dreamt up—a clear roof with a slight incline. It catches all the rain, feeds it down through drainage in the wall, and then underground and out to the Gulf of Nevada."

So that's the blur . . . the rain, rushing across this overhang.

"Place looks good!" Bhili says. "Garden's twice the size as when I last saw it."

A garden . . . like Thara's garden.

Everything and nothing alike.

"Come on, now!" Bhili says, walking down the slope. Thara steps forward, pulling me and Taim. We scrabble down a few feet of rock, and then I step onto a soft expanse of grass, my weight pressing down on the dirt as blades slip between my toes.

I lean toward Thara. My chest feels like an ocean's on top of it, and there's one thought in my mind. "I wish Dad was here," I say. "He would have loved this. A lawn—a *real* lawn."

Thara looks up at me with eyes so wet and round. Her

hands move behind her neck, and she removes her necklace, pinching the Lakshmi medallion between thumb and fore-finger. "I've got both of them right here," she says. "Mom's necklace, the one Dad gave her." Wet streams glisten off Tha-ra's cheeks. "Maybe we let them rest in this place—together."

Thara kneels down, and I do too. Gently, her fingers flow through blades of grass, until she finds a small pocket of open soil. With her thumb, she drives the medallion into the earth, the thin chain nestling on top. Her hand lingers over the ground, and I cup mine on top of hers. "Do you remember the prayer Dad used to say when you tended *your* garden?" I ask.

Thara has the most peaceful smile as she says the words. "That spirit, that went far away, to the waters and the plants, We cause to come again, that it may live and sojourn here."

I swallow and squeeze her hand. "You chose a good place for them."

We stand, and Bhili and Taim are behind us. For once, no wisecracks from Bhili. All she says is, "Why don't we walk in some."

Thara leads the way, and at first we step in silence between the trees. I have no idea what any of them are—never seen a real tree. Before long, Thara's running between them, tracing her fingers along leaves, trunks, mumbling about "oaks" and "pines" and "maples."

"These are all miniatures," she says at one point. "Miniatures require less light. The ancestors of these trees—they grew over a hundred feet toward the sky."

Over a hundred feet? That thought almost knocks me to the ground. I hold myself firm, though. I won't let anything, not even history, belittle this moment. These trees may be miniatures—but to me, they are larger than life itself.

As we step farther through the Garden, my nose is assaulted with smells. Not normal smells—not the salty, sour, putrid smells I'm so used to from our coastal living. These smells are different: something sweet, like barley malt syrup; something sharp, like re-dried timber; something fresh, like an approaching squall; something floral, like the water lilies that the Huynhs grow in buckets of rainwater.

Thara veers off, clearly needing some alone time with the Garden. Behind me, Bhili scratches her back on a tree's trunk. I grab Taim's hand, and we walk through long, thin strands of green that hang like cut netting from a branch.

In front of us is a beautiful bush with clusters of bulbous blue flower heads, each head stuffed with tiny, four-petal flowers. I lean down, sniff, and the intoxicating smell rolls through my body. When I glance up, Taim's holding his head, looking like he might crumble. "Didn't know a place like this was possible," he says.

"Glad we found out," I whisper, and I reach out for his waist with both hands. I pull him close, our bodies pressed together, my hip nestled into his. He's been after me for so long: to dream, to strive, to take something for myself. Now I have, and I'm here, and he's here, and it's like months of craving rising from the depths of my body.

"Hello," Taim says, raising his eyebrows, but before another taunting word can emerge, my lips are on his, my eyes close, and he groans as I pull the breath straight out of his mouth. This kiss is no delicate thing of pecks and cheeks and eyelashes. This kiss is swollen and hungry. This kiss is full body, with Taim's hand pushing on the small of my back, my fingers in his hair, his tongue searching, and my knee riding up his thigh. I grab a palmful of his back and shove myself in harder, while the heady smells of the flowers and him descend like a cloud, thick, powerful, and penetrating. My hands shift down Taim's body. Those new cords of muscle he built in the Guard are taut and firm. I wrap one leg around his, still standing, not knowing what I'm doing. Not caring, either. Rust take me, I want him. I want him *now*. Which is not convenient at all as a raspy voice shouts back toward the road.

"What kinda flowers they put in this Garden, Yuri! These two done lost they minds."

Swamping Bhili. Go away!

"All right, then, Jinny! They be time for that later. Nyala don't like to be kept waiting."

* * *

339

Bhili had to pry me off, but she did, and now we're back on the road, lacing up our boots, with my body still strung tighter than a forestay. Thara won't take her eyes off the Garden, demanding that we come back immediately after meeting Nyala. Taim still looks flustered, which is all kinds of satisfying. Then, boots on, we hop in the jeep, I wrap my hand in Taim's, my pulse keeps racing, and we drive off through the last stretch of the Garden.

"Can I meet the person who's in charge of upkeep?" Thara asks.

Yuri looks back from the front seat. "Yes, if you're staying with us. The Garden Curator teaches at the Rocky Mountain Institute for Agriculture. She'll be back in a few days."

"Why do you want to meet her?" Taim asks.

A soft smile lingers on my face. I know why, and Thara turns to me. "Jin, I know this sounds crazy. I'm sure you think it's too soon, and I need to relax and breathe, but—this place—it's everything I ever dreamed of. I can't go back to Coconino after seeing this. I know I promised to see the sun with you, and I will, but"—Thara pauses—"after that, I want to come back *here*. I want to work and live *here*. I'd do any job they offered. And I know this isn't my decision, and you think I'm just a kid, and—"

I cut her off. "You're not just a kid. I treated you like that after Dad passed, and that was wrong. That was because of my own fears. I've been so scared to lose you, to lose anyone." I glance at Taim. "But you were right about Taim and me. You were right about Bhili. You were right about us needing this adventure. You're the wisest younger sister I could ever have, and I'm the one who's in awe of *you*." I tuck a strand of Thara's hair behind her ear. "You deserve every dream. If that means you want to work here, then we will find a way to make that happen."

Thara throws her arms around my neck, and my whole spirit glows. I wouldn't trade this moment for every coin in Treasure Island. The jeep rumbles on, and finally the Garden ends about a thousand feet past the wall. Yuri tells us that the grow lights only carry so far.

Massive black pillars hold up the overhang where it stops, and from there, the familiar pattering of rain resumes on the jeep's roof. The road descends down a slight ramp, over a massive grate, up a modest incline, and we park in front of several large concrete buildings. We exit the jeep, and Thara almost slips beside me, while Taim kicks something that skitters across the paved ground, clinking. All three of us bend down, and Thara picks up a tiny glass ball, about a half inch in diameter. She holds it up, and it sparkles in the headlights of the jeep. Then she draws out Luz's bead from her pocket. They look identical.

Yuri comes up behind us. "We attempted a cloud dispersal

a few days ago. Packed a drone with chemicals and blew it up in the clouds. Nothing happened, but Madame Nyala likes to try them all the same. Always causes a huge mess with the beads."

A cloud dispersal?

"So the beads—they *are* in the clouds," Thara says.

"Yes. They fall whenever we attempt a dispersal. Pain to sweep up."

Thara shoots me a look. *Another thing she was right about. This could get annoying.* Still, I have no idea how to interpret this. Maybe that Maxwell Theory about cloud technology is true? Although in that story, the sensors are microscopic. These beads are the length of my fingernail. I pick one up. The thing is so clear and light and hard. I knew that from holding Thara's, but it feels almost impossible—and that old Coaster saying plays in my head:

Water makes its own plans.

"Do you know what they do, Yuri?" I ask.

He shrugs. "Boss studies them some but doesn't say much. This way now." Before we have time to probe further, Yuri leads us toward a wide building, two floors, with giant red double doors, and the word *Musée* in white script across them.

Yuri throws the doors open, bright light pours out, and I'm blinking as I take in my surroundings. The building is a single massive room, with hundreds of paintings, drawings, and photographs hung from gleaming white walls. Across the floor are dozens of statues and pedestals with glass cases. Four security personnel with earpieces are in the back. The old bones of a gigantic animal ten times my size hang from the ceiling in the center of the room, and just to the side of that animal is a woman sitting in front of a small round table. She's in a charcoal suit, dark-brown skin, legs crossed, maybe sixties, and tall with a back that's perfectly straight. Her long, thin, gray braids are swooped to the side, and in her nose is a single diamond stud.

She beckons us forward, very formal, but Bhili jogs up, lifts her by the armpits, squeezing. "Nyala! You lookin' like a stick shoved up your ass, same as I last saw you."

Thara barks a laugh beside me. A few of the security personnel in the back shift, but none approach, and the woman pats Bhili across the back before she's set down. "Good to see you too, Bhili. It's been what—ten years?" Nyala flattens out the creases in her suit from Bhili's hug.

"Somethin' like that," Bhili says, pulling a chair from the table and pouring herself tea from a fancy glass pot in the table's center.

"Won't you introduce me to your friends, Bhili?"

"Aye. Everyone, take a seat. This here Nyala. She has many businesses and is a dealer of antiquities, as you can see." Bhili waves her arm around, then knocks the giant calf bone of the animal we're next to. "What you call this one again?"

"A Tyrannosaurus rex," Nyala says smoothly.

"Always liked that name," Bhili says. "Ferocious." She bites the air, and her teeth clunk. "I helped Nyala recover it from the Somethin' Somethin' Museum in Chicago-Below."

"The Field Museum of Natural History," Nyala says. "But yes—it's a favorite of mine as well. A reminder that monsters roamed these lands long before we arrived. And monsters will swim these seas long after we're gone."

I shudder, and Nyala notices. "Had encounters, have you? With the things in the deep?"

I nod, my mouth glued shut.

"Girl was in Vegas-Drowned today," Bhili says.

Nyala considers this, drawing a finger down the ridge of her nose. "Did you see a large cephalopod there? A color changer?"

Clouds above, how does she know that? I nod again.

"Were you scared?" Nyala asks.

A single word eeks out of my mouth. "Yes."

"Good. The bravest of us always admit to being scared." Nyala taps a finger against the table, once, twice, three times, and at last, she says, "Now, Bhili—introductions, please."

This woman is both terrifying and very used to keeping Bhili on track.

"So that's Jin and Thara Haldar. And that there's—"

"Taim Mazatlán," Taim says. "I'm a lieutenant with the Coast Guard's Eleventh."

Nyala smiles. "Pleased to meet you all. Now then, what can I do for you? A member of my security detail rode ahead and told me it's about seeing the sun?"

Bhili takes that as an invitation to launch into a ten-minute-long story about her life over the past eight months. Living with us in Coconino, the trip into the Gulf of Nevada, Silva taking us hostage, how she saved us (lot of time spent there). I fill in a few bits on the dive, and Nyala sits quietly, hands clasped. Finally, Bhili concludes, and Nyala simply says, "Good to know the seascapes are still on the *Bandeira*."

"She want those bad," Bhili whispers. "Real bad."

"Now then, Jin—you sound like quite the diver," Nyala says. "And Taim and Thara—you've been diving from a young age as well?"

Bhili answers for us, like she's the proud parent herself. "Right on all accounts! Jinny's a shark if I ever saw one, bite your face off."

Strange, but that makes me feel all warm and fuzzy.

"And you want to see the sun?" Nyala says.

"Yes," I manage to cut in. "How much does it cost? And what's the route?"

Nyala steeples her fingers. "The best way is through the Himalayas. We have many government contacts in the Tibetan Plateau. We can ensure a very smooth journey. As for payment, well—the price is normally fifteen thousand ounces a person."

Fifteen thousand! That's more than twice my share.

"But I'd be willing to do it for free," Nyala says.

"And how's that?" I scoff.

"Well, my last dive crew had something of an—accident. I'm looking for a crew to take their place." Nyala stares directly at me. "If you really bested Silva and four of his people, then you may be one of the best divers in the Archipelago."

"She is!" Thara says, and I'm shining all over again with that compliment.

"And if you're willing to do a wrecking job for me," Nyala says, "then I'll take all of you to see the sun personally, free of charge." Nyala pauses, scanning my face.

I draw a deep breath. Should have known this wasn't going to be some meet-Bhili's-friend, sail-right-above-the-clouds kind of excursion. My eyes shift across Thara and Taim, both of whom are wide-eyed and clearly interested, both of whom are also waiting for me to respond.

There's a part of me thinking, forget this woman. We just recovered sixteen thousand coin! I'll see the sun later. For now, I'll get Thara this job. Then I'll head back to Coconino. I'll polish up the inn. Maybe I'll buy a new inn. I'll get one in Nevada. Thara and I can still live together. I'll see Taim when he's stationed in the Gulf. I'll pay off the conscription tax—permanently. Life can be so simple. So safe.

But there's another part, a newer part, a part that has my heart thumping and my saliva flowing. It's the part of me that rose up during those final moments blasting out of Treasure Island. The part that went back for Silva. Not because he deserved to be saved, but because there is a part of me now that roars with desire. It yearns and needs. It *wants*.

I won't be happy back at an inn. I haven't been happy there since Dad died. I've been scared. Taim knew it, Thara knew it. But beneath the scared—there's someone else. Someone who's been diving into the deep since she was five years old. Someone who's bold. Someone who's brave. Someone who's more like Dad than she's ever admitted.

What would Dad do if he found five hundred coin lying on the ocean bottom? Dive down the next day in search of five hundred more. For so long, I thought that was a problem. That he was greedy, selfish, reckless. But he wasn't. He was hungry. He loved the search. And all that striving, all that wanting—it made him strong.

"So what do you think?" Nyala says, prodding me again.

I meet her eyes and ask the only question there is. "What's the job?"

Acknowledgments

In 2018, I left my job to stay at home with our second baby. It was a big leap, but I thought it would be a fun, special experience that I'd never regret. As it turns out, I underestimated just how profound the experience would be. Staying at home with Caleb changed my entire life. It made me into a better partner to my wife, as I learned about the mental load of running our home. It made me into a more patient father. AND—it helped me launch a new career.

I started writing during nap times and at five a.m. (before the baby woke up . . . usually). At first, it was just reflections on life, work, and being a dad. I read *The Artist's Way* by Julia Cameron, and I started penning my "morning pages." Those pages gave way to a gag book that I wrote to celebrate my cousin's fortieth birthday.

So that's where I'll begin. Thank you to my larger-than-life cousin, Arul. You were my first muse. You embraced

Gio Powers with your big, hearty, contagious laugh, and I so appreciate you for being such a great sport, the ultimate family loyalist, and a truly kind, good person.

To my best friend, Naveen, thanks for reading countless early snippets from Gio Powers. For sending me endless lols, for keeping it real when I wrote some trash, and for being there through everything. Boyz II Men continues.

To my sister, Kavita; brother-in-law, Vikram; Mom; Dad; and my mother-in-law, Priya; thank y'all so much for reading the first novel I ever wrote. I can't imagine the persistence it took to get through that terrible thing. It will always remain unpublished, but I'll never forget that Zoom where you gushed about it on my birthday.

To Vikram Bisarya, my nephew, who was the first family member to ever read one of my novels in full. Thank you!! I was floored when you did that.

To Mom and Dad (again), thanks for encouraging Kavita and me to write skits, performances, songs, inappropriate holiday cards, for listening to my weird experimental poetry in college, and for generally raising us in a loving, open-minded, and deeply sarcastic household. You two really set the bar on parenting— one that parent-Dinesh finds to be annoyingly high.

To my father-in-law, Michael, who passed in 2014. Jin works through a lot of grief in this book. I was thinking about you. We miss you.

To Julie Eshbaugh and Erin Young, who read *Into the Sunken City* and/or other early unpublished novels of mine—thank you!! My writing grew leaps and bounds because of your thoughtful words, critiques, motivation, honesty, and care—I am in your debt!

To all the early readers and friends who gave feedback on my writing, especially: Soumya Santhanakrishnan, Sarah Sutton, Julie Shetler, Dave Kornfeld, Kaitlyn Johnson, Katherine Locke, Jon Michael Darga, and Eric Wyman—thank you so much for your insights! They improved my writing tremendously.

To my amazing agent, Claire Friedman, who quite literally plucked this "bonkers book" out of the query pile. Wow. Thank you for believing in me and in this book, for getting it so deeply, and for being so calm, thoughtful, responsive, and motivating. Every week, I feel beyond fortunate to be working with you.

To my editor Kristen Pettit, who saw everything this book needed. I've gone on long monologues with my family about how much I've learned from you, and how you're truly a master of craft. Thank you for seeing the potential here. I hope I've done your wisdom some small justice.

To my editor Alice Jerman, who's been an incredible champion for *Into the Sunken City*. Thank you for being on top of everything and for bringing me onto your team with such a warm reception. I'm so lucky to have been scooped up by you!

To the entire HarperCollins team, including (but not limited to!): Clare Vaughn, Caitlin Lonning, Alexandra Rakaczki, Catherine Lee, Jessie Gang, Kate Lapin, Meghan Pettit, Allison Brown, Cara Norris-Ramirez, Audrey Diestelkamp, and Abby Dommert. Thank you for all the hard work, careful readings, kind emails, copy edits, thoughtful designs, marketing and publicity support, proofreads, and so much more!

To Diana Dworak for that stunning cover! Wow. You found a way to capture the heart of this book. I can't thank you enough. And to BMR Williams for the map! Since first imagining the American Archipelago, I hoped we'd have a stop-and-stare map like this.

To my kids, Isaac and Caleb, you two light up my life, and I consider myself the luckiest dad in the world. Every day with y'all is filled with: joy, laughs, snuggles, tears, fun, singing, racing, jumping, shouting, and it's sometimes exhausting, and you're always-always the favorite part of my day. I love you with three hearts, like a colossal squid.

To my other kid and forever puppy, Charlie (the chocolate lab). You're the sweetest, most loyal goof any work-from-home writer could ask for. You deserve to lick my jeans as much as you want, even if your breath stinks.

And finally, to my wife, Ruch, the absolute love of my life, who recently told me, "I'm just really surprised at how you turned out!" Lol. Thank you for taking a chance on a super gangly kid wearing an upside-down visor. Thank you to fate for moving you next door during our junior year at Penn. Thank you for being the most thoughtful person I know. Thank you for being the breadwinner and supporting our family while I was home with the kids and exploring this new career. Thank you for reading every book I've written, multiple times, and unfailingly giving the best advice. Thank you for making me a better person every day. I love you.